The Sacrifice

of One

Book One in the Camilla Crim Series

Edition: 1/2022

ISBN: 978-0-9966824-7-3

Cover Design by: www.ebooklaunch.com

Editing by: www.ayersedits.com

Find Emily online at www.emilyfortney.com

TO MY DARLING PHILIPPE (THE CAT)

The Sacrifice
of One

CHAPTER ONE

THE ROAD CURVES as my eyes catch a glimpse of the twisted black iron gate that opens to Governor Leo's farm. My thick legs keep pace with the mass of hirelings. The man next to me coughs violently into his tattered sleeve. We mosey together almost in a uniform marching formation, but there's nothing stately or grand about us. I brush a frizzy dark curl out of my face and tuck it behind my ear.

My gaze is trained to the damp ground. Worn boots pop out from under my gray wool dress. I crunch a couple of dried leaves as the line moves forward. It's autumn, harvest time, and the farm has a fresh frenzy about it. This is the time of year when new workers pour in from all corners of Elmyra. The work is plenteous. The pay is reasonable. At least that's what we're told.

The crowd ahead of me slows and we're reduced to a painful shuffle. Two soldiers guard the gate, checking that each worker has his credentials before entering the farm. I'm jostled into the mass of filthy workers in the same way a river is forced over the waterfall's edge. Neither I nor the river has a choice in the matter.

My eyes drift to the ten-foot wooden wall that branches out from the gate. It's made of tree trunks, the tops of which have been sharpened to a point. To an outsider, it may look like a giant cage, meant to hold us all inside. But I've become quite content between these walls.

I approach the gate. We're funneled together so that only two of us can pass through the gate at a time. The guards are Warwick soldiers. Tight black leather vests cover their middles, a red W stitched into the breast. It's my turn. I step up to the threshold. The one soldier peers down at me with narrow eyes. Raising my arm, I flash the symbol that's branded on my skin. He nods his approval.

Before me sits the grandest estate in my home territory, Bear Gap. A path of small pearly white stones snakes through the courtyard. From the pinnacle flies a flag made of leathery black fabric with a deep crimson W burned onto both sides. Out of habit, my fingers reach over to brush the matching mark on the inside of my forearm.

I break from the path, jogging around some lingering workers. Time is precious here. We get paid by our quantity of work, so every minute missed is less time to harvest. I continue along the right arm of the building. As I turn the corner, I'm met with miles and miles of farmed land. First are rows of vegetables, then behind them, the fields of corn, wheat, and barley. Beyond them the farm continues with rows and rows of raspberry bushes, fruit trees, and grape vines. The fields roll and curve so I can hardly see the orchards from where I'm standing, but I'm familiar enough with the property that I know they're there.

Leo Harras is governor of Bear Gap and the owner of all of this. He was appointed to his position by our Supreme Ruler and charged with bringing this farm to fruition. Bear Gap is home to the largest farm in the whole kingdom. From here, we supply food to nearly every territory.

Despondent bodies dot the field in multitudes. I hear a whip crack and turn to see a man falling to his knees. No work is disturbed or delayed by this event. Even I hardly take a glance before moving on.

I have work to do if I'd like to eat later.

I approach the field supervisor booth, a wooden box with just enough space for one man to stand up and look out a small window. I'm jittery as I wait, anxious to get started.

"Next."

The woman in front of me steps out of line and I take her place, ready to get my work assignment. The man in the booth doesn't look at me. He's wearing a pair of spectacles that balance precariously on the end of his nose. The booth is guarded by three more Warwick soldiers. One of the guards restrains a man about my age. His hand grips tightly around the man's bicep. I turn to look, curious why he's being held here. The man's skin is a deep olive tone, smooth and nearly perfect in quality. I look down at my own calloused hands and frown.

"Name."

My gaze jolts back to the supervisor.

"Crim, Camilla," I say quickly.

Supervisor Benedek runs a bony finger down his ledger. He looks at me with a wrinkled nose, then turns to his book. He flips back a few pages before finding my name. I've known this man since I was a child, yet he still plays this silly game with me, pretending like he must remember who I am. I'm just hoping he doesn't hate me enough to assign me to Mac today.

"Ah, yes. I have a special job for you today, Miss Crim." I tense with irritation. "You'll be taking this fellow with you."

Benedek peeks out his little window to signal to the soldier. The man with the light brown skin is tossed a few paces forward.

"See that he's put in the system," the supervisor continues.

Anxious flutters torment my body. I don't have time for this. I feel jumpy all of a sudden and without thinking I blurt, "Why do *I* have to take him?" I look at the new laborer full on. His hair is a shiny black. He runs his fingers through his shaggy tendrils as if to shake off the guard. I inspect his outfit too: nice riding pants that look dirty but not worn and a finely stitched canvas jacket. I'm certain of one thing—he's not from Bear Gap. Usually new workers come here because they have nowhere else to go. They're homeless with no families and not a ring to their name. I can't imagine a scenario where this man would choose to come to a place like this.

"By our great Supreme Ruler, Miss Crim, you should be grateful to share this institution with a new member!" Benedek says. "And until he's fully trained, your harvest will be combined and your pay will be split evenly between the two of you."

This is not fair, I think to myself. I'm diligent with my work every day. I shouldn't have to share my earnings with someone else.

"But I'll be late to my field assignment."

"It'll be a small sacrifice for you, and besides, Foreman Mac will understand."

I grind my teeth together.

"You'd put me with Mac after forcing me to be late?" I step forward, wrapping my fingers around the edge of the booth window. Benedek's eyes flash, the black center growing to an unnaturally small size. Quickly, I pull my hands away and turn my gaze downward.

"Go on now, Miss Crim, I have a line of people that are just as eager to work as you are."

Benedek clicks his fingers at one of the soldiers. He grabs both me and my charge by the scruffs of our shirts and pushes us down a short embankment. I land on my knees but stand up quickly, brushing the dirt from my dress. I feel anger steaming up through my chest. I clench both my fists and don't even have the patience to look at the new inductee.

"My name is Lawrence," the man speaks.

His clear, cheerful voice sends me further on edge. I look at him and he smiles at me, warm and pleasant.

"Camilla," I say. "Let's go."

I lead Lawrence to the back corner of the estate. It's a place I haven't been in a long time, but I will never forget where it is. The smell of burning coal touches my nose as we approach. Cave-like brick structures were built under the house as the ground slopes. This is where I take Lawrence. We turn the corner. A man in a black leather apron is pounding away when we approach.

"He's new," I say when the blacksmith looks up.

I glance over at Lawrence, who's smiling. I stare at him in amazement. What a fool. He has no idea what's coming.

"My name is Lawrence." He sticks his hand out to shake with the blacksmith.

"Show me your wrist," the blacksmith says, his voice as dark and gruff as his hands. He sets his hammer down and walks back to the stove. He pulls a long ash-covered rod out of the coals.

Lawrence stands awkwardly, holding out his arm so the top of his wrist is showing. I'm tempted to look away, but I don't. Years of working on this farm have hardened my stomach.

Back from the stove, the blacksmith grabs Lawrence's hand and flips it over so the tender skin underneath is showing. He takes the pole in his other hand and firmly presses the smoldering brand to the inside of Lawrence's forearm. Lawrence screams so loud that my ears seem to blister. But I keep watching as the white hot brand is pulled back and a blazing red W eats away at Lawrence's skin.

"Warwick . . . " I mutter to myself, clutching at the raised brand on the inside of my own arm.

Lawrence's cries reverberate through the stone cave and I wonder if the field workers can hear him too. The blacksmith plunges Lawrence's arm into a dirty bucket of water and goes back to his work. Sweat forms on his face and he weeps as he hugs the bucket. I stare, dead-eyed, until Lawrence pulls his arm out of the water to look at the burn. My scar has stretched and grown. It doesn't hurt anymore, but the pain is still fresh in my memory, even after seven years.

The blacksmith ignores me as I rummage through his shop, pulling out the drawer of his workbench. I find a scrap piece of linen and take it over to Lawrence.

"Here." I toss the fabric so that it falls onto Lawrence's lap. "Bandage yourself up. We have to get out to the fields."

"I can't. There's no way . . . I can't . . . move." Sweat and saliva drip from Lawrence's face as he struggles to speak.

"You have to." I fold my arms across my chest. "You have the mark now and that means you work no matter what."

Lawrence looks at me in disbelief. I feel my patience growing thinner and thinner. I pull him to his feet, feeling this tall, strong man go limp from the pain. We exit to the sound of metal hitting metal.

Lawrence crudely wraps his raw brand as I lead him through the vegetable rows and past the orchards. His eyes widen at the sight of children and elderly people working alongside men like himself. I wonder what it must be like to see this place through fresh eyes.

Just as we reach the edge of the grape field, the barley stalks come into view behind the wooden posts that supported the grape vines in summer. Terrible shouting wafts through the edge of the rows. A short round-bellied man with a bald head paces up and down the barley field, spitting a mixture of profanities and other words meant to encourage faster production.

"Come meet Mac," I say, but I don't think Lawrence catches my humor.

Sweat glistens on Mac's face despite the coolness of the late season. His eyes lock onto me. He barrels toward us with heavy steps. I always fear his stubby legs will give out and he'll roll down the fields until he's caught in a thorny bush. Despite that thought, my body still tenses as he draws closer.

"Sorry we're late, sir," I say quickly, keeping my eyes on the ground. "Supervisor Benedek asked me to get him branded."

"What did you say?" Mac shouts. He skids to a stop, his red face inches from mine.

"Supervisor Benedek asked me to take him to be branded," I repeat, louder this time.

He looks Lawrence up and down. "Did you say you're late cuz your mamma made you eat a bowl of porridge this morning?"

Spit flies from his mouth, spattering my face. Two guards standing by the edge of the field chuckle at Mac's insult.

Lawrence's forehead creases with concern. "No. We were just down with the blacksmith and—"

I shoot Lawrence a warning gaze, hoping he'll understand that it's best if he just keeps his mouth shut.

"No?" Mac sucks in a labored breath. He shifts to face Lawrence, pressing his hands hard on his thighs. "It looks like we have a gentleman with us today!" He turns toward the guards, wearing a sloppy smile. They laugh, if only to please their boss. "You must be a spoiled runaway from LilyAye. I want everyone to call this one Gentleman." Mac straightens his back and takes Lawrence's hand, shaking it violently. "Let's make sure we respect him like he deserves. Now listen here, Gentleman, we start work at dawn. Somethin' she should've told ya." Mac turns to one of the guards. "Three lashes for her."

"What?" Lawrence shouts.

I drop my hold on Lawrence's arm and take a step back. I press my lips tightly together. Thin scars already line the length of my back.

"For the gentleman's tardiness," Mac says.

A few pairs of eyes leer at me from among the barley stalks but quickly turn away as Mac hobbles toward the field. The guard unhooks a coiled cord from his belt and marches straight at me. Covering my chest with my arms, I feel as though I'm shrinking in size.

"Wait!" Lawrence shouts. "You can't strike a girl." His voice is confident but still buried with the pain of his arm. In unison, Mac and his guards explode with laughter.

The guard grabs me by the wrists and pulls me toward the tool shed. I know better than to fight back.

"Hey! You can't do that." Lawrence says, following us closely.

The guard instructs me to kneel down and hold onto the edge of the shed. I grip the corner, already feeling my breath quickening. Unsatisfied with my stance, the guard grabs my hands and stretches them up higher.

"Stop it." Lawrence shouts, but the guard ignores him, and so do I.

Before stepping into position, the guard brushes my long wavy hair off my back and tears the top seam of my dress so that my back is exposed. This is the worst part, the silence as the torturer positions his body and cocks his arm. I look at Lawrence. He's holding his wrapped arm close to his chest and staring at me, helpless.

The whip whirrs through the air. A lightning bolt of pain strikes the middle of my back and snaps over my shoulder. Lawrence twitches and closes his eyes. I suck in air as the whip is pulled away. The second strike hits across my back and up the length of my right arm. My eyes scrunch tightly closed. The third hit shakes my body as the cord wraps around my stomach.

My breath cracks and I heave for air. Slowly, I let my hands fall down the shed and into my lap. Behind me, the guard's footsteps fall away. Lawrence comes to my side. He looks at me as if he were looking at a complicated knot he is trying to untie. He places a gentle hand on my shoulder. I shudder violently, shoving his arm away and giving him a look that leaves his mouth agape.

"Sorry . . . " he mumbles.

"Don't . . . put your hands on me."

"You didn't even scream."

I cough onto the ground, trying to catch my breath. My hands dig into the grass as if doing so will suck away some of the pain.

"They . . . do it . . . harder . . . when you cry." I take a deep, labored breath and look at Lawrence. Ignoring the pain for a moment, I fling my arm back and pull my dress together where it was ripped. Blood seeps through the wool, congealing and holding the fabric in place. My hand makes its way to the spot on my belly. When I pull it away, there's blood.

"What can I do to help?" Lawrence asks, his eyes glistening with what I think must be tears.

"Nothing."

I pull myself to my feet. Lawrence follows my every move like a sheep dog. Running a hand through his hair, he says, "I can't believe what they did to you."

"We were late." My voice snaps as hard as the whip. "What did you expect to happen?" I push past him, marching toward the rows of barley, then stop suddenly and turn around to face him. "I was ten years old when I got my brand." I hold my arm out to show him. "But unlike you, I didn't come here because I *wanted* to work, or even because I needed to. My father brought me." Lawrence's eyes are big and glossy as he stares at me. "He became too much of a drunk to be able to support us." I take an angry step closer to Lawrence. "Today we work so tomorrow we can eat."

CHAPTER TWO

THE BARLEY FIELD looms before us like a great beast that must be tackled. One of Mac's soldiers shoves us into a row and chucks a couple of garden sickles at us. Lawrence struggles with his work and I know it's more than just the pain of his brand. I sigh, take his hand in mine, and show him how to curve the sickle around the base of the barley stalks. Then I explain that he'll want to build a bushel so we can get paid for what we harvest.

It's well past dawn and the two of us still haven't harvested even one bushel. Lawrence moves at a ridiculously slow pace. At one point his blade slips and he nicks himself in the leg. I bite my lip and force myself to be patient with him.

"Gather a few stalks like this," I say. "Then pull it hard. It's one quick motion. Toss the stalks and keep moving."

Lawrence nods. The supervisor's idea to split our pay is working. I'm shackled to this man until he can learn this simple skill.

"I . . . I'm sorry," he says. "I've never done work like this."

Mac paces a few rows away. "Move faster, Gentleman!"

"You have to learn quick. They'll toss you out if you can't keep up."

Pulling hard on the handle of the sickle, I feel a shock of pain run up my back. I pause my work and glance in Lawrence's direction. His eyes are trained firmly on his hands as they move with a new swiftness. He's trying, I realize. He's at least trying.

Lawrence's arms are thick with muscle and he's clearly strong. It's not a matter of bodily strength that holds him back. Curiosity pulls me in. "What kind of work then?" I ask.

"Huh?"

"If not farming, what kind of work *are* you used to?"

"Oh." Lawrence wipes his brow with the back of his hand. He hesitates but says, "I'm rather good with a sword."

A sword? My eyebrows knit together.

"Then why don't you join the militia? Why come and work here?"

"Well . . . " Lawrence doesn't meet my eyes.

I return to my work. "My brother's in the militia," I say. "I'd be with him right now if they'd take girls."

Lawrence moves his arm quickly, taking stalk after stalk off at the base. He's finally getting it. "Warwick's Militia's not for me." There's an ironic smirk on his face. "I'm looking for a new life in Bear Gap. I always heard, since I was a kid, that there were opportunities here, that anyone could work at Governor Leo's farm."

"That's true," I say. "But you have to be strong enough to do it."

Lawrence breaks from his work, leaning back on his heels. His face is damp with sweat, but I can tell it's not from the sun. He looks down at his poorly bandaged arm and shakes his head. "The farm's not what I thought it was though. The stories never talked about being branded."

I scoff. "What did you think it was like?"

He pauses, considering for a moment. "Honorable . . . I guess. In school, at home, we were always taught that it was this great thing to work at the national farm. Peasants have a way to earn rings and have a part in feeding people."

I twist my body to throw a handful of barley stalks onto a pile. Each move stretches my cuts farther open.

"It's not honorable," I say flatly. "It's just a way to make some rings."

I never thought much about how other people in Elmyra lived. My brother, Tuor, has told me about the people he's seen up north in the capital, where he's stationed. They're all wealthy up there. Most of them work for Warwick. They eat our food. I look down at my hands caked in dark, sticky soil. *This* is all I've known.

Mac staggers past our row. I whisper to Lawrence to work faster and he does while still keeping his branded arm close to his body. The rest of the day hardly a word passes between Lawrence and me. He's quiet and focused. Both of us work as if we hadn't been impaired: him with his brand and me with my whipping wounds.

Soon laboring hours come to an end. Late afternoon settles across the farm. I show Lawrence how to get paid. I explain to him that each stack of barley we produced gets recorded and we get paid on current value. Of course, for today, our production has been combined and our pay will be split.

I wipe the dirty sweat from my brow and dry my hands on my even dirtier dress. I'm herded, with Lawrence, into the mob of workers, all heading to the same place. Guards with canes corral us like cattle. When it's my turn, I show my scar to Supervisor Benedek in the booth.

"Name."

"Crim, Camilla." I sigh.

He flips through his large leather-bound book and makes a mark next to my name. He pulls six small rings from a brown bag and places them in my hand.

"More than your normal, Miss Crim. Next."

I'm pushed out of the line by one the guards and sent on my way. The supervisor is right, I think as I roll the smooth rings around in my hand. I earned more than I usually do. Glancing behind me, I watch as Lawrence accepts his pay all while cradling his branded arm like a baby. I feel a twinge of guilt.

"Wait up!" Lawrence calls as he jogs toward me.

I watch him carefully, a goofy smile still on his face despite his pain. I can't figure out Lawrence's place in this world. Perhaps I should have asked. In truth, I hardly care. I have my own work and my own life to worry about. He received enough training today, I think. He'll be fine on his own and then we won't have to work together anymore.

I try to stick myself in the flow of people leaving the farm. I pass through the large iron gate and step onto the road that leads to town. Reaper's Way is what it's called, named many years ago when the farm first opened. Everyday the farm workers walked this path to the farm to harvest the crop. People started calling us the reapers and eventually this road received its name. I look behind me, confident I've lost Lawrence in the crowd. Then I feel a warm hand on my shoulder. My body tenses as I spin around, flinging off his touch.

"I'm so sorry," Lawrence says quickly. He runs a shaky hand through his hair. "I forgot about your back."

I pull my arms across my chest.

"I-it's okay." Even though it wasn't the cuts on my back that initiated that response.

"Thank you for helping me today."

I bristle slightly at his kindness. "It's nothing. Try not to be late, or you'll be whipped next time." I keep pace with the crowd.

Lawrence jogs up next to me and says, "Hey, Camilla." I'm forced to pause on the road.

"Yeah?"

"Take this."

Lawrence's smooth hand slips a piece of parchment into my palm. Instinctively, I clasp my fingers around it. He smiles at me, places a finger to his lips, then jumps into the flow of people. I watch him for a moment as he seems to wash away down the street.

My body feels oddly immobile. I fight the urge to look at the parchment that moment. Half uncurling my hand, I peek at the note, then decide I can't wait. Breaking from the main road, I drift into the trees that surround the farm until I'm far enough away that I feel safe. My hands are shaking, but I don't really know why, the unknown, I suppose. I unfold the paper as soon as I'm out of eyesight from any other departing workers.

Scrawled across the page are the words:

Camilla,

I'm in serious danger. I need your help. Meet me at the church on Twenty-First tonight.

Tell no one.

Mind the key.

CHAPTER THREE

THE TIPS OF my fingers tingle as I hold the note. I fold it quickly into a crumpled ball and shove it into my jacket pocket. Jogging to the road, I merge back into the crowd of bodies.

Mind the key. The phrase is not new to me, but I haven't heard it in many years. There's only one person who understands what those words mean to me. So I have no doubt whose hand wrote the cryptic message: Tuor. It has to be from my brother, Tuor.

Another worker bumps into me as I walk the tree-lined road that leads into town. She looks at me oddly, and I get the feeling that *I* may have bumped into her. I don't apologize but push past her and break into a brisk walk.

Mind the key. I repeat the phrase in my head over and over. It was a saying only between my brother and me. We started using it as children when we played with a small wooden chest that our mother left at our house before she abandoned us. There was nothing special about the box except that it had a brass lock on it, which Tuor and I loved because we could hide things that we didn't want our father to find.

We kept the key to the chest on a piece of twine that one of us would wear around our necks at all times. Tuor would always say to me, "Mind the key." It was his way of saying be careful or watch out. Tuor was paranoid even then about our father. Actually, he was paranoid about *everything*. Sometimes when we were children, we'd buy food from a vendor in Rande Square and Tuor would end up spitting out the food because he'd say he didn't trust the man that sold it to us.

Reaper's Way opens into the village of Rande. I rush past what's left of the thinning crowd. This note means Tuor is in town, and as much as I want to run and throw my arms around him, Tuor being in town is bad, very bad.

Rande Square is a collection of eager vendors desperate to sell food to workers returning from the farm. A posting tree sits in the very center of town along with a scattering of Warwick soldiers. The streets are lined with rows of uniform houses shaped like apple crates with squat chimneys on top. These are Warwick-owned homes, built to house all the farm workers. The workers pay a tariff to live in one of these homes and they're promised a sturdy roof and a fire to keep them warm. By the end of the day, most only make enough rings to pay their rent and buy some food. Some of these people have been living day to day like that for a decade.

The smell of yeast bread and boiled eggs reaches my nose. I'd normally stop to eat something, but instead I hang a left at the posting tree. Getting to Tuor is more important than anything else right now.

Soon the sound of heavy footsteps falls away and I'm left alone in a rarely visited part of Rande. I hear the sound of something tinkling in the distance. The dirt road broadens even farther. Nestled neatly among the trees are a couple of tall stone-built mansions. The grass and flowers are well kept, and one house has a white wooden fence encircling it. One building has a curved balcony with a Warwick flag draped reverently over the railing. The people who live here work for Governor Leo. They're foremen or advisors or treasurers or some other government job that I don't understand. I stare at the red W as the wind ripples its fabric.

My eyes widen at the sight. I never walk down this street. I'm fairly certain I'm not welcome here. I pick up my pace as I pass two Warwick soldiers patrolling the street. Instinctively, I put my hand on the crumpled-up parchment in my pocket. They both look my way. One soldier raises an eyebrow at me, but I keep moving.

The stately homes dissipate, and the street begins to die out. Trees and vegetation take over the road. Before long it's nothing more than an overgrown trail. The streets and alleys become so vacant that there are no longer signs. I start counting the street numbers in my head: nineteen, twenty, twenty-one.

I pull out the parchment and look at it again, the church on Twenty-First. I make a sharp turn onto what should be Twenty-First Street. It's a dead end marked by an overgrowth of forest and a stone structure that was once a church. The church is circular like a hut. It looks vacant, something that's been abandoned for years. Long tufts of grass peek out of every crack and crevice.

My stomach twists into nervous flutters. Why here? Why does Tuor want to meet *here*? I start to doubt myself. Maybe I shouldn't go in. Maybe Lawrence handing me this note is a trick of some sort. It's been almost a year since I've even seen Tuor. He joined the Warwick Militia when he was sixteen years old and has been stationed in our capital city ever since, only given leave once a year. What could have brought him back?

I take my first step to conquer the yards standing between me and the church. The street is quiet. I glance around to see if anyone is close by. I place my hand on the knob. It has a thumb-sized lever on the top that I push down to unhook the latch. The door opens noiselessly.

Candles burn all along the inside of the curved wall. My eyes dart back and forth, searching for the worst. But all I see is a man sitting in the front row of wooden pews. His head is bowed as if he's praying. The dim light flickers, creating deep shadows on everything in the room. I release the door and it closes behind me with a gentle *click*. The man's head pops up and spins around to look at me. My body jolts in response.

"Camilla! I knew you'd come. Thank you, thank you." Tuor staggers down the center aisle. His tall bony frame embraces me with relief. "The note, you understood."

I wrap my arms tightly around his thin waist. I'd forgotten how much I missed my brother. "Of course, the wooden chest that mother left behind."

"You came alone, right? Did anyone follow you here?"

Tuor brushes past me and pulls a dirty curtain aside to look out the window. His wild eyes scour the vacant road. I breathe deeply. He's in one of his moods.

"I don't think so," I say. "Who would have followed me?"

"Shhh!" Tuor says quickly. His whole body tightens like a soldier. "Do you hear the horses?"

I listen hard, but there's no sound in the hollow air of the abandoned church.

"There are no horses, Tuor."

"Are you sure?" He turns back to me, his face drawn and desperate.

"Look for yourself."

Another quick look out the window and Tuor seems somewhat confident there isn't a cavalry of horses coming for us. He turns from the window and looks into my eyes. His dark curly hair is an untamed mess.

He sighs. "I'm so happy you're here finally." Tuor wipes a film of sweat from his forehead, then squeezes me into another hug. When we pull apart, I stare at his Warwick uniform, a black leather vest with a W on the left of his chest. It's the same symbol that's burned into my arm. Tuor grabs my face and squeezes it in the funny way he used to when we were kids. "I've missed you, little sister." He kisses me on the cheek.

"I missed you too," I say, and I start to wonder how I've gone about my days without him here. I can't blame Tuor for joining the Warwick Militia. If he hadn't, he'd be working at the farm like me. Tuor's smile dissolves. He backs away from me, hanging his head as if he's praying again. "Tuor, why are you . . . *here*? Why aren't you in LilyAye?"

"He's after me, Camilla."

"Who?"

"Three days I've been here, three, waiting for the right time to contact you." Tuor's feet take three fevered steps up the aisle, then turn and take the same three steps back toward me. "I didn't know who I could trust, but when we found this place and it seemed safe."

"Is someone else here?"

I had not missed the part where he said *we*. Tuor doesn't have friends. I've always been the only person he could truly depend on. And he has always been mine.

"I'm in hiding." Tuor lets his voice drop.

He paces the aisle and mumbles to himself. Ringing his hands together, he brings them up to his head and pulls tightly on his curls.

"Who are you hiding from?"

"Eight, nine, ten, eleven. One is missing."

"What's missing?"

"Look at the candles." I glance at the rounded walls. There are eleven candles sitting in their holders, lighting the room. "There should be twelve, see? Do you see?" Tuor takes a step toward me. "There are six holders on either side from the door to the pulpit, but there are only eleven candles. One is missing! Eleven, ten, nine, eight . . . " Tuor returns to his pacing.

"Who are you hiding from?" I ask again, keeping my voice steady.

"I escaped my prison cell in LilyAye, and then he hunted me like an animal. I think the whole army might be after me."

"The Warwick Militia? Why would they be after you?"

I try to stay calm. I'm certain the only thing really at stake here is Tuor leaving his post in LilyAye, not . . . whatever it is he's hiding from. My mind starts racing with ways they may punish Tuor for leaving LilyAye: time in the dungeons or maybe a beating.

"Tuor," I say firmly. He stops his pacing. "*Who* is after you?"

"Who?" Tuor looks down at me with glassy eyes. "Who?"

He returns to his pacing. I sigh, realizing this is all the information I'll be able to get from him right now.

"We need to get you back to your captain." I place a hand on Tuor's shoulder, an attempt to steady him. "I'll have to arrange for someone to . . . "

"No!" Tuor's eyes blaze with horror. "No, Camilla!"

"You have to go back."

"You don't understand." Tuor grasps me with both of his hands. "He's the one who's after me. I think Captain Thatius is here in Bear Gap looking for me."

"Why?" I ask, trying with all of my mental muscle to get the truth out of him.

Tuor's body clams up and he's suddenly silent.

"Tell me," I scold.

Tuor's bottom lip quivers. "I'm accused of murder."

My head twitches at his statement. I don't believe him, obviously, but this is more absurd than I'm used to with Tuor. Perhaps the Warwick Militia is not as good for Tuor as I used to think. I exhale slowly and place a calming hand on his arm. Tuor shrugs it off.

"I'm speaking truth," he says, his voice cracking. "One night they barged into my dormitory and arrested me. They locked me away, Camilla. When I escaped LilyAye, all I wanted to do was come home and see you. I thought, if I made it to Bear Gap, then this would all go away." He covers his face in anguish and turns toward the front of the church.

I need to get him back to LilyAye. The longer he's gone the worse his punishment when he finally makes it back. But Tuor is in bad shape, and right now, there's no way he'll go himself. Bear Gap is riddled with Warwick soldiers. Once word is out that Tuor Crim has fled his post and may be hiding in his home territory, it'll be impossible for me to protect him. I start to feel a little frantic myself as if Tuor's ill humor is passing to me.

"What will I do?" he asks.

Tuor walks the rest of the way down the center aisle, then plops himself in the front pew. I follow, sliding in next to him as he brings his hands over his face.

"You could come home with me for tonight," I say, my attempt at a terrible idea.

"No." Tuor rips his hands from his face as his whole body goes rigid. "I don't want to be anywhere near him."

He's referring to our father.

"Then you'll just have to stay here until I can figure this out."

"You won't stay with me?"

"I can't."

"You have to. I can't stay here another night by myself," Tuor says, bringing his fingernails to his mouth.

"If I don't go home tonight, father will ask where I was. What would I say then?"

Tuor has nothing to say to that because he knows that as aloof as our father can be, gone for days on drinking binges, our father also likes to control what's rightfully his: me. If I'm home late tonight and Father is there, I'll be hit with a barrage of questions and likely the back of his hand.

"Just stay here tonight." I stand from the pew and I can already feel Tuor's temper rising again. "Don't go anywhere and I'll be back as soon as I can tomorrow. Hopefully, I'll have enough rings to get you a room at Lindon Place."

"You'll come back the first chance you get?" Tuor asks.

"I will. It'll be okay."

I pull Tuor into a hug even though I can sense his disdain over me leaving. I try to make a swift exit to the door as if I'm a mother leaving her child in the care of someone else for the first time. I need to get out before Tuor has too much time to think about what's going on.

"Do you have food?" I ask. Tuor is close on my heels as I walk the center aisle.

"Yes."

"Good." I place my hand on the door knob and open it just a crack.

"Lawrence got me enough the first day we were here."

I pause, turning around to look at him.

"Tuor." I hesitate. "How did you manage to get that note to me?"

"I sent Lawrence to find you."

I release the door and let it ease shut.

"How do you know this man Lawrence?"

"We were stationed together in LilyAye. He got me out, Camilla. He got me out and fled with me to Bear Gap."

"But why?" I shift hard on my right foot. "Why would he risk his life like that?"

Tuor furrows his brows in confusion. "Because... because he's my friend... I think."

CHAPTER FOUR

THE SUN SLOWLY starts to sink behind the trees as I pass through Rande Square. This time I go straight through town and enter the woods on the other side. I hate leaving Tuor alone. He just doesn't do well by himself, which is probably why he needed Lawrence's help to get to Bear Gap. Who is Lawrence? A best friend to my brother? Can't be. A friend would never put Tuor in this position with the Warwick Militia. Tuor may be teetering on the edge of treason, a crime he could die for.

The ground quickly turns into a steep drop-off as I descend deeper into the trees. My legs are used to this, though, and I take the decline with ease. My feet shuffle the blanket of leaves covering the forest floor. A fresh wave of cool, damp air prickles my arms. Soon the silhouette of a little village comes into view. Tiny shack-like homes speckle the ravine where a river flows and all other water gathers to make a cesspool of creatures and peasants. Welcome to the swamps, home to the poorest in Bear Gap, including me.

It's four steps up to my front door. I can see a flicker of light through the wood slats. I open the door cautiously, never quite sure what I'll see behind it. The room reeks of dank earth. It's a smell I hardly notice anymore since I've lived here my whole life.

Malcolm Crim lies passed out on the floor. I feel a constriction in my throat when I look at him. His lumpy body shifts so that his bulbous nose is facing me.

"Camilla . . . " he moans.

"Yes, Father?" My body tenses. I wait for a response. Nothing.

Our home is little more than one room with two straw mattresses, a tiny table with chairs, and a stove. I reach for the candle on the table. Gingerly, I sidestep Malcolm, who's lying with his face pressed against the wooden floor. I relax when I'm safe on the other side of the room. I place the candle on the floor and slink onto my bed.

An empty liquor bottle slips from Malcolm's grip as the muscles in his fingers relax. He rolls over so that he's facing me. I sit motionless. My father's eyes slowly open. He looks at me, then pulls himself onto his hands and knees until he finally rises to his feet. Our eyes connect.

He takes a heavy step toward me, holding out a hand in front of my face. I reach into my pocket and I pull out the six rings, dropping them with a light tinkling sound into his hand.

"Supper?" he asks, his voice deep and hoarse.

"I missed the street vendors today. They closed before I could get out of work." It's a small lie, but Malcolm won't know the truth.

He shuffles the rings with his finger, counting my day's pay. "You got nothin' for me to eat?"

"No." I hang my head. I knew I should have stopped first, but I was too distracted by Tuor.

Letting out a long sigh, Malcolm drops his hands to his side, cocks his head, and stares at me.

"What did I tell you about gettin' out of there on time?"

"Sometimes the checkout line is long and . . . "

"What . . . did I tell you?" Malcolm leans in closer and I jolt slightly.

"I'm sorry."

Malcolm sighs again. "It's *your* fault when we don't eat."

"I know." I nod.

"Here." Malcolm tosses me a ring from the pile I just gave him. It bounces on the wood floor and I scramble to grab it. He turns around so that his thick broad back faces me. Crossing the room, Malcolm reaches for the door, the remaining five rings now in his pocket.

"Thank you," I say, my voice small and weak.

"You'll do better tomorrow."

I nod in agreement even though he can't see me. Malcolm *is* right. I wasn't paying attention and now we'll both be hungry tonight. I feel bad about that, but he didn't hit me this time, which means I must have done okay.

Malcolm's heavy steps pass over the threshold and lumber to the ground. He'll be out all night spending those rings in places I don't want to think about.

Unhooking the buttons on my jacket, I toss it on the floor next to my bed. Then I add my boots to the pile. Brushing my hair to the side, I carefully peel away my dress from my fresh cuts. The dried blood tugs on my wounds until I get my dress all the way off. My body is spent and exhausted. I manage to rinse some of the blood away with water from the basin before pulling on a new dress. I sit cross-legged on my bed. Gently, I lean against the wall and close my eyes. I can feel a thousand stings on my back. Mind the key, I say to myself. Nostalgia erupts within me from just those three words.

My eyes pop open and I begin rummaging through my stuff. I toss my jacket aside, move my pillow out of the way, and dig out a dress that somehow got shoved under my mattress. A stale liquor bottle rolls out from under the pile of junk. I grab it and set it upright. I stop. Where could the box be? Then I remember our hiding spot.

I pull myself to my feet and run outside. Darkness is heavy in the swamps. I crouch down under the house, which is propped up on stilts to keep it from floating away when the river floods. It sits up from the ground about half my height. As I bend over I feel my cuts slowly opening again. This space seemed so much bigger when I was a child, I think to myself.

Using my hands, I feel along the edge of the house. There's a small shelf here, perfect for storing secret things. Then I find it. Tucked away under the house for who knows how many years, the wooden chest Tuor's note was talking about. The key is still stuck in the lock.

I grab it and run back inside, taking a seat on my straw mattress. I hold it with both hands and stare at the splintered wood. It's smaller than I remember, only about the length of a corn cob. It's been years since I opened this box. I can't even remember what's in it.

The candle flickers eerie circles on the ceiling. I place my thumb on the rusty key and turn it with a firm push. The lock clicks open. My heart jolts as I slowly open the lid.

Nothing. I laugh audibly. The only thing inside is a doll made out of sticks and twine, a thimble, and one ring. What did I think would be inside? Maybe an answer to what I should do with Tuor. Maybe just an idea on how to get him out of this mess. Maybe I thought remembering our past would give me insight on how to deal with him now. It doesn't.

I pocket the ring from the box before closing the lid and setting it aside. Rolling onto my side, I blow out the candle and lie in darkness. Only a tiny stream of moonlight reaches past the trees and through the cracks in the ceiling.

My body lies sprawled across the narrow bed so that my feet and arm extend onto the floor. I try to focus on Tuor. I'll have to convince him to go back to LilyAye, but that won't be easy. I need to change his mind before things get too bad. More urgently, I need to find a place for him to stay so that he's not close to any Warwick soldiers or our father. I drift off to sleep before any good ideas come to me.

Dawn arrives in what seems like a moment. Malcolm's already home when I sit up in bed. He sits lazily on the wooden chair, a leg propped up on the table as flakes of dried mud sprinkle off his boot. One hand scratches at the back of his neck while the other holds a bowl of something.

"Have some," he says stretching out his arm to offer me the bowl.

I stand, my bare feet touching the cool floor. "I shouldn't. I'll be late."

Malcolm retracts his arm and takes a big spoonful in his mouth. He digs into his pocket and flicks me another ring.

"Then take that. You can get something on your way."

I smile gratefully. It's been nearly a day since I've eaten. Malcolm's eyes follow me as I pull on my boots and don my jacket before slipping out the front door. The grass near the swamps is cool and plush. I sink ever so slightly as my feet hit the ground. A few yards away is another house like ours, a wooden cabin propped up on stilts. My neighbor, a portly woman with brown hair, is already seated on her three-legged stool. She stares across to the hundreds of other identical homes just like ours nestled among the boggy earth. She nods at me and I nod back. She'll sit there all day.

Without a backward glance, I jog through the low brush until all that surrounds me is trees. My breath evens, and I drink in the familiar smell of pine. It's only a twenty-minute walk into town and then another five to get to the farm. Bursting through the tree line into Rande Square, I bustle past some villagers. I stop to buy two boiled eggs and a yellow apple from a street vendor before crossing the center of town and turning onto Reaper's Way. I'm anxious to get to the farm this morning so I can talk to Mirabelle. She's the only person I can imagine that could help with Tuor.

I funnel into the dusty road that leads up to the big iron gate and start searching for Mirabelle. I didn't see her yesterday, probably because I got stuck helping Lawrence. A sigh escapes my mouth just at the thought of him. I drift off the road and face the workers as they enter the farm so that I can hopefully spot Mirabelle.

I consider what I'll do if I see Lawrence. If I see him, I'll approach him. I'll ask him why he took my brother out of LilyAye and if he realizes how dire that decision may have been for him. I've thought of a couple of other things I'll say to Lawrence when I realize most of the workers have already passed through the gate. I'll be late if I don't go now. That's two days I haven't seen Mirabelle at work. I start to feel a terrible sinking feeling in my stomach when I realize I may not have anyone to help me.

CHAPTER FIVE

I'M ASSIGNED TO work with Mac again today. Fortunately, he pays me no attention. At checkout I'm pushed into a thick line of workers, all of us waiting for our pay. I search in front of and behind me for Lawrence. I look for his dark, silky hair and his finely stitched clothes. But he's not here.

"Name."

"Crim, Camilla." I hold out my wrist.

I pocket five rings and hope I have enough to feed Malcolm, Tuor, and myself without Malcolm growing suspicious.

"Governor's giving a speech today." A guard catches me by the arm as I wander toward the exit.

He's right. With everything that's been going on with Tuor, I'd forgotten about Governor Leo's speech. He makes one every few weeks to encourage his people. But today is not a good day. I'd hoped to leave right away to see Tuor.

I circle back toward the manor, where the crowd is gathering. At the back of the governor's house is a balcony that overlooks the field. The terrace is made of white marble and conveniently located above the prison stocks. I always imagine that Governor Leo enjoys stepping out and peering down at those of us laboring over his fields.

A mass of people huddle around me as we wait for the governor to appear. The man next to me is sifting rings through his fingers. In front of me an elderly woman rubs her sore shoulder. I turn around. A boy stands, wearing a face so blank I wonder if he's forgotten where he is.

Governor Leo Harras steps onto the balcony, his chest swollen. He's greeted by mingled applause as he takes several imposing steps toward us. I clap along, hardly even aware that I'm moving my hands. The governor takes a moment to survey his land and his people. Gracefully, he places his hands on the wide railing encompassing the balcony. He spreads his fingers and lifts his chin upward, closing his eyes just for a moment.

"Thank you," Governor Leo says, pausing to let the words echo. "Thank *you*. It's because of each of you that we are able to deliver shiploads of food to many cities in Elmyra." Governor Leo pauses, allowing people to clap. "We are now supplying food to five out of the six territories in Elmyra! And that's all because of you, and your hard work." This time Governor Leo steps back and claps to congratulate us. "We're adding new workers to this farm every day, and people are now flooding into Bear Gap for a chance to work and live in the fastest growing territory in our country." We clap again.

"Let us not stop there and become complacent. We shall never forget the terror we lived through twelve years ago. When our Supreme Ruler, Quinten Warwick, came to power, he started what I believe to be the most important campaign of his reign. People all over Elmyra were dying because of a disease that was spreading through our . . . seed."

My mind begins to wander. I've heard this story hundreds of times. I was only five years old when Quinten Warwick came to power. I don't even remember what life was like before the seed crisis, but it's still profoundly important that I'm reminded of it over and over.

"Our Supreme Ruler put all of his best scientists in LilyAye on the task of figuring out what we could do to stop the disease and protect our people. Now, after much research and a lot of hard work, we have been using a new kind of seed, and the presence of that disease barely exists anymore. This is why we need to keep working until everyone is eating from our farm. This territory is special, and each one of you has been carefully chosen to save the lives of many."

The onlooking guards glare until the crowd erupts in applause. I turn to leave, trying to stay ahead of the mass of people.

***

I need to get to Tuor. Being alone in that church is sure to drive him mad. It sets me on edge just to think about the state he'll be in when I finally get there. I quicken my pace, bursting through the crowd into Rande Square. I'm about to veer left toward the church when a hand grabs my arm and yanks me under the shade of the posting tree.

"Camilla."

"Lawrence?"

His hair, although still sleek in texture, is a tousled mess over his ears and forehead.

"Did you go to the church yet?" he whispers. Lawrence's forearm hangs limply from his body. He still wears the linen wrappings I used to cover his brand.

"What are you talking about?" I ask through gritted teeth. Around us people bustle about, but no one seems to be paying us any attention.

"The church. Have you been there yet?" Lawrence leans in closer. "Did you see your brother?"

"Yes. I saw him." I rip my arm out of Lawrence's grasp.

"Good," he says. "Look, I'm sorry I had to leave you yesterday. It's just—"

"Who are you anyway?" Unlike him my voice cracks as my volume rises.

"I-I'm Lawrence."

"No, I mean who *are* you?"

I stare at him as if I'm digging for a long-forgotten secret. Lawrence steps a pace away from me and moves so his back is almost against the posting tree. Behind him is a littering of messages and announcements fixed to the tree by the Warwick government. I keep my gaze locked as he struggles for words. A thin sheen of sweat glistens on his forehead. I'm not sure if it's from my inquisition or the pain he likely still has in his arm. Lawrence opens his mouth, but I speak before he does.

"How do you know my brother?" I cross my arms impatiently.

"Camilla, it's . . . "

"It's what?"

"There's a lot to tell, and I'm not sure if here is the right place." Lawrence scans the street around us as all the farm workers flood the square.

"Why did you bring my brother home? Do you realize the danger you've put him in?"

"He was in danger in LilyAye."

I throw my hands down. What kind of person did Tuor get himself mixed up with?

"Camilla, I promise I'm helping your brother."

Lawrence purses his lips, runs his fingers through his hair and shifts so that my gaze catches a large piece of parchment posted on the board behind him. I squint, blinking my eyes as I step forward to push Lawrence out of the way. My mind tumbles as it tries to catch up with what I'm seeing. The words at the top of the parchment say *In Pursuit* and in the center is a crude drawing of . . . Tuor.

I rip the poster from the iron nail that's holding it to the tree. My hands grip the parchment tightly, wrinkling the edges. The bottom reads: *The Warwick Militia is currently in pursuit of Tuor Crim, believed to be in this territory. He's suspected of several crimes, including the killing of a Warwick Militia member. If seen, keep distance and inform nearest Warwick soldier. One hundred rings granted as reward to the finder.*

"What?" I breathe.

Tuor was telling the truth? It feels like the world around me is spinning. He said they accused him of murder . . . He said they were hunting him down . . . I suddenly feel a rush of guilt and I have the sensation that I could vomit.

Tuor has spoken fanciful stories his whole life. Once, he thought that Mirabelle poisoned our chicken stew. His story had elaborate details, like the yellow vegetable in our soup was supposedly gathered from deep in the woods and caused horrible stomach cramping if eaten. He convinced me to dump out the stew. It turned out the yellow vegetable was corn kernels. How could I possibly know he was telling the truth this time?

"What's wrong?" Lawrence asks. He turns to look at the poster, but I crunch it closed before he gets a look.

"Nothing."

I stumble into the street, the poster still in my hand. Lawrence steps toward me. "I can help."

"Stay away from my brother."

I'm firm, holding Lawrence's gaze so he knows I'm serious.

"Camilla, I just want to help your brother. In LilyAye he and I were friends. And . . . "

"Tuor has never needed anyone in this world except for me." My fingers curl tighter around the poster. "And that hasn't changed."

I walk away before Lawrence has a chance to say one more thing. After that encounter my mood is off and I struggle to get my thoughts straight again. I feel a sharp stinging on my back and realize my cuts have reopened. Warm blood oozes down the small of my back.

Returning to the church now is no longer an option. It's too risky in the daylight. Every Warwick soldier in this territory is looking for Tuor. If they found out that I knew where he was and didn't turn him in, I'd be arrested too, and then who would help him?

My feet take me to the other edge of Rande. I brush past bodies shrouded in gray and brown tones and barely notice them. What am I going to do with Tuor when I do see him? I'll just have to convince him to come forward and give his side of the story. If Tuor is found hiding out, they'll think he's guilty. And with accusations like this, sometimes there isn't even a trial.

He could be executed.

The road dies as it turns into a field of waist-high grass overgrown with brambles. I push on, the burrs catching on the bottom of my dress. There is only one place I can go now, only one person I can trust to help me.

CHAPTER SIX

THE NARROW DIRT path intersects with another road. I cross it and continue into the forest on the other side. A cobblestone path is laid among some of the oldest trees in the territory. Mirabelle's house looks like a castle compared to the shack that I grew up in. The house was passed down to her from her father, who many years ago was quite wealthy. Mirabelle is no doubt wealthier than me, but the only people in this territory now that have a lot of rings are those working for the Warwick government, which she most certainly doesn't do.

Vines snake across the red brick facade of Mirabelle's great house. A tower winds up toward the trees, marking the topmost point of the house. The outer brick has worn and crumbled to create a porous-looking wall. I take the path to the front door and walk inside without knocking.

"Mirabelle." My voice reverberates through the high ceiling. "Mirabelle!"

Dust catches in my throat. Sun rays pierce the tall windows, lighting a cloud of particles. I walk to the center of the room and yell up to the exposed floors that lead all the way to the building's roof. Books cover every wall and shelf in Mirabelle's house. They form mountains of written works with peaks that extend almost as high as the ceiling.

"Mirabelle!"

Every layer of the house can be seen from my vantage point. Balconies and landings scatter the upper floors, revealing shelves and shelves of books that Mirabelle's father collected for decades.

"Camilla dear." A soft voice floats to my ears. Mirabelle peeks over one of the railings. "I'll be right down," she says, her body disappearing again.

I pace the soot-covered floor, removing my jacket and tossing it on a nearby chair. She'll be down soon, I tell myself. I'm gripping Tuor's poster so firmly, it feels like my hand might meld into the parchment.

"How are you, darling?" Mirabelle crosses the lobby to meet me. Her light hair creates a wispy wreath around her face.

"We need to talk."

With determined steps, I march across the floor toward Mirabelle. She pulls me into a hug, as is our custom.

"Now," I say, my mouth close to her ear. My voice is muffled by her chubby embrace. "It's about Tuor."

Mirabelle pulls back and looks me in the face. "All right," she says, her cheerful spirit falling slightly. "How about some tea?"

Mirabelle leads me through a door that takes us into a back room and then down a set of stone steps into her basement kitchen. There's a rustic wooden table in the middle of the room that can easily seat twelve people. A fire whirs quietly behind the cast iron door of Mirabelle's stove.

"Take a seat, dear," Mirabelle instructs.

I feel too jittery to sit down, but Mirabelle gives me a warning gaze that I feel I must obey. So I plop down on the long wooden bench, tossing the poster onto the table, and drop my chin into my hand. A shriek escapes Mirabelle's lips. I turn around quickly. She's staring at my back.

"What?" I ask.

Mirabelle takes a step closer. She reaches her hand out toward me.

"Were you whipped today?"

"Oh." I turn back to the table. "Yesterday, yeah."

"Why didn't you tell me?" Mirabelle rushes back to the corner of the kitchen where the water basin sits. She picks up the wide porcelain bowl and carries it and a few kitchen rags over to the table, placing them in front of me. "I think I have some ointment I can use," she mumbles, bending down to look in a basket on the floor. I watch as she holds the small of her back where her apron is tied into a sloppy bow.

"Why weren't you at the farm today?"

"It's not down there . . . " She reaches up to a high shelf, pulling down a glass tincture filled with dark brown liquid. "There we go."

She sets the tincture of ointment on the table next to me.

"Mirabelle?" I cock my head to look at her. "Why weren't you there today?"

"Oh, it's my back," she says, pushing aside my hair to reveal what I can only guess is my blood-soaked dress. "Great Warwick, Camilla! Why didn't you come to me yesterday?"

Without asking, she unbuttons the top clasp on my dress and pulls the straps off my shoulders. Quickly, I hold the fabric to my chest to keep it from falling down.

"They're going to kick you out, Mirabelle," I say. "You can't keep missing work."

"Oh, hog tail!"

From the corner of my eye, I see her fling a hand at me, laughing off my remark. She dunks one of the rags in the water basin. My eyes flicker to the scar on Mirabelle's arm. It's the same symbol that resides on my own forearm. Nearly every able-bodied person in Bear Gap works at the farm, but the rules are strict. If you get hurt or too old to work, they'll kick you out and make it so you can never return.

I have seen the banning for myself. Once someone is kicked off the farm permanently, if they don't have anyone to look after them, they'll either be thrown in the dungeons because they have to steal food, or they'll simply die. No work means no rings, which means nowhere to live and nothing to eat. The farm is all I have. Sometimes I shudder when I think about what would happen to me if I got banished.

"Don't you worry about me, dear. Now what's that on the table?"

Mirabelle's gaze falls to the rolled up parchment. She runs the soaking rag down my back. I flinch as fresh stings pierce my skin.

"Have you been in town today?"

"Not today."

I unroll the poster flat on the table. Mirabelle's eyes grow big as she leans over my shoulder and stares at the sketched drawing of my brother.

"This was posted in town today."

Mirabelle stops nursing my back. She leans in even closer to get a better look at the image. Her lips move silently as she reads the notice.

"I don't understand . . . " Mirabelle's voice quivers.

"Tuor is being accused of murder. They think he killed someone and now they're looking for him."

"Oh, dear . . . "

I feel the beat of my heart trip and tumble. Mirabelle's face is one of horror, and that leaves me feeling worse. She's supposed to know what to do about this. She's supposed to be able to fix it and make everything all right.

"Perhaps he's been mistaken for someone else?"

"I've considered that," I say, tilting my head to look at her straight on. "What if there's someone else who looks just like Tuor who did this? But how do we prove it wasn't him? Tuor couldn't hurt anyone. That's why he makes arrows and cleans swords for the militia. It doesn't make sense."

Mirabelle pushes my head forward and begins dabbing my cuts with the dry rag.

"It is strange that they're putting up posters in Rande. LilyAye is a two-day journey from here. Do they think Tuor will come back home?"

I hold my lips together and sigh. Mirabelle reaches for the tincture of ointment. She wets the corner of her rag and blots the acrid-smelling liquid onto my open wounds. She stops halfway down my back. Her hand slowly lowers to the table.

"Is Tuor here?" she whispers.

I nod as if saying the words aloud can be heard by a soldier. Mirabelle's face morphs from confusion to understanding. She takes a step back to think. Pausing, she brings her hand to her mouth and turns to face the wall where a crate of potatoes sits. She rubs her hands together to warm them, then turns around to face me again. It's like she knows something, a secret, that I'm not aware of.

"What should we do?" I ask.

"I'm very concerned for you and Tuor."

"Me? Why?"

"The Warwick Militia has their eye on Tuor, and I'm afraid it might get very dangerous for the two of you."

I pull my straps back over my shoulders and reach around to button the clasp of my dress.

"Not if I get him to turn himself in," I say, my voice firm. "With the farm in Bear Gap, this place is crawling with soldiers. He's going to get caught eventually, and it would be better if he came forward."

"Camilla, I don't think Tuor turning himself in is a good idea." Mirabelle bristles like a hen ruffling her feathers. "If he's arrested, they'll put him through a trial. I can't imagine Tuor withstanding a trial. He could never take all the questions. I'm afraid the poor boy would fall apart."

"What other choice do I have?"

Mirabelle touches the tips of her fingers to her forehead. "Heavens child, I can't believe I'm saying this, but I think you should leave Bear Gap."

"What?" I spin around on the bench, flinging my legs onto the other side. This is the solution that Mirabelle has come up with? "That's impossible. We won't make it past the village gate. They'll just arrest me too."

Mirabelle takes a panicked step closer to me. "You must try. I have seen too often what happens to people that are arrested by those men."

"I don't have a horse or any rings to take with us!" My hands ball into fists.

"I know you're scared," Mirabelle says. She talks as if she's taming a wild horse. "I just don't think we should leave this in the governor's hands."

A moment passes as Mirabelle takes my hands. I consider her, then say, "You think he might have done it, don't you?"

Mirabelle holds her lips tightly together. Tuor and Mirabelle are not as close as they once were. After our mother left us, Mirabelle would keep an eye on Tuor and me while Malcolm looked for work. But when Tuor joined the Warwick Militia, they grew apart, and Tuor became more suspicious— even of Mirabelle. She still cares for him, I think.

"You truly believe he could have *murdered* someone?" I practically spit the words.

Reluctantly, Mirabelle meets my gaze. "I don't know." Her voice is a whisper.

"He didn't." I break my hands free from Mirabelle's grasp. "Leaving town is terrible advice. Tuor and I would die a day after crossing the border."

"It's better than the alternative. Camilla dear, please don't willingly put your brother's fate in the governor's hands."

"Tuor didn't kill anyone."

I swipe the poster from the table. Rising to my feet, my heartbeat picks up pace, and it feels like pressure is building in my head.

"Camilla," Mirabelle says calmly. Gingerly, she takes a step closer to me. "If that's true, then why is he being accused? He must have done something."

"Because this is just a lie!" I screech.

Crumpling the parchment into a ball, I throw open the stove door and shove the poster inside. I swing the door shut as ashes form a cloud as hot and angry as my temper. Mirabelle's eyes flash and her chest rises with a deep breath. She doesn't have to say what she's thinking. I know what she's thinking; that I'm acting crazy and irrational like Tuor. But I don't care.

"Tuor did not commit the crime of which that poster speaks." I hold my teeth tightly together as I speak. "Tomorrow I'll take him to the Justice House so he can turn himself in. He's innocent, and they'll discover that he's innocent. You will see."

"Just stop and think, please. We'll come up with a better plan." Mirabelle reaches out to touch me. I push her hand away as if it were a nasty spider.

"Don't put your hand on me," I say. My jaw is set tight. The words creep out of my mouth.

"Camilla—"

"Stop. Stop! Don't touch me."

My arms fling about like they're not a part of my body. I push Mirabelle hard. She flies backward and hits the stone wall. She yelps out in pain, her hand clutching at her back. My face twitches before I dart out of the kitchen. I storm up the steps, grab my jacket, and slam the front door. Running down the cobblestone path, I push myself to get as far away from Mirabelle as possible.

***

The cold air brushes past the trees icing my temper. I trudge through the woods and down the hill toward home. I'm not going to make the same mistake I did yesterday by not checking in with Malcolm after work. I'm already pushing my luck by visiting Mirabelle.

The swamps come into view. Tiny houses dot the valley. My eyes flicker up quickly to see five Warwick soldiers on horseback scaling the hill into town. It causes me to stop. Soldiers don't like to come down here. With the feeling of Tuor's wanted poster still tingling in my hand, I start to panic.

The soldiers crest the tree line and pass into town. I bolt down the hill. I notice a commotion among my neighbors when I settle on the soft grass around my house.

Lina, my portly neighbor, calls to me with the wave of her hand. "Camilla!"

"What happened?"

Lina and her kids, the old man that lives on the other side of us, and a few other people from the area are all gathered awkwardly around my house.

"I think they were doin' a raid," Lina says. "Looking for illegal producers."

"Where? My house?"

"Yes." she screeches. I run past her. "They left," she calls after me. "They must not have found anything."

My heart beats fast. I take the steps and bust through my front door. My chest flutters as I see all my clothes flung about and my mattress flipped and thrown across the room. Everything else in the house is turned over, dumped out, or wrecked in some way.

Malcolm's lumbering footsteps scale the steps behind me. He pushes me out of the way as he stomps into the middle of the room. When he turns around, I see his face seething with anger.

"Warwick scum came lookin' for my liquor!" Malcolm's eyes follow me as I try to casually walk to my bed. "I know they didn't find none," he says, answering a question I didn't ask. "They don't expect me to be smarter than them." Malcolm picks up a chair and sets it upright. He plops down and leans back, propping his feet up on the table as if he's gloating.

"They didn't find anything, huh?" Lina stands at the threshold.

"Warwick's men got nothin' better to do than bother me," Malcolm says.

"What happened, Lina?" I take a step closer to her.

She puts her hands on her wide hips. "Well, I was sittin' outside and I see all the Warwick horses traipsing down the hill. I stood up and called to William and told him to go inside because I didn't know what was going on. A few of them soldiers went inside your house and started makin' a wild amount of ruckus. Then they came over and asked me if I'd seen your father."

I take my eyes off Lina. They only asked about Malcolm. Is it possible that this really was just an alcohol raid and has nothing to do with Tuor?

"They asked where you were too."

I spin around to look at Lina. "They did?"

Malcolm's feet fall from the table as the legs of his chair slam into the floor. "Governor thinks he's going to get to me through my daughter, does he?"

"Did they say it was an alcohol raid?" I ask.

A voice calls from outside the shack. "Mother!"

Lina shifts to look out the door. "Oh, that's my William. I must be going," she says as she waddles out the door. "Stop shoutin' at me like that."

Leery, I turn to look at Malcolm. "Do you think it was an alcohol raid?"

Malcolm pauses. "I'm no idiot."

"I didn't say you were . . . "

"What else would they be looking for?" he shouts.

I step away from my father and bend over to turn my mattress on its right side. I'm not feeling hopeful. There's no way Warwick soldiers did a random alcohol raid on the same day that they posted a wanted poster of my brother. They were looking for Tuor. I'm sure of it. Malcolm stands abruptly from the table, and my body flinches. Keep your mouth shut, I tell myself. I can't risk another cut or bruise. The marks on my back are still fresh and sore.

"Give me the rings," Malcolm says. "I've been waiting all day for you to get back."

I hesitate. His glossy eyes stare at me as he steps over and holds out his fat hand.

"How much do you need?" I ask cautiously. I need to hold on to as many rings as I can so I have enough to feed Tuor too.

"All of them."

I sigh, reaching into my pocket, feeling the five rings I earned earlier today. I pull out four of them and put them in his hand. He fingers the rings, flipping them over his palm, but keeps his hand out in front of my face.

"All of them," he says again, more sternly this time. Malcolm's body towers over me. I reach into my pocket and place the last ring into his hand. He glowers at me without even looking at his palm.

"That's all of them." I say.

Satisfied, he trudges out the front door, letting it hang open. I'm not sure how Tuor and I will eat now, but I'll figure that out later. Unfortunately, I have bigger concerns. I wait painfully for the amount of time

I think it will take Malcolm to leave the swamps before running out the door to get to Tuor before anyone else does.

CHAPTER SEVEN

TWENTY-FIRST STREET is quiet except for the
chirping of crickets. The darkness of evening falls on
Rande and a cool autumn breeze tickles the back of my
neck. The street is empty, abandoned even. At the
front door of the church, I'm about to click open the
knob when I hear a rock tumble across the road. I spin
around and scan the street. It's empty. Seeing the
poster of Tuor has put me on edge, and I feel I'm
growing paranoid like him.

Turning back to the door, I take a deep breath and
prepare to be calm inside. What I say next is pivotal to
Tuor's outcome. I must convince him to turn himself
in, and I can't risk showing my nerves in front of him.
The door swings open, and I step inside. Only a few
candles are lit on the wall tonight.

"Tuor?" I call.

My voice is shaky. The church looks empty. Have
they already found him?

"Tuor?"

I say it louder this time as I rush down the aisle, checking every pew for my brother. I hear a noise and look up to see Tuor pop out of a cupboard at the front of the sanctuary.

"Shhh!" he scolds me. "Don't scream in here!" Tuor runs down the aisle toward me. I exhale in relief. "What took you so long?"

Tuor gives me a quick hug before moving to a window and checking the surrounding street.

"No one's out there," I say, not fully convinced of that myself.

Tuor throws the curtain across the window before turning to me.

"I've been waiting for you for so long."

"It's only been a day."

Rubbing his hands together, Tuor says, "I can't stand it in here any longer."

"I know. I know. I'm sorry. I was at Mirabelle's. Listen, Tuor, we need to sit down and talk."

"Mirabelle? You didn't tell her about me, did you?"

Shuffling down a pew, Tuor meets me again in the aisle. He has brown splotches under his eyes. He hasn't been sleeping.

"Tuor."

"She works at that farm too. She could easily tell one of those guards where I am."

"Why would she do that?"

Tuor pinches the bridge of his nose while he squints his eyes shut. "I don't know," he moans. "She might do it on accident."

"Tuor, look at me." Rolling his head to stare at the ceiling, Tuor's eyes finally settle on my face. "Tomorrow," I start. "I want you to give yourself up to Governor Harras."

His eyes grow big and round. I wonder momentarily if I'm the insane one.

"Listen to me." I keep my voice firm, steady. "If you keep running from them, they'll think you're guilty."

"I'm not guilty!"

"I know. But hiding out here makes you *look* guilty. You need to come forward and tell them you're innocent."

Plus, I think to myself, they've already searched our house and they may be closing in on this place too. But I can't tell Tuor that. Tuor moans as he wraps his head in his arms.

"The longer they have to search for you, the worse it will be when they find you—and they will eventually find you."

I shudder slightly when I say those words. They will find my brother. Eventually they will catch up with him, and if they think he's guilty, it won't be good.

"They'll kill me! They will kill me, Camilla."

"They won't."

"How do you know?"

I unwrap Tuor's arms and take his head in my hands.

"I won't let them hurt you. The Warwick Militia is just and right. They will see that you're innocent. They will see that you're the sweetest, most faithful person in all of Elmyra."

A faint smile cracks on Tuor's face.

"They are lucky to have a soldier like you in their ranks. They would be fools to treat you poorly."

"What if they don't believe me?" Tuor asks, the tension starting to leave his body.

"We'll have to convince them. I'll help you decide exactly what to say."

Tuor's body straightens. "Do you promise?"

"I promise."

He smiles, and I pull him into a hug.

"I'm going to take you to the swamps tonight," I say.

"No!" he shouts, pushing me out of our hug. "I can't go there."

"I don't want you spending another night here. You'll be much safer in the swamps."

That's the one thing I'm confident of now. They've already searched our house, so it's the last place they'd expect him to be. But if I tell Tuor that Warwick soldiers have already been there looking for him, there's no way I'll convince him to go.

"No, no, no . . . " he mumbles. "There are soldiers looking for me everywhere."

"There are always lots of soldiers here, remember?" I move my hands to Tuor's shoulders, trying to keep him focused on saying yes to me. My fingers dig into his arm harder than I'd like to. But I need him to listen.

"I can't go out there," he weeps.

"We have to."

"What if *he's* there?"

He's talking about Malcolm. He's actually right about this. I can't let Tuor and Malcolm see each other.

"He's already gone for the night." My eyes burrow into Tuor's. Trust me. Trust in *me*.

Tuor walks away from me toward the front of the church. He puts his hand on the pulpit, bowing his head and rubbing his eyes with his other hand.

"We can do this," I say, moving to stand next to him.

I start rubbing his back, but the motion is more to calm me than him. Silence engulfs the little country church as Tuor agonizes over my suggestions.

"All right," he says finally.

I exhale. "You're doing the right thing. Now, let's go."

This puts Tuor into a new kind of panic. He rushes around the church, getting ready to leave. I walk to a window and push the curtain aside to look out onto the street. I can hardly see anything. Even though it's dark in here, it's darker outside. I console myself by saying that I would at least be able to see movement outside if someone was there.

We have to stay ahead of these soldiers. If I can control Tuor's surrender, then I think they'll eventually release him. My skin feels tingly, and to say I'm nervous would be an understatement. I just blew off the only real mother I ever had and made the terrifying decision to surrender my brother to Governor Leo.

Tuor throws a burlap bag over his shoulder and blows out all the candles on the wall. I nod, and we slip out the door. Outside the church, Tuor is quiet. We turn off Twenty-First Street, and voices echo in our direction. I stop suddenly. My calm demeanor melts away.

"What was that?" Tuor whispers.

"Nothing. Keep going."

When we reach Rande Square, I see a few soldiers loitering near the posting tree, right by Tuor's picture. But I tore down that poster. Then I realize, that quickly, they've mounted another one. I need to keep

Tuor away from the posting tree. If he sees his picture, he'll really lose his senses.

"This way," I say, nudging Tuor away from Rande Square.

I take him to the outskirts of town, where I go when visiting Mirabelle. But instead of going to her house, we dive into the woods to avoid the streets altogether. I take Tuor's hand, and he takes mine, squeezing it tightly. We move silently past trees that look like ghosts shrouded in dark capes. The only sound is our feet rustling the dead leaves on the forest floor. My body is tense. It's an inky black in these thick woods. We veer ever so slightly to the right, pushing farther and farther toward the swamps.

"Did you hear that?"

"Keep walking," I snap.

Tuor's hand tightens around mine and goes sweaty.

"I think we're being followed."

Tuor is talking at a normal volume now. Although I'm confident we're the only ones in these woods, I also know that voices carry well up and down these hills.

"Keep going, no one knows you're here except for me," I hiss.

An owl sings its morose warning hoots as we tumble the rest of the way into the swamps. The smell of mold and stagnant water reach my nose. Firelight flickers through the windows of this vast impoverished village. The outline of our leaning shack comes into view.

He looks around our old house in awe. I made sure to tidy up from the raid to put Tuor at ease. It probably looks exactly the same as when he last saw it.

"We'll stay here tonight," I say. "Malcolm will be out all night. And then tomorrow we'll go to see the governor and plead your case."

I cross the room, light a candle, and pour two cups of water from the pitcher on the table. Taking a sip from mine, I offer Tuor the other cup, but he declines.

"It's going to work out just fine." I keep saying this in the hopes that Tuor will actually believe it. "We'll get it all sorted out tomorrow."

He doesn't say anything but drops his burlap bag on the floor and takes a seat on my bed. I swallow a large gulp of water.

"They just arrested me one night," he says, dropping his face in his hands. "There was so much blood . . . "

I pause. My body turns stiff, and Tuor has made his point. I'm listening.

"It was a mistake, right?"

"I was so confused about what had happened. But even Captain Thatius said that I killed him." Slowly, I walk toward Tuor and take a seat next to him on my bed. "They had me in jail, set for execution and everything."

I never know when Tuor will choose to speak and open up. So I sit and listen and bid him to share as much as possible.

"You didn't know why you were arrested?"

Tuor's head, which had been facing the front door, turns suddenly and he looks me in the eyes. He doesn't answer my question.

"How did you get out of the LilyAye prison?"

Tuor shifts on the bed and turns back to face the door.

"Lawrence, the one who gave you the note." I nod in understanding. "He worked as a jailer. Got the key to my cell and snuck me out. He knew I didn't do it. We escaped LilyAye that night, but Warwick's men caught up with us just at the Bear Gap territory border. We ditched our horses and went on foot, hiding in the woods until I saw the church. After a couple of days, I sent Lawrence to find you. I told him not to come back to the church in case he was followed."

It makes sense now why Lawrence started working at the farm. He probably knew it was the safest way to find me without drawing attention. And it would have been the only place that Tuor knew for sure that I would be. If Tuor's story is true, then I can't help but feel a touch of guilt for the way I'd treated Lawrence. Maybe he *was* just trying to help my brother.

But Tuor doesn't have friends. *I'm* his friend. Growing up, we used to survive together. Before Malcolm took me to the farm, Tuor and I would wander the streets of Rande scavenging for food or begging for rings. We had fun though. When Tuor wasn't in one of his worrying fits, we would trick the food vendors to get free food. Tuor would pretend to be stealing an apple or a loaf of bread to distract the vendor. Then I would run up from behind and snatch as much food as I could.

"Lawrence said you were in trouble." I pull my arms in close to my body as the cool of night begins to chill the room.

"Hey! Our box."

Tuor's eye catches the little wooden chest that I dug out last night. He leans forward, picking it up and pulling it onto his lap. He riffles through the things inside. I ignore him though. I don't have time to think on memories right now.

"How many days did you say you were at the church before you sent Lawrence to find me?"

"Three. Three days."

I rub my arms briskly to try and generate some heat. Tuor's poster was only put on the posting tree today. That means that Tuor's captain knew he was likely in Bear Gap for three days before he put it up. Why would Tuor's captain do that?

Tuor tosses the box aside and seems to relax as he leans back and rests his head on the wall. I want to relax with him. What I really want is to go to sleep and focus on taking care of this ordeal tomorrow, but I can't seem to get this thought out of my mind. Why did Tuor's pursuers wait to put up a wanted poster today? If they're so desperate to find him, why didn't they post it the night they chased him into Bear Gap?

Something feels queer about this. I didn't trust Tuor from the beginning, and I turned out to be wrong. Perhaps I'm wrong, too, about forcing him to give himself up to the governor. Tuor closes his eyes and starts to drift to sleep. I pull my hand to my mouth and begin to gnaw at my fingernails.

"What if this was a trap?" I whisper. I sit up straight on my bed.

Mirabelle was right, I realize. Maybe we should have left town. Someone is determined to get their hands on Tuor. I get a sick shaky feeling in my stomach.

"Get your things," I say.

Tuor's eyes flicker open. "Why?"

"Because we're leaving."

Tuor scrambles for his bag. I stand, grabbing for

my jacket on the floor when the shack's door swings open. Screaming, I jump back against the wall. The candle on the table casts an ominous shadow on the figure of a Warwick soldier standing in our doorway.

CHAPTER EIGHT

TORCHLIGHT SPLITS THE dark room. Two more men march up our front steps as the first soldier lunges toward us.

"C'mon!" Tuor screams, ripping me from the wall. He opens the wooden flap that hangs over the back window and shoves my body through feet first.

"Go around back," the soldier barks.

My stomach flips as I dive ten feet into darkness. Tuor lands beside me and grabs my wrist. I hear the other two soldiers round the house. We take off at a sprint into the black forest. The trees and houses barely show their outline as we whip past, breathing in the bitter fall air. Leaves and branches brush past my head, so I stretch out my arm in front of my face to try and block the blow. My other hand is holding firmly onto Tuor's.

A shout echoes past us. "They went that way! South, toward Hanover."

My lungs burn. We twist through the dense woods. I hear another shout behind us, then one to my right.

A whizzing sound hurls past my ear as an arrow sticks in the tree next to me. I scream as another arrow flies past.

"Run!"

I push my legs faster as a burst of arrows thump on the ground behind us. The shouting begins to fade. I chance a look at the soldiers but see dark forest.

"Don't . . . slow down," Tuor breaths. "They've just gone back to get their horses."

My legs struggle to keep up with Tuor's long gait and superior physical strength. Our hands break apart as we continue to run parallel to the river past a scattering of houses. We stop only when our feet sink into a bog. We've run downhill to a low-lying plot of land that's been taken over by the swamp. My feet feel heavy as I struggle to place one foot in front of the next.

"Keep going," Tuor urges, taking my hand again.

The soft earth latches onto our legs like there are demons below pulling us downward. One of my boots pops off in the mud and I decide to abandon the other shoe before we finally reach steadier ground.

"This way," I say to Tuor. I pull him west, away from the river.

"We can't slow down."

Tuor's voice cracks from a dry throat, but he's still not breathing as heavily as I am.

"I know these swamps . . . " I gasp for air. "Better than they do . . . Follow me."

I am familiar with this area and the people who choose to reside in the muckiest part of the swamps. They may be our only chance at evading the soldiers. Tuor and I use the trees to lead us until I nearly collide into the side of a log house. My weary legs take me along the outside wall until I feel a door. I push it open and step inside. I'm hit by the overwhelming smell of stale alcohol.

"Camilla." Tuor grabs my arm to stop me from taking my next step.

"It's abandoned." I cough and stub my toe on an overturned chair as we move inside the house. "Ouch."

"How do you know it's abandoned?"

"Vincent and his crew used to live here. They left when Governor Leo got word that they were producing." I pause, feeling desperately for anything to anchor myself in this inky pit. The air has a thick yeasty quality. "Malcolm helped them find a new spot before this place was raided."

My hands finally touch the wall opposite the door. I reach for the window where a light blue glow emanates behind a thin sheet. I pull the sheet over to peer into the woods. It looks bright outside compared to this house. Tuor joins me at the window, but he doesn't look out. He turns his back to the wall and slides down, keeping his knees pointed upward.

"I don't hear them out there," I say. Tuor doesn't say anything. I follow his lead, taking a seat on the floor next to him. "I guess we'll hide in here until they grow tired." Although I have no idea what our plan will be after that.

I look intently at the side of Tuor's face. He stares emptily at the front door before closing his eyes and resting his head on his knees.

Mud cakes my bare feet and legs and my hands are bleeding where I scrambled out of the window. My body starts to shake as we sit. Is it the cold that leaves me shivering or the thought that Tuor could be taken from me tonight?

I wait to hear the sound of footsteps, to hear voices echo through the cracks in the walls. My muscles are so on edge that I can barely keep my body seated on the floor. Time seems to melt away one painful moment after another.

"Mirabelle was right," I whisper. Tuor doesn't look up when I speak. "She told me to take you and leave Bear Gap. She said we were in danger." I shake my head slowly, then look over at Tuor again. He still has his head buried in his knees. "I was so foolish," I say, my voice quieter than a whisper.

Beside me, quiet sobbing breaks through the tension.

"Tuor?"

Tuor's body convulses. His weeping grows louder as he lifts his head and knuckles away a tear.

"I can't live like this," he says. "I don't want to spend the rest of my life running."

"You won't." I touch his arm, pulling away the hand he's using to shield his face. "I know you didn't kill that man, and soon they'll figure that out." I feel as though I'm running out of affirming things to say to my brother. "Maybe we can still leave Bear Gap, like Mirabelle said. We can steal a horse tonight . . . get some food for the road. We can do it. You don't need to run away forever, just until they catch the right man."

Tuor's glassy eyes turn to bore into mine. Warm moonlight pours in from the window, making his face look ghostly.

"It would do no good to leave town," Tuor says. His face is wet with tears and struck with agony. "They already know I didn't do it."

"What do you mean? If they know you didn't do it, then—"

With a crack, the door flies open. The three soldiers crash through the house, tearing away the rubble that sits between us. I scream and turn to fumble with the window behind us, but it's shut tight. By the time I turn back around, we're already face-to-face with the men.

"Get up," the first soldier says, pushing me aside and grabbing Tuor by the collar of his shirt.

"Leave him alone!" I shout, but I'm completely ignored.

I shove one of them with both my hands as hard as I can. I'm nothing but a nuisance to him. Two of the soldiers hold Tuor by either arm while the third holds the torch.

"You've been slippery," the one soldier says as he pushes Tuor out the front door. "But we always find the traitors."

Find something, do something! I tell myself. My hands skim the splintered wood floor in search of anything I can use as a weapon. I feel the smooth surface of a glass jug. I pick it up by its dusty handle, run, and smash it into the back of the third soldier just as he's walking out the door. Amber glass shards sprinkle the floor and his body crumples into a lump.

Just past the threshold, Tuor turns around to see what I've done. His eyes light with hope for the blink of a moment. With the other two soldiers distracted, Tuor wriggles from their grip, elbowing one in the face. He breaks into a run and I brush past the soldiers to follow.

Ten yards out from the house Tuor comes to a skidding stop. I trip, falling on the ground next to him.

Why is he stopping? The grass around me flickers with the light of many torches. I brush away my hair and look up to see an army of twenty soldiers, mounted on horseback.

A man, front and center, speaks. "No need to run anymore." His voice is smooth like honey. He wears the same black leather vest that all Warwick soldiers wear, but his is adorned with pins and ribbons, trophies from battle. Another soldier approaches Tuor.

"Please don't take him!" I beg. "He hasn't done anything wrong."

I force myself to my feet and pull Tuor into a strained grasp that resembles a hug. Tears glisten in his eyes. Before the soldier has a chance to take him, Tuor pulls my hands off him and turns around without being told.

"No!"

"Stay back," the soldier snaps. He pulls out a thin cord from his belt and begins wrapping it around Tuor's wrists.

Perhaps it's because of the shadows cast by the tall trees, but the captain's face looks evil, almost devilish. His jaw sharp and his hair, as black as pitch, is slicked back into a tiny ponytail.

"Did you search the house?" he asks when the three soldiers appear behind us, two of them holding up the soldier I knocked out.

"It's clear, sir."

Once his hands are secured, Tuor is pushed forward, toward the band of soldiers. Tears blur my vision. I stare at these men, all deployed just to retrieve my brother. Without needing to be told, all the soldiers begin a silent ascent up the hill that leads into town.

"Stop!" I shout, but no one turns around, not even Tuor. "Stop! You can't take him. He hasn't done anything wrong!"

I scream and thrash until the last bit of torchlight is eaten up by the shade of night.

CHAPTER NINE

STANDING ALONE IN the forest makes my skin prickle and my mind turn mad. It's the last thing I feel like doing but I begin groping through the trees, searching for the swamp where I lost my boots. I pull them out of the mud, knowing I'll still need to work at the farm even if my brother has been arrested.

Boots in hand I start heading for home. Every step feels like a mile. I follow the sound of the river, knowing eventually I'll stumble across something I recognize. When I find the steps to our front door, I feel so heavy, I have to force my feet up them. Malcolm isn't home. I feel so alone it makes me shudder.

A candle continues to burn on the table. I mosey toward it, staring into its wispy flames. My bed is crumpled where only an hour ago I sat with Tuor. I still believed everything was going to be okay. I still believed I had the strength to help him. I still believed they'd find Tuor innocent.

I don't believe any of that anymore. Staring at this hollow room, I realize it will be impossible for me to sleep here tonight.

I button my jacket and blow out the candle. The darkness outside feels like pressure on my body, but I focus on walking and nothing else. I move without thinking, letting my mind remember the steps I take everyday that lead me into town. My bare feet feel nothing. They're numb, just like my mind.

Rande Square is eerily quiet right now, only a few lanterns still lit. It's a stark comparison to its typical busyness in daylight. The air grows cooler as I step into the field that leads to Mirabelle's house. My heavy breathing starts to chap my lips and my voice croaks as I enter Mirabelle's and call her name.

The front hall is peaceful. Moonlight flecks through the tall windows, reflecting off the dusty books. I run to the spiral staircase at the back of the house and climb the steps to the room where I know Mirabelle sleeps. I yell for her again. She's sitting up in bed when I enter. I drop my soaked boots on the ground. My hands reach out for the wall behind me to steady myself.

"What's going on?" she asks, swinging her legs over the bed.

"They got him. They got him!"

Tears appear in my eyes out of nowhere. They pour down my face, creating streaks along my skin. "They arrested him. He's gone!" My lungs labor for air. "I tried to do the right thing. I tried . . . " Mirabelle rises, rushing to my side. She pulls me into a tight hug. "I've always followed the law and they still took him!"

She pulls me out of the hug and holds my head between her hands.

"Calm yourself, dear," she says, but her voice is shaking, like mine. "Tell me exactly what happened?"

"There were so many of them. I . . . I . . . just couldn't stop them. I'm a fool!"

"Shhhh . . . child. Shhhh . . . "

Mirabelle wraps me in her arms again so that my face is pressed tightly to her bosom. I close my eyes and bury my whole body into hers.

"Why did they take him?" I moan. "Tuor said he didn't do it. I don't understand!"

The tears slow their raging. I back out of Mirabelle's grasp and step farther into her room. A large four-poster bed sits in front of me. My weary body collapses on top of the blankets.

"What do they want with him?" I ask, my voice now barely a whisper.

"I don't know."

"He's never hurt anyone."

To this Mirabelle doesn't respond, and I'm tempted to bristle because she's not agreeing with me. But my energy is spent. Mirabelle moves toward me, taking a seat on the other side of the bed. She begins raking her fingers through my tattered hair.

"Why would they do this?" I ask one more time as the tears start their march down my cheeks again. I raise my eyes to look at Mirabelle. She brings a hand to her mouth and weeps softly with me. I'm not sure how long we lie like this, but at some point in the night, I fall asleep. I don't bother to pull a blanket over me or even take off my jacket.

***

No amount of blinking seems to help. My eyes are hazy and sore from either crying or lack of sleep, possibly from both. I sit up on Mirabelle's bed and stare at the forest through her bedroom window. The room looks different in the soft glow of daybreak. Warm sunlight fills the room as a breeze shakes the tree branches outside. I turn around to rouse Mirabelle awake.

"I'm going to the Justice House before work," I say.

Mirabelle sits up, rubbing her lower back.

"I'll come with you."

"You don't have to."

The rims of Mirabelle's eyes glisten with tears. She massages the bottoms of her feet and her calves before finally standing up to dress. "Of course I do, dear. You and Tuor are all I have in this life."

For a long time I have known Mirabelle's statement to be true. Mirabelle was actually married once when I was very little, and she had a daughter named Devika. But her husband died during the Battle in Bear Gap, and her daughter died years later when she caught a terrible illness.

Devika and I played together. She was my only friend aside from Tuor. I was old enough to remember her death vividly. After the tragedy of Devika, I think Tuor and I were the only ones to ever visit this house.

"I'm sorry about yesterday," I say. Mirabelle looks at me from under heavy eyelids. "I shouldn't have pushed you."

She sighs while slipping on her worn shoes. "I forgive you, dear. I just wish . . . " Mirabelle moves back toward the bed, taking my head in her hand. "You seem to lash out when you get . . . upset." She tries to meet my eyes, but I keep my gaze on her shoes. "Like your father."

"He can't help it." My eyes flicker up to Mirabelle's face.

"Why not just come and live with me?"

Mirabelle strokes my hair. I brush her hand away as I stand from the bed. I'm regretting my apology. As usual, it has led to a lecture.

"I can't leave Malcolm."

"Sweetie, you don't owe your father anything. I have plenty of space here. You could have your own room. We could walk to work together and eat dinner together." Mirabelle smiles at me meekly.

"He'd be alone. How would I get him his food?"

"Your father can take care of himself." Mirabelle takes a step closer to me. She reaches out and takes both of my hands in hers. "I know you worry about him, but, Camilla . . . you don't see him for who he is." Her voice is calm. Her words are spoken slow and steady. "He uses you. Your father can go at any time to the governor's farm and get a brand and do the work, but he doesn't." My gaze veers to the floor. Mirabelle painfully tries to keep my attention. "I know that not all of these marks on your body are from the farm."

Tears glisten in my eyes even though I try so hard to push them away. "Malcolm has always been there for me. My mother left when I was practically a baby. But *he* kept me. *He* raised me."

"What your mother did wasn't your fault."

"I know. I know that . . . But my mother still left, and she left my father too. And then Tuor was such a disappointment to him. The last thing he ever wanted Tuor to do was join the militia." I brush a tear from my cheek. "I'm all he has."

"But he strikes you." Mirabelle's voice is practically a whisper.

"It's not all bad." I drop my hands from Mirabelle's grasp. "Most of the time it's fine. We can sit together and be normal." Mirabelle opens her mouth to interrupt me, but I continue before she has a chance. "I know how he can be. I'm not blind to his vices. But he's my father. I can't leave him like everyone else has."

I turn around and busy myself by pulling on my boots. Chunks of dried mud crumble onto the floor. I stand, bring my hand up and watch as I flex my fingers in and out. Mirabelle doesn't understand. Malcolm has been through a lot in his life. He's not without fault, I know that, but he has never left me. He's always been there. If I ever turned my back on him, our relationship would be over. He would banish me in the way he banished Tuor. And then who would I have?

"I'll be downstairs," I say, passing through Mirabelle's bedroom door without a backward glance.

I wait for Mirabelle in the front hall while she dresses. My feet can't stay in one place, and without realizing it, I'm pacing furiously. Going to the Justice House isn't something a person could feel pleasant about. I've never been inside myself, but on the farm I've seen people carried away by Warwick soldiers. Sometimes they return; sometimes they don't. But everyone knows where their fate is determined—the Justice House.

Thoughts ramble through my head like they might for a mad person. How had things gone so wrong over the last couple of days? What bit of information am I missing to make sense of it? But the biggest question is, why do they think my brother killed someone? The thought pounds in my mind, and it's the first thing I ask Mirabelle when she meets me in the hall.

"I don't know, dear." Mirabelle's voice is sullen. She's as baffled as I am. "Have you eaten?"

I reach for the front door. "I'm fine." I can't even think about food right now.

Mirabelle pulls an arm through her coat. She shakes her head at me in disapproval.

"I'll be right back." She ducks downstairs to the kitchen and returns with a hunk of bread for herself and a mushroom cake for me. Mirabelle makes great mushroom cakes because the mushrooms grow right in her back yard. I still don't want to be bothered with food, but I immediately take two bites.

"I thought you weren't hungry."

I shrug my shoulders as we pass through Mirabelle's front door.

"Why aren't you eating one?" I ask, my mouth garbled with chewy dough.

"That's the last one."

Mirabelle leads the way down her front walk, the tall trees swaying in the morning's cool breeze. I shove the rest of the mushroom cake into my mouth, feeling just a little guilty for eating the last of it.

"They're not going to be helpful at the Justice House," Mirabelle warns as we step onto the front cobblestone path.

"I just need to know what evidence they have against Tuor. If I can find a way to prove they have the wrong person, then—"

Tuor's words ring in my ear: they already know I didn't do it. We cross the field that leads into town. My eyes feel as though they've swollen to the size of apples.

"He didn't kill anybody." I mumble as if I'm trying to convince myself more than Mirabelle.

"Camilla." Mirabelle pauses, reaching out her hand to stop me just as we step into town. "Tuor is in trouble."

"I know."

A village woman crosses behind Mirabelle, a large woven basket tucked under her arm.

"No, I mean, he's in very serious danger." Her fingers wrap tighter around my arm. "If Tuor has already been arrested, then there'll be no talking to them." She shifts her body so she's facing me. "You know that I care deeply for Tuor, but . . . "

"What?" I snap, pulling my arm away from her. An old man sits propped up outside a Warwick-owned house. His eyes dart when he hears me yell.

"I don't want you getting hurt. You're walking toward a pack of wolves."

"He's my brother!"

"I know." Mirabelle's eyes fall slightly. "Besides you, he's the only family I have."

"I would do anything for Tuor," I say. "Even get myself hurt." Mirabelle takes a deep breath. Her eyes focus on mine. "What do I have if I don't have my brother?"

It will be both of us or neither of us. Living in this village of Rande, with so many Warwick soldiers present, it has always been about blending in. The outspoken people were the ones who got locked up in the dungeon. The quiet people were the ones who could go to work, get their rings, and go home without ever being noticed. How had I been one of the quiet ones for so long when right now I feel like ripping the doors off the Justice House just to get to Tuor?

"Please, Mirabelle. I can't get Tuor back on my own. I need your help."

Mirabelle nods. She rubs absentmindedly at her lower back.

"It feels like I'm sacrificing you," she says. Her eyes glisten with tears. "You two are like my children."

I'm surprised when she pulls me into a quick hug. As she leans back, Mirabelle wipes a stray tear from her cheek.

"Let's get going to the Justice House then," she says. "We'll do whatever it takes."

CHAPTER TEN

THE STRUCTURE BEFORE us is wide and squat and would probably be very unassuming if it wasn't for the great Warwick flag flying from its pinnacle. It's a hideous place built of a mineral called Catahli, named after the Catahli Clan that used to harvest and sell the substance.

At one time, it was so abundant that our money rings were forged out of Catahli. The mineral is gray and smooth and incredibly strong. It can withstand the harshest of elements: wind, storm, flooding. The only way to destroy it is with direct flame. There's a saying in Elmyra, only a fool stores his Catahli in the stew pot.

"Have you ever been inside?" I ask.

"No . . . " Her sigh is distant and tortured as if she never wished to go inside for the horrors she might find. "Everything is underground I'm told."

"Underground?"

Mirabelle's cheeks are flushed red and her eyes are focused. She nods.

"The Justice Room is where the trials are held. It's large enough to hold the governor and his council, the accused, a host of witnesses, and I'm sure plenty of soldiers."

I squint my eyes at the square building. A set of long steps lead to the front door. Two soldiers guard the entrance dutifully.

"And then there's all those prison cells," Mirabelle continues. "They scatter farther underground through tunnels and passageways, probably as far as we're standing."

"How do you know all that?"

Mirabelle looks at me for the first time during this conversation.

"You live in this territory long enough, and you hear the rumors."

I stay quiet, letting Mirabelle continue. One thing I can depend on from Mirabelle is a story, or a lesson depending on how you look at it.

"Grueling trials that last for days," she continues. "People who have been imprisoned since the day they were arrested and have never even been out to see the sunlight." I suck in air, quickly thinking about Tuor rotting below the earth for years, or the rest of his life. "I'm sorry, dear. I shouldn't have said that."

"It's just the truth," I say simply. I brush off her comments as if they don't bother me.

"We'll get him out." Mirabelle gives me a weak smile. I nod to make her feel better, but my stomach feels twisted and hollow at the same time. "What are you going to say to the guards?"

I take a deep breath and fix my eyes on the Justice House. "I have no idea."

Mirabelle sighs as I walk away. She hates it when I say I don't know or I'm not sure or I think so. Uncertainties make her worry. I'm worried too. I can feel my hand shaking inside the pocket of my jacket. But there's no planning for a moment like this. There is only action.

The soldiers shift on their feet when they see me take the long Catahli-carved steps. The one reaches for the sword on his belt, then pulls his hand away as if he realizes I'm not a threat. I stop abruptly on the top step. I hear Mirabelle's timid steps behind me.

"I want to see my brother."

I try to sound firm, but instead my voice comes out defiant, like a spoiled child. The soldier to my right meets my gaze even though he's a head's length taller than me. The other one, young and dark-skinned, won't even bother to look at me.

"He's a . . . " I stumble now, struggling for words. "I think he's been imprisoned here."

The two guards exchange a contemptuous look.

"Truly?" the soldier on my right says, his voice dripping with sarcasm. "You're quite the little idiot if you think you can just walk through this door."

He laughs lightly while the other guard smirks to himself.

"Please, I—"

"Move along!" he barks.

Mirabelle touches my shoulder to pull me back. She can see as well as I that they're not going to be helpful.

"He's innocent, you know." I say, spinning around. My arms feel shaky and somehow detached from my body.

"Innocent you say?" the one on my right speaks. "You should have told us that first off."

The dark-skinned soldier smirks again but still keeps his eyes trained forward.

"I have a right to see my own brother."

The dark-skinned soldier looks down at me for the first time. His mouth looks likes it's been permanently set in a straight line. "Trust me," he says. "You don't want to go down there." He then turns his head back to look out at the street. "Forget about your brother."

"The only right you have is to shove off," the other soldier adds. "This is the governor's land." Straightening his shoulders, the cocky soldier reaches for his sword and raises an eyebrow at me. "Don't make me force you off these steps." He says it in a way that makes me think he'd enjoy such an opportunity.

I feel Mirabelle's hand on my arm, pulling me away. This is absurd. Tuor has been arrested with not one piece of proof that he killed the man they say he did. I start to take the steps leading away from the Justice House. No one has ever kept me from Tuor before. I didn't see him nearly as much when he was stationed in LilyAye, but he was still able to come home from time to time. And if I ever really needed to speak to him, I could have traveled to LilyAye. I know deep down that I probably wouldn't have done that. I've never even stepped outside of Bear Gap, let alone taken the two-day journey to LilyAye.

"This isn't right," I say, pausing midway down the set of steps.

"I know, dear, but we're going to have to think about this in a different way."

"Tuor has been arrested unjustly. And they . . . " My breathing quickens. "They can't keep me from him."

I turn around and march back up the steps, reaching directly for the door when I get to the top. Both guards are so stunned I manage to turn the knob and stumble inside. I feel a pair of hands on my waist.

"I have to see my brother!"

My scream echoes through the hollow Justice House as I'm pulled outside. I fight back, scratching and grabbing for anything. A set of arms reaches up and hooks under my shoulders so that I'm held upright, face-to-face with the stoic dark-skinned soldier. My scraggly hair covers my face in pieces.

"Please . . . " I beg, pathetic and exhausted.

The soldier takes a step toward me. He raises his arm and strikes me hard across the face with the back of his leather-gloved hand.

"Camilla!" Mirabelle shouts. "Okay, okay. It's okay. Let's go."

Mirabelle grabs me as I slip on the steps. She holds me up by my shoulders, waiting for me to orient myself. I touch a cool hand to my cheek.

"We need to go." Mirabelle speaks directly into my ear as if the hit has kept me from hearing.

The door to the Justice House opens. Both guards step aside and salute as two men walk through. Leading the way with a brisk, almost jolly walk, is Governor Harras. He wears a long maroon cape that ripples in the wake of his stride. Behind him follows the man who was in the woods last night when Tuor was arrested. He wears his Warwick vest speckled with awards. His skin looks smooth and tan and he walks with a fluidity that matches his tone.

"You boys seem to be having trouble keeping the riffraff outside," the governor says. He glances at me and I realize he must have heard me scream a moment ago.

"Our apologies, sir."

Two horses stand waiting for the governor and his friend. Governor Leo tugs at the knot that keeps his horse tied to its post.

"Well, go on then," Governor Leo says to me when he notices I'm staring. My hand still rests on my cheek. "You'll be late for work."

I hesitate. I don't want to leave, knowing that Tuor is still trapped inside this horrible building.

"C'mon, we'll help Tuor another way," Mirabelle says as if she has read my thoughts.

Her hands still clutching my shoulders, she turns me around like a wheel turns a ship.

"Tuor?"

We both turn our heads to look. The governor stops his work on the knot and speaks my brother's name again.

"Tuor Crim?"

"Yes," I say.

"What a coincidence," he exclaims. His friend waits patiently as Governor Leo takes a step toward me. "That is just the fellow I have gone to see this morning."

"He is here then?" I ask, hoping by some chance that maybe he's being held in different, better conditions meant for Warwick soldiers.

"Oh yes, I made sure of it myself. How do you know of Mr. Tuor Crim?" The governor takes another step toward me as if I'm the most interesting subject he's ever beheld.

"He's my brother."

"Ah! You're the sister."

He turns around to look at his friend, who gives him a courteous smile.

"You have been quite important to us the last day or two. You led us right to your brother."

"What?" I ask. I feel my heartbeat picking up pace again. Is it my fault that Tuor was arrested?

"I had gotten word that our fugitive had a relative in this territory." Governor Leo adjusts the round gold clasp just below his neck that holds his cape together. "When you checked in for work, my men recognized your family name, Crim. So we put up the posters and sure enough, you took our bait!"

"What do you mean, bait?" My forehead grows warm.

"We were hoping you'd panic and decide to move your brother somewhere presumably safer. Of course, we thought you'd try to leave town . . ." His voice trails off. "Regardless, you led us right to him. And Ridley here, I mean, Captain Thatius, was able to bring him into captivity." Governor Leo gives the other man a fraternal smack on his back.

The governor carries a laugh on the tip of his tongue, and he smiles, looking as if he's just married the prettiest girl in all of Elmyra. The governor and Ridley exchange a look of satisfaction. I wonder who this Ridley is and why Governor Leo seems so overjoyed at capturing Tuor. But more than wonder, I start to seethe. My cheeks feel hot, and I know it's from more than just the slap.

"Go on now," Governor Leo says as the two men turn to their horses. He waves his hand at me as if he's shooing away a cat. "Off to the farm with you."

"Are you proud of yourself for hunting down my brother like a harmless doe?"

Silence settles in the air for a long moment. I swallow hard. The governor's and Ridley's backs still face me. Governor Leo acts as though he didn't hear me speak, continuing on with untying his horse. But Ridley pauses. He turns around slowly, giving me a look of utter indifference.

"Your brother is a dangerous criminal," Ridley says.

"C'mon, good fellow!" The governor yells as he mounts his horse. "I want to take you to Lindon Place. Have you ever had waffles with chicken atop?"

Ridley looks at Governor Leo, giving him a slow nod. He then turns to me.

"Remember, a dead doe can feed many people."

CHAPTER ELEVEN

WHOEVER RIDLEY IS, I'm confident he rode to Bear Gap straight from LilyAye. My stomach has that same queasy feeling it had when I met Lawrence.

"Who is that man?" My voice is hoarse and red with anger, like the stinging wound on my cheek.

Mirabelle puts her hands on my shoulders and leads me away from the Justice House.

"He looks LilyAye, doesn't he?"

"I don't know *who* he is." Mirabelle's voice is low.

She glances back to the Justice House as the governor and Ridley urge their horses toward Rande Square. Reaper's Way opens up before us, and we join the other haggard people heading to work. Mirabelle finally releases my shoulders as if she's confident I won't say anything stupid that could get me slapped.

"He was in the swamps when Tuor was arrested." Mirabelle and I are squeezed together as the workers are funneled closer to the gate. "And Governor Leo said that *he* was the one who found Tuor," I add. I look up at Mirabelle, desperate for her to answer my questions.

"I'm not sure, sweetie," she finally says, reaching over to stroke my hair. "But he has something to do with your brother's accusations." Her hand leaves my head and folds neatly on her lap. "I would stake my life on that."

***

My eyes are glassy as I stare at Supervisory Benedek's long wrinkled face. I give him my name, then Mirabelle gives hers. We're both assigned to winterize the tomato field. It's a great relief that I won't be working under Mac again. After the ordeal at the Justice House, it's also nice to know I'll have Mirabelle close by all day. I need her right now. I just wish I had the courage to say that out loud.

The tomato field has been cultivated and cleared of any stray rocks or old roots. We're instructed to cover the freshly tilled dirt with a thick layer of straw and manure. Mirabelle scoops big clumps of manure onto the field with a pitchfork while I work on my hands and knees to spread it. The pungent smell only bothers me for an hour or two, and then I get used to it. Even the clingy paste that gets stuck in my fingernails isn't bothersome after seven years of working these fields. I move ferociously, laying out the manure, then sticking the hay on top so thoroughly that the field looks powdery and soft.

"Are you feeling all right, sweetie?"

The field foreman paces twenty feet away from us.

"How am I supposed to work when I know Tuor is locked up?" A bee flies past my face and I swat it away. "I can't even stop for one day to help him because then Malcolm will ask why I'm not bringing any rings home. Then I'll have to tell him about Tuor."

"Your father doesn't know that Tuor has been arrested?" Mirabelle leans on the handle of her pitchfork. The hem of her long dress has been scooped up and stuffed into the waist.

"He doesn't even know Tuor's in Bear Gap."

I scoot backward, letting Mirabelle drop another pile of manure in front of me. I'm careful with what I say to Mirabelle. If I tell her that Malcolm would have a fit if he knew that I was helping Tuor, she'd worry. And worse, she'd force me to explain everything. Mirabelle just doesn't understand Malcolm.

"Hasn't he seen the posters?" Mirabelle gapes at me.

"Malcolm hates going into town."

"You need to tell your father what's going on."

I look up from my kneeling position. Dirt is caked on my knees and in the crevices of my fingers. Every time I wipe the sweat from my brow, a little soil attaches to my pale face.

"I can't," I say. I'm out of breath, and I don't feel like explaining this to her. "He doesn't care anyway."

"I've known your father for many years. I know he's not pleased that Tuor joined the militia, but I'm sure he cares that his son has been arrested."

"No, he doesn't. It'll just cause more trouble to tell him. He'll get mad and just take it out on me."

Mirabelle knows what I mean and it quiets her temporarily.

"Don't you think he'd be more upset to see Tuor's picture on the posting tree and realize that you didn't tell him about it?"

Her voice is softer now but still scolding. I stand up and place a hand on my hip, stretching my back.

"He never goes into town, and soon it won't matter."

"What do you mean?"

"Back to work!" the foreman barks.

I drop to my knees. Mirabelle joins me on the ground, clutching her lower back as she bends. I specifically told her I would do this work so she didn't have to bend over, but she plunges her hands into the manure and starts helping me with the spreading.

"Camilla, what do you mean it won't matter?" Mirabelle whispers.

I keep my head down, focusing on the quick movements of my hands.

"Because," I snap. "They're soon going to realize that Tuor is innocent." I pause, waiting for Mirabelle to rebuke some part of what I've said. "They're going to realize he's innocent and send him back to his post in LilyAye. He'll be punished. He'll have to be punished for fleeing. But eventually they'll release him, and it will be fine."

Mirabelle is quiet for a moment. She sits up on her heels, rubbing the tops of her thighs and looking out across the field. Her eyes narrow. She's thinking, intently.

"What is it?" I ask.

The boots of the field foreman march past us. His walk is slow and steady as if each step is scolding us. Mirabelle returns to the dirt.

"I hope you're right," is all she says.

***

At the end of the day, Mirabelle and I are herded to the checkout booth. We stand in line, a mob of filthy workers that smell of horse excrement encompassing us. The line inches forward. A man bumps into me.

"Watch it," I warn.

From the corner of my eye, I see a head of silky black hair appear. It's Lawrence. He pushes through the line of grumbling people before placing a hand on my arm. I flinch. I've never known a person who touches others so freely.

"Where have you been?" I ask, folding my arms across my chest.

Mirabelle's eyes grow big and look just a touch terrified.

"Your brother said I should stay away for a while." Lawrence's olive skin flushes red from a day of hard work. His face glistens with sweat, but he still wears what seems to be a permanent smile.

"What happened in LilyAye?" I whisper. I've been thinking up all the questions that I wanted to ask Lawrence if I ever saw him again. "Do you know the danger he's in?"

"Yes. Yes. I've been wanting to talk to you since we met at the posting tree. I . . . I just want to help." Lawrence leans in close to whisper my brother's name. "Tuor is my friend. If we work together, maybe we can hide him somewhere better—"

"Tuor was arrested last night."

Lawrence's mouth gapes. He tilts his head and our eyes connect.

"Oh no," he says, lifting both hands to his head. I can see his arm where he got his brand still wrapped in crude bandages.

A hand curls around Lawrence's shoulder, pulling him away from me.

"To the back of the line with ya!" an old man shouts.

"Sorry. Hold on." Lawrence drops his arms, begging the man for another moment.

"You have to wait like the rest of us!"

"Why are you trying so hard to help Tuor?" I ask. "How do I know you didn't commit the murder, and now you're blaming it on my brother?"

A gap opens in front of us, and Mirabelle and I move closer to the checkout booth.

"No! No. That's not it at all." The old man tugs on Lawrence's arm. "Please, can I just explain myself?"

I look to Mirabelle as if I'm asking for her advice, but she is completely dumbfounded.

"Give me a chance to explain myself, and I'll tell you everything." Lawrence's eyes are wide and carry with them a note of innocence. "I promise."

"Fine," I say. Lawrence's body relaxes. "Meet me at Lindon Place."

"Thank you." Lawrence's eyes light with relief. The old man pulls him back a few paces. "Wait," he yells. "Where's Lindon Place?"

"In the square, you stupid Lilyite!" the old man screams.

Lawrence looks back at me one more time before finally succumbing to the hungry crowd. "I'll meet you," he says.

Lawrence is pushed back so far I can't even see him after a few moments. I can't decide if Lawrence wants to help Tuor or use him for something else, but if he has information about Tuor's time in LilyAye it might help to get him released.

"Next!" The man at the checkout booth yells.

I give my name and receive my small stipend of rings.

"Who in all of Elmyra was that?" Mirabelle asks after she gets her payment.

We move away from the booth toward the front gate. I can't help but roll my eyes.

"His name is Lawrence," I say. "And I don't trust him."

CHAPTER TWELVE

IT TAKES THE whole walk down Reaper's Way to explain to Mirabelle who Lawrence is, and what his involvement is with Tuor.

"Apparently Lawrence broke him out of the LilyAye prison."

Hordes of people mosey past us.

"How did he manage that?"

"Tuor said he was one of the jailers, so he had a key or he could get a key, I guess."

Mirabelle scrunches her eyebrows together.

"You don't believe it?"

Street vendors shout their offerings for the day as we enter a noisy Rande Square.

"I just don't think they'd put a soldier that young in charge of other prisoners. He's practically a child. He looks hardly much older than you."

Mirabelle folds her hands in front of her as we pause in front of Lindon Place. Its windows are coated in dust. The front door is faded and worn. Lindon Place is a public eating house in Rande. The food is good, and it's the only place you'll see peasants and Warwick soldiers mingling together passively. Food has a funny way of pulling friends and enemies into the same room.

"Why didn't you tell me about this boy?" Mirabelle asks.

"It just happened so fast. Tuor was back, then we were being followed, and the next thing I knew he was arrested. I don't know what to think of him."

I glance at her with a look that I hope communicates everything I'm too proud to say.

"When he gets here, let *me* talk to him," she says.

Mirabelle points her chin up ever so slightly, and I have one of those moments where I feel like I have a real mother, someone who'll defend me. I actually start to feel a little giddy inside at the thought of Mirabelle having it out with Lawrence.

"All right."

"I think I see him coming." Mirabelle taps my arm.

Mingled among the weary workers, Lawrence staggers down Reaper's Way. He looks up and catches a glimpse of me, then breaks into a jog, coming to a breathless stop in front of us.

"Thank you so much for meeting me," he says, practically gasping.

Dirt speckles Lawrence's face. His clothes are filthy and threadbare. He barely looks like the same person I met two days ago.

"This is Mirabelle," I say, nodding my head in her direction.

"Oh." Lawrence's mouth is agape. Although surprised by the introduction, he flicks on a pleasant, happy countenance. "Hi!"

"Nice to meet you, dear." Mirabelle gives Lawrence a sweet smile but keeps her arms close to her body. No hug for him, I suppose.

The three of us leave the sunny street for the damp, dimly lit cover of Lindon Place. Five girls stand in the front hall. One of them with slick blonde hair directs us, with the flick of her finger, down a few steps into the dingy dining room. Her long braid bounces as she weaves through the tables with a resolute walk.

We're seated at a squat round table with four chairs. I rest my elbows on its sticky surface. Almost every table in the dining room is filled with patrons. The sound of laughter and raucous chatter mingles with the smoke that's settled on the ceiling. Mirabelle knows I have no rings to spare as Malcolm will notice a shortage, so she orders me and her a mug of cider.

"This looks like a fine place," Lawrence says, flashing our petite waitress a smile. Her eyelids are heavy, and her face speaks great disinterest.

"It's quite fine," she says, standing up straight and letting her hands come together in front of her. She purses her lips. "We have an inn upstairs as well that is equally as fine."

With a few long strides, the girl is gone. Lawrence looks after her before turning to face Mirabelle and me.

Mirabelle is the first to speak. "Explain your dealings with our Tuor." I give Mirabelle a sideways look. "Don't leave out any details," she adds.

"Oh, I knew him in LilyAye. We were stationed in the same dormitory, bunk mates actually. A few months back... or maybe it has been a year... " Lawrence bows his head as he thinks.

"Be certain about your information," Mirabelle warns.

"Yes, right. It was about a year ago we became friends. He wouldn't even talk to me for so long, and then finally one day he just opened up."

"What do you mean, he opened up?" I ask.

Sometimes I can't even get Tuor to open up to me. How could he have ever been comfortable enough to just start talking to Lawrence?

"I saw him one night in the training yard, well after dark. I was passing through there to deliver some papers to another dormitory. I almost walked right by him, but I noticed he was studying the sky. He was trying to map the stars on a piece of parchment."

The fire behind us pops, spraying embers onto the scuffed floor. My eyes shift to Mirabelle. We don't say it out loud, but we've both caught Tuor staring at the sky before. Something about it always seemed to calm him.

"So?" I ask.

"Well, I studied astronomy during my schooling as a child. Tuor was pacing back and forth. It looked like he was having a really hard time figuring it out, so I asked if he wanted help."

"And he let you?"

"No, not at first." Lawrence brings his arms onto the table. "I asked him if he knew the name of the constellation he had sketched on his parchment. When he said no, I told him that the ancient astronomers had named it The Dragon almost three hundred years ago."

I look at Lawrence a bit dumbfounded. I, like Tuor, know nothing about the light that pierces through our dark sky at night. Our waitress returns and places two mugs of warm cider in front of Mirabelle and me. The strong smell of apple emanates from the foamy liquid. I take my first sip, savoring the sharpness.

Lawrence continues. "Later that night, he leaned over his bunk and asked if I knew anything else about The Dragon, which I did. From then on, Tuor rarely left my side. I showed him how the constellations move throughout the year. I helped him draw the stars and told him what their names were. Whether I liked it or not, I had found a companion."

"What did *you* get out of this?" Mirabelle asks.

"What did I get out of it?" Lawrence stumbles over his words. "I got a friend. And I actually had something to do in LilyAye besides combat training."

My eyes connect with Mirabelle's. Slowly, she takes a drink from her mug, then sets it down, letting her arms fold softly across her chest. Her fierce motherly countenance is thawing. My feelings toward Lawrence are changing a bit too. I always imagined Tuor wasting away his days in LilyAye all alone. To know that at least for the last year he's had a friend leaves me both pleased and a little . . . jealous.

Mirabelle looks at Lawrence intently. "Tell us about the murder."

"Right, okay. It was probably about two weeks ago now," Lawrence runs a hand through his hair and shifts in his chair. "Everything has changed since then . . . for weeks I noticed Tuor wasn't quite himself. He'd sneak off outside for hours, and he'd come back to the dorm looking . . . "

"Looking?" I ask.

"I don't know, shaken?"

Something about that word sends a tingling feeling up my spine. "Did you ever ask him what was wrong?"

"I did. He'd never give me a straight answer. Then two weeks ago was when it all happened. It was right after supper time. I came back to our dorm, and Tuor was being arrested."

"Did anybody say why he was being arrested?" Mirabelle asks.

"I asked our captain. He said he arrested Tuor because he'd killed one of the men that worked in our dormitory. I tried to talk to Tuor, but they told me to keep back. I didn't see the body or anything. And I know Tuor wasn't with me when the man was murdered." Lawrence's hand connects with his hair as he bows his head to the table. "I don't know where he was that night." Lawrence looks back up at Mirabelle and me. "But I know he didn't kill anybody."

"How do you know?" Mirabelle asks, hopeful.

"Tuor and I have become close. You don't know who I am, I understand that. But when Tuor gets upset or angry, he closes in on himself. He doesn't become brutal."

I shift, leaning back in my chair. He's right. *I'm* the one who lashes out, not Tuor.

"It's why I broke him out of prison. I knew he was innocent."

"You risked everything for my brother though. I don't understand it. You must have had a life in LilyAye, and now you're a fugitive too."

Lawrence pauses, struggling for words.

"Tuor insisted on coming to Bear Gap to be with his sister, and I agreed." He glances around the dining room, then leans in closer to Mirabelle and me. "There are a lot of soldiers stationed in Bear Gap, but . . . " he shakes his head. "It's a different world down here. These soldiers that work the farm and guard the territory gate have no idea what's going on up north. Everything's more connected up there. There's no letter post in Bear Gap. In LilyAye we have a press that prints news and other information every day. People can buy the parchment and read at their leisure instead of walking to a posting tree." He stops abruptly, staring at his open hands. "I thought Bear Gap was safe. I thought no one would know who we were here."

"But why would you want to come to a place where no one knew you?" Mirabelle's voice is soft, sympathetic.

As if tortured by the question, Lawrence moves his head back and forth in such a way that looks like he's in pain. His voice is quiet. "I despised my life in LilyAye," he says. "I was born there, under the shade of the great Warwick castle . . . but I loathe the place." Silence fills the space between us. All I hear is the clanking of dishes and muddled chatter. Lawrence lifts his gaze back to Mirabelle and me.

"Tuor and I often spoke of running away from the militia. I think he said it just to humor me because he knew how badly I wanted out. Growing up in LilyAye, it seemed I was always a member of the militia. My captain had me promoted to be one of the jailers. So when Tuor was arrested . . . " Lawrence smiles broadly, bringing his hand up in front of him. "I held the key." He laughs lightly to himself and drops his hand. "I bet my captain regrets that decision now."

"So you really did break him out of the LilyAye prison?" I ask.

"It wasn't easy. But I saw our opportunity to get out of there, and I took it."

Lawrence seems to have shed the innocence that he held the first day I met him at the farm.

"But you don't think my brother murdered anyone?" I ask.

"I *know* your brother didn't do it."

CHAPTER THIRTEEN

"I DIDN'T BRING Tuor all the way to Bear Gap just to have him arrested again," Lawrence says as we step into the now dying sunlight of Rande Square. "I'm not a jailer here. I can't sneak him out again."

"I know," I say, feeling useless. Looking up at the dimming horizon, I remember that Malcolm will soon be wondering where I am. "I have to get home."

Mirabelle nods. "Why don't we meet at my house tomorrow? We can talk things out. See if we can come up with some ideas on how to help Tuor."

"Yeah, okay."

"I'll be there," Lawrence says.

I'm not used to having other people around to help me. The loneliness I'd felt before starts to dissipate.

"Lawrence, dear, you looked practically starved. How about I fix a stew for the two of you as well? How does that sound?"

"Thank you," he says, shaking his head like a puppy receiving a scrap of meat.

"I can always spot a hungry one." Mirabelle winks.

All I can do is smirk. We part ways from Lawrence just outside of Lindon Place. I watch him for a few moments as he staggers down Reaper's Way.

"Do you trust him now?" Mirabelle asks, pulling me out of my stare.

I nod. "He seems to actually care for Tuor."

I think about what Lawrence was able to teach Tuor about the stars and the sky. I couldn't have done that. Somebody else in this world besides me has found a connection with Tuor. That's good, I tell myself.

"I was thinking . . . " I say.

"Yes, dear?"

"Lawrence said their captain arrested Tuor in LilyAye." We cross Rande Square. "And when I first saw Tuor a few days ago, he said it was his captain that was hunting him down. What if Tuor's captain has a vendetta against him?" I look down at my feet as we move under the shade of the posting tree. "Maybe Tuor did something to upset him, and now he's pinning this murder on my brother."

"It does seem odd." Mirabelle folds her hands in front of her as we come to a stop.

"I bet that's it. I bet they argued, or Tuor did something stupid that he didn't like."

"Accusing someone of murder is awfully harsh for just a disagreement, though."

"Well, it seems personal if the captain himself is the one who arrested him and chased him to Bear Gap. His captain probably resides over, maybe hundreds of soldiers?"

"I suppose."

"Tuor said they were chased to the Bear Gap border. That means his captain left his post in LilyAye just to find Tuor."

Mirabelle looks at me skeptically until her eyes light with understanding.

"What?" I ask.

"If his captain chased him to Bear Gap, then his captain is probably in Bear Gap right now, don't you think?"

My head tilts to the ground. "That man at the Justice House," I shout.

"Ridley Thatius, yes. He must be Tuor's captain."

I gnaw on my fingernails, thinking about what Tuor could have done to warrant this much attention from a Warwick captain.

"Camilla . . . " The worry in Mirabelle's voice does not go unnoticed by me.

I look up quickly. "What?"

"Look."

Mirabelle turns to the posting tree. She touches a hand to a small piece of parchment nailed to the tree, pulling it forward.

"Tuor's trial," she says.

I push past Mirabelle to read the parchment myself.

"A trial shall be held for Tuor Crim," I mumble, "Six days hence from the day of this posting at the Justice House of Bear Gap."

I step away from the posting tree, feeling slightly nauseated.

"Six days."

Mirabelle nods, her face speaking its sympathy. I have six days to prove my brother is innocent.

CHAPTER FOURTEEN

I PLOD THROUGH the farm gates, still reeling from yesterday's news. How am I going to defend Tuor at his trial? A strong hand wraps around my arm. Fear pulses up my spine. The farm and all of its workers fall away as I turn to face my attacker.

It's Lawrence.

"Hey." His face is flushed but full of energy. "I asked the supervisor to assign me to wherever you're working today."

"Oh." Lawrence drops my arm. I coil it in close to my stomach. "And he allowed it?"

Lawrence shrugs his shoulders. "He waved me on."

"All right." I try to maintain my composure. "I'm supposed to throw hay."

"Throw hay?"

"C'mon, I'll show you."

Lawrence steps up beside me and we start the walk across the rolling hills. It's chilly today, so I pull my jacket tighter over my arms. I feel Lawrence's eyes peering in my direction.

"It's too bad we're not doing barley again." I shoot Lawrence a sharp look. He reciprocates with a goofy smile. "I just started getting good at it."

My smile is weak and forced.

"Is something bothering you?" he asks.

"I didn't sleep well last night, thinking about Tuor."

Lawrence nods. The cool breeze pushes long strands of hair off my face. We walk together in silence toward the corner of the Harras Manor. There sit piles upon piles of hay that've already been cut and dried.

"Our job," I explain, "is to fill up these wagons and deliver them to the workers that are preparing the fields for winter." I point toward the brown and barren plots. "We'll still grow winter vegetables, like squash and pumpkins, but we just don't grow hardly as much as we do in the summer. The empty fields have to get covered with hay to preserve them during the snow."

I toss Lawrence a pitchfork and show him how to shovel globs of hay into the small wooden wagons. After several moments of quiet hay-throwing, he glances at me sideways. His dark eyes seem to look through me.

"Tuor talked about you all the time in LilyAye," he says. "You're not what I pictured."

I roll my eyes. "It's frightening to think how my brother would describe me."

"He was very kind in his description, just not accurate." A piece of golden hay falls on top of Lawrence's head. I can't help but smirk. "For instance, he said you were caring." I raise an eyebrow at

Lawrence. "He doesn't know that you're only caring to him. To strangers you're quite . . . disagreeable."

Our eyes stay locked for a moment as I remember the day Lawrence and I met. The corner of his mouth creeps up slowly. He's teasing me, I realize. I allow myself to laugh. I'm not used to being teased.

"I'll concede that there's some truth in what you say." I pause, adding a big pile of hay to the wagon. "I know my brother. I know how he can be. He once went a whole week without saying the word fire."

Lawrence chuckles. "He did that in LilyAye too, except it was the word pillow that he was compelled to never say."

"How did you not grow angry with him?"

Lawrence stops with his work, jamming the tips of his pitchfork into the ground. "I'm sort of used to it."

"What do you mean?"

"My elder sister, Jazelle, she was born crippled. Her legs never worked." I pause, too, looking on with unblinking eyes.

He shakes his head. "Growing up, I watched her be excluded from life. She couldn't do things. No one wanted to be with her because they saw her as freakish. Even my own father . . . " Lawrence turns his gaze downward. "Tuor just reminded me so much of my sister. Jazelle barely had any friends. She almost never ventured outside. I was her only companion."

"But you left your sister. You left her in LilyAye all alone."

Lawrence sighs, leaning forward on his pitchfork. "Jazelle died last year."

A gust of cold air catches the top of our hay pile, scattering strands among our feet.

"Oh."

"It's one of the reasons I left LilyAye. No one resides there that I care for anymore."

A foreman approaches. I lift my pitchfork and reach for more hay.

"This wagon's full. Get it out to the field," he says without stopping his march across the field.

"Yes, sir."

I jump in front of the wagon, picking it up by two handles while Lawrence pushes from behind. We follow the dirt paths that twist between the fields and leave the wagon sitting with a batch of workers.

"Do you think you'll ever return to LilyAye?" I ask as we walk back toward the hay piles to fill another wagon.

Lawrence scratches at his scruffy chin. "Perhaps someday, when I'm an old man. But only to visit Jazelle's tomb."

***

Lawrence sits across from me at the table in Mirabelle's basement kitchen. He shovels stew into his mouth at an incredible speed.

"How's your arm?" I ask, remembering his brand.

Lawrence shrugs. "It feels better."

Instinctively, he looks at the burn, pulling the wad of bandages back. His skin is fiery red and overrun with soft blisters. He tries to touch the marred image of the Warwick crest but flinches when he barely makes contact. Mirabelle's ears perk up at the sound of Lawrence's pain.

"Oh, honey! Let me look at that."

Like a thirsty horse galloping to a cool stream, Mirabelle leaves her spot by the stove and holds Lawrence's arm like one would cradle a baby.

"When did you get your brand?" she asks.

"Couple of days ago."

Mirabelle removes the dirty rags from his arm. Carefully, she inspects the burn.

"It doesn't really hurt anymore."

"Mmm hmmm . . . "

I roll my eyes at the proceedings before me. It's silly how Mirabelle fawns over a grown man like Lawrence. Although I realize, to her, he's only a boy.

"I think I'm fine."

Lawrence tries to shift away as embarrassment flushes his cheeks, but Mirabelle is completely oblivious.

"Oh, you poor thing . . . I hate, hate, hate this barbaric practice of branding us like cattle."

Mirabelle taps her tongue against the roof of her mouth before patting Lawrence on his head. Lawrence's face blushes almost as red as his arm. I consider telling Lawrence that she talks to everyone like that, but my pleasures are few, so I decide to sit back and watch.

"This is infected," Mirabelle exclaims, bringing her hands to her hips. "Let me see now, I'm going to need some garlic . . . " Mirabelle turns about and starts riffling through her root cellar. "And ginger root . . . " She moves through her kitchen like a bee at his hive.

Lawrence smirks, winking at me from across the table. Perhaps he doesn't find this embarrassing. Could he be relishing her attention?

"That's not necessary," he calls to her.

Mirabelle ignores him, exiting the root cellar with a bulb of garlic, a gnarled looking piece of ginger root, and a small wooden bowl. She vigorously chops the garlic and tosses it with the ginger root shavings.

"Then I'll mix in—"

"The clear part of an egg?" I ask even though I know the answer. Lawrence looks at me curiously. "I've seen her make this concoction a million times."

Mirabelle presses her lips together and reaches for an egg from the counter behind her. She drops in just the white part and starts whipping the mixture furiously. Soon it turns into a disgusting looking paste, which Mirabelle insists on applying herself to Lawrence's arm.

"I want to make sure it's on there thick enough," she says. "You know, I used this same mixture on Camilla's arm many years back."

"Oh?" Lawrence says with a devilish grin.

"I was only ten years old, if you'll recall."

Lawrence holds his gaze with me until Mirabelle slathers on the egg mixture. His face contorts in pain, but Mirabelle continues to pile on the cool sticky paste.

"I see too many workers out there with horribly disfigured arms." Mirabelle shakes her head as she puts fresh wrappings on Lawrence's arm.

"Not everyone is so lucky to have a nursemaid like you," he says, patting the top of Mirabelle's hand.

She smiles in pure delight as she grabs Lawrence's hand and gives it a squeeze.

"What a kind boy!"

I take a bite of my stew. "So can we talk about Tuor?"

"Yes, dear. Of course."

"He's the one who's trapped in the dungeons at the Justice House. Who knows what it's like down there?" I pick up my bowl of half-eaten stew and deliver it to the basin. Mirabelle trails behind me and begins cleaning the bowl immediately. I find it hard to care about Lawrence's brand or anything else when I don't have Tuor with me. "We have five days," I say, leaning against the stone wall to face Mirabelle and Lawrence. "What am I going to do to get Tuor out?"

"I actually have an idea," Mirabelle says. She dries her hands on her apron. "It may prove wise to spend some time in study of Elmyra law. I have all of these books on Elmyra history, and no one bothers to read them."

I furrow my brow and turn my gaze downward.

"If we're diligent," Mirabelle continues, "we could learn how the courts work. It might help to get Tuor released."

No one in this room would doubt my love for Tuor, but the idea of studying Mirabelle's history books makes my head ache.

"Do you really think that would help?" I ask, hoping to dissuade Mirabelle from her idea.

"Knowledge holds far more power than you believe it does, Camilla."

I'm skeptical, not just because I'm keenly aware of Mirabelle's unnatural love for her books, but because this route seems far too tedious. We only have five days, and Mirabelle's home holds hundreds of books.

"Why do we have to read about Elmyra law? You probably know everything already. Haven't you sat in a trial before?"

"No, I haven't, dear."

I sigh, equally surprised and annoyed by Mirabelle's answer. Reluctantly, I look to Lawrence, hoping that maybe he has an idea that I haven't thought of. He looks as me with doughy eyes.

"What about you?" I turn to Lawrence. "Were you ever part of a trial?"

"No, not really."

"Not really?"

"Well, I know how trials work," he says.

"How would you know that if you've never sat in one?" Mirabelle asks.

"Study," he says simply. Lawrence pauses, giving us a leery eye. "My father kept me apprised of that sort of thing."

"Perhaps you'd enlighten us then, dear."

All eyes in the room settle on Lawrence. He shifts in his seat as if sensing the sudden attention on him. "Well, the Justice House has one judge, one person that makes the final decision of innocence or guilt."

"Who is it?" I ask.

"It's whoever the leader is. So in Bear Gap, it would be Governor Harras."

My heart sinks. The one person in this world who will decide if my brother lives or dies is that buffoon we call a governor—Leo.

"No one else makes the decision?" I ask.

"The judge will always have a council," Lawrence adds. "He appoints people, sometimes it's his militia leader. Sometimes he chooses a trusted assistant, or he could pick a family member, or even a servant if he wanted. But he's required to choose seven council members. The Seven are supposed to advise him, and then he can take up to three days to consider their thoughts and make a decision."

The prospect of waiting three days to hear of Tuor's outcome seems almost worse than having to riffle through a bunch of boring books. I lean my head against the rough brick wall, feeling more and more like I did when Tuor was arrested—helpless.

I keep waiting to hear a contradiction from Mirabelle, something that will set Lawrence right and make our prospect seem better. But all she does is stare blankly at the floor. She's realizing what I'm realizing: Tuor has gotten trapped in some sort of sick system, and it may be harder to get him out than we had planned.

"The thing is, every judge is different," Lawrence continues. "They have their standards they're supposed to follow, like choosing the seven council members, and they're all required to listen to testimony from anyone who wants to defend the accused. The accused can actually speak for himself if he chooses, but ultimately the judge decides."

"So if Governor Leo hears logical testimony in favor of Tuor, he might be inclined to set him free?" I ask.

"Yes, if you cater to his likings. Or if . . . "

"If?"

"Well, past court cases can be cited during a trial if the offense or situation is similar. It can help persuade a judge if he sees how another judge ruled. And often, if it's a revered governor or Supreme Ruler who made the decision, The Seven will advise the judge to do the same. It's a way of matching their likeness to that previous ruler. So I'm afraid Mirabelle's right. Research into Elmyra history may help."

I don't dare look next to me to see Mirabelle gloat.

"Thank you for that well-told lesson," she says, turning on her heels and wrapping an arm around Lawrence's shoulder. "How about some tea before we head upstairs?"

CHAPTER FIFTEEN

WE LEAVE THE damp basement kitchen and ascend one, two, then three flights of stairs. Mirabelle is quite jolly despite the seriousness of our task. She has always been thrilled to find me with a book in my hand. When Tuor and I were kids and we stayed at Mirabelle's house, she spent hours teaching us to read. Tuor took a little more time and patience to teach than I did, but Mirabelle never seemed to mind.

"This way," Mirabelle says as she leads Lawrence and me up the fourth and final set of steps.

The three of us reach the pinnacle of Mirabelle's library. Each floor gets smaller and smaller, so this part of the library is just a little room with a square window looking out to the back yard. There are only a few bookshelves balanced on the scuffed wood floor. A long railing runs along one side of the room. I lean half of my body over the railing, staring down the spiraling spindles that lead to the lower level.

"Oh, Camilla dear, please stop that!" Mirabelle chides.

I feel like a little kid again. I used to slip my legs through the spaces between the railing and dangle my bare feet over. Looking through the dusty haze of Mirabelle's house calms my mind. I turn around and give Mirabelle a teasing look.

"I like the rush I get in my head."

"You'll be the death of me, child."

Mirabelle wags a hand at me. Lawrence creeps slowly along the wall as far away from the balcony as possible.

"Lawrence," I call. His head pops up with a jolt. There's a flush in his face. "Take a look at the view."

"I saw it," he says with a tight jaw. His hands clutch desperately to the stone wall as he inches farther and farther away from the balcony.

I turn my back to the railing and lean lazily against it. "You're afraid."

"Hardly." With a shaky laugh, Lawrence forces himself to free one of his hands and run it through his soft dark tendrils.

"Leave that poor boy alone."

Mirabelle pulls a thick book from the shelf and then tops it with two other books. I sigh, already finding this to be a boring event. I mosey toward the shelves. The books look centuries old. I pick one up, a light-blue-covered book, the binding of which is almost completely deteriorated.

"These books look ancient," I say.

I open the cover, and a chunk of pages falls out.

"Be careful," Mirabelle says, rushing, with her arms already full, to pick up the parchment.

Gingerly, Mirabelle slips the paper back into the book and closes it shut. I pick up another book, turning it over in my hand.

"Where did you get all of these books from?" Lawrence asks.

"My father." Mirabelle runs her finger along the book spines, searching for her next treasure. "He owned this house and acquired most of what's in it. My father was a collector. We'd make trips to Billage and Hanover and sometimes even LilyAye to shop for printed works. That was a long time ago. Bear Gap was rather different then."

Lawrence takes an unsteady step closer to the window and peers out with an innocent look.

Mirabelle sighs. "That was before Warwick came to power, before the farm was built. My father used to make the sweetest bread cakes you could buy in Bear Gap. He'd sell them by the dozens along with his apple juice, which he made from these trees out back." Mirabelle smiles to herself as she shelves one of the books in her stack. "It was always just Pa and me. His whole life he always wanted to live in LilyAye so he could be at the center of learning. He waited until I was grown and married, put the house and most of his books in my care, and then went to follow his dream." Mirabelle pauses, her hand resting on the rickety bookshelf. "He has since passed, but it's comforting to know he touched nearly every book in this place."

"You're married?" Lawrence asks.

"*Was* married," Mirabelle corrects. "Only briefly."

She grabs one more book from the shelf and drops it in my arms. It's heavier than I thought a book could be.

"You can start with this one," she says.

The book is a deep brown color and written in large, gold-flecked calligraphy is the title *A Collection of Elmyra Records Vol. VII.*

Mirabelle leans in close to me. "Is your father expecting you at home?" she whispers.

I shake my head. "He's doing something with his buddies tonight."

Mirabelle nods, then crosses the room to hand volume four of the same series to Lawrence. I move to the wall and slide down its bumpy surface to sit on the hard floor. Mirabelle makes herself comfortable in the room's only chair. She has a stack of books next to her and a mug of tea. I watch her happily crack the cover of the first one in the pile. I'm doing this for Tuor, I remind myself.

Lawrence walks slowly across the floor and takes a seat only inches from me. His leg brushes against mine. Instinctively, I start to shift away, but I stop myself, keeping my legs still, and set my book down between my knees. I take a deep breath as I open the cover. I wonder how anyone could have bothered to write every tiny word on these pages. I glance over at Lawrence. He looks engrossed but also confused.

There's nothing but silence between us, yet somehow it's comfortable and almost . . . ordinary feeling. As a child, Tuor was always my friend. We stuck to each other like fleas on a cat. Our lives were a game we were desperately trying to win. We'd sneak away from Malcolm and spend hours wreaking havoc in town or surviving in the woods. When Tuor joined the militia, I found myself alone. I've never really made any other friends. I'm not sure I know how to.

I'm surprised how easy it is to feel close to Lawrence. I understand now why Tuor felt drawn to him. He's kind and sensitive, and as much as I don't want to notice, his presence sends a calm, warm feeling through my body. Lawrence catches me staring. His eyes flicker to mine and I feel a breath catch in my throat before I finally set myself to actually reading the beast in front of me.

***

"Well, this one won't help."

Mirabelle's voice is like a clap of thunder in the middle of the night. I realize I've been staring at the same page for the last ten minutes. I rub my eyes vigorously and decide to blame it on the dust if Mirabelle asks.

"All it is, is the history of old Elmyra Supreme Rulers, most of which I already know. Are you finding anything in there?"

"Not really," I say.

Mirabelle sets down her book and pulls another one off the pile.

"How are you faring, Lawrence?"

Lawrence looks up, almost as bleary eyed as me.

"Mostly just a bunch of records about wheat yield, a cattle disease that caused starvation in some small towns, and a minor famine that affected some northern territories," he says, turning a page.

It's silent again. I'm not sure I can take another session like this, sitting quietly, rifling through books about things that happened well before I was born. I force myself to sink further into the book, flipping through pages and pages of law changes, like the year that women were permitted to sell goods on public streets. Or when Supreme Ruler Manhew, who reigned a mere 260 years ago, caught a terrible fever and died in the span of half a day. As heir to his wealth, Manhew's son was appointed the new Supreme Ruler before word had reached the rest of Elmyra of the original Manhew's death.

It was only a few years later that one of the castles that sits in LilyAye was built. Supreme Rulers before that time lived on handsome manors, but nothing like the castle that was built during the younger Manhew's reign. He was a wicked ruler, it seems. He collected exorbitantly high taxes from his people in order to have the finest marble harvested and built into the flooring of the new castle. Doors made of solid silver with crystal handles were also luxuries he insisted on.

Of course, word from LilyAye is that the Manhew castle which was later inhabited by the Bradac Supreme Rulers is cute and darling compared to the castle that Quinten Warwick built for himself when he rose to power. I've never laid eyes on either. Without even realizing it, I scoff audibly.

"Did you find something?" Lawrence asks.

"Oh, no."

Lawrence returns to his book. "What was it like living in LilyAye?" I ask in a hushed tone that I hope Mirabelle can't hear.

Lawrence sighs, shifting his position on the floor. "It's a big city, lots of people. Every other person you pass on the street wears the black Warwick vest."

I always thought Bear Gap held a lot of soldiers. I can't imagine feeling outnumbered by them.

"And our houses don't look like the ones here," Lawrence continues.

"What do they look like?"

"Well, nearly everything in LilyAye is made of Catahli. There are crafters that take the Catahli, buff it, and dye it so that it's smooth and iridescent. It can look quite beautiful."

I see the memory of Lawrence's home in his face as he smiles.

"Your family is wealthy then?"

Lawrence hesitates as I stare at him. "Yes, I suppose they are."

I shake my head, turning my gaze to my book.

"Does that bother you?" he asks.

"You must have had servants and plenty of food, fine clothes . . . I just don't understand how you could be so unhappy living there."

"Being rich was nice," Lawrence admits. "Although I didn't truly become grateful until I moved here. But having a comfortable bed isn't everything. I'm far happier sleeping on the streets in Bear Gap than living in the same house as my father." He runs his hands along his thighs until they rest on his knees. "I don't even want to be in the same territory as him."

"How terrible could your father have been when you had every need supplied for you?" I don't want to be upset right now, but I feel the heat rising in my cheeks.

"He wanted me to live the life that *he* desired. It doesn't matter how many rings you have, Camilla. Do you want someone deciding your future for you?"

My eyes fall to my book. I can't help but think of Malcolm. In his own way, my father has decided my future. There is nothing else for me except a long life working at the farm and providing for Malcolm until he dies. It's the future I've always seen.

"I'm sorry," Lawrence says, stroking his hair with his hand. "That all came out wrong."

"I don't understand." I speak quickly. "My father is sort of the same way. He's . . . mean sometimes. But we're family. I just couldn't imagine leaving him like you left your family." I fiddle with my fingernails. "I've never even left Bear Gap."

I look up at Lawrence through heavy eyelids. His brows furrow. "Why not?"

"What?"

"How come you've never left Bear Gap? I've traveled all over Elmyra. You wouldn't believe the other worlds that are out there."

My face is hard, set like a statue. Why not? Why have I never left Bear Gap? It seems like such a stupid question. How ever could I? I have no rings. I have no knowledge. For a moment I thought I could flee with Tuor, but I knew it'd be a death sentence. Leaving Bear Gap just doesn't make sense. It's impractical. It's *impossible*. Yet as I look hard into Lawrence's eyes, his words ring loud in my head, *why not?*

***

"I think I've found something."

Mirabelle's voice strikes me from across the room. I jump to my feet and join her, looking over her shoulder at the wide book in her lap. She leans forward and points to the middle of the page.

"Do you think it will help Tuor?" I ask.

Lawrence comes to the other side of Mirabelle.

"There was a trial that was held in LilyAye about eighty years ago where a girl drowned the son of a noble family."

My face twists in horror. "That's awful."

"Yes, dear, I know. But they put her to trial, and the family claimed she had a disease of the mind where she would go into blind fits and didn't know what she was doing. The Supreme Ruler himself stood over the trial, and they promised him on their own lives that they would keep her with them always, not even leaving her side for a moment, if he would let their daughter live."

"Which way did he rule?" Lawrence asks.

"Guilty."

I exhale, feeling the last bit of hope for Tuor dwindle away.

"But he let the girl live. It seems he forced the family to move a day's journey into the wilderness for the townspeople's safety, but told them that if he never saw the girl again, he'd allow her to go on living."

Mirabelle looks a bit astonished.

"This may work," she says. "We could convince Governor Harras that we can look after Tuor. We'll tell him that he suffers from an illness, and it's not his true character."

"For that to work, I'd have to admit Tuor's guilt," I say. I feel a touch of anger creeping up in my gut.

I glance from Mirabelle to Lawrence. They both give me a look of reluctant agreement.

"Yes, dear, that's right."

Shifting away from Mirabelle, I feel betrayed. "I don't know if I can do that."

"Camilla dear, at this point it's our only option."

I take a step back swiftly. "No, I don't believe this is our only option. I still have five days to think this through."

Mirabelle straightens in her chair as she clutches her lower back.

"We're all tired," she says, closing her book. "Why don't we end our study here, and we can pick it up later?"

"I'm not going to admit that Tuor killed somebody when he didn't."

Mirabelle stands. "I know, dear. It's just something to consider. Let's not fret anymore about it today."

I sense that Mirabelle is coddling me. Perhaps she

see's that I'm growing angry. But she's right—I am exhausted. I concede. Mirabelle directs Lawrence and me down the steps to her front hall. She gives both of us a hug and makes sure I button my jacket before going outside where darkness has already fallen around our little village. Lawrence and I split ways at Rande Square, and I wonder briefly if he really does prefer sleeping on the cold, dirty streets of Bear Gap.

CHAPTER SIXTEEN

THREE NIGHTS OF arduous study have passed as quickly as it takes an acorn to become a tall oak tree. At least, that's how it feels to me. It was actually my idea to keep searching Mirabelle's books. I'm simply not able to admit to Governor Leo, or anyone for that matter, that Tuor is guilty. There's a twisting feeling in my heart every time I think about letting those words pass over my lips.

Reading late into the night and studying texts so ancient that the papers had to be turned with a delicacy I didn't possess had done nothing to weaken my resolve. Tuor is pure of heart, and the innocent are always seen for who they truly are, just like the guilty.

Lawrence and I walk the cobblestone path away from Mirabelle's house. We enter the dark, cool night to the unsettling sound of rustling leaves and swaying tree trunks.

"Don't tell me again why we should admit Tuor's guilt," I say, tugging my thin jacket over my chest.

"You told me at Lindon Place that you knew he didn't kill anyone."

"I still believe he didn't do it, but—"

Mirabelle calls out a final goodbye from the threshold of her front door. We both turn and wave before disappearing into the field that leads to town.

"Why would I testify that my brother is a murderer when I know he's not? Then I would be lying."

I chance a sideways look at Lawrence. His head is low. Why can't he see how impossible it is for me to say that Tuor killed Aiden Brookes? That's the man's name, we recently learned, that Tuor supposedly killed. Getting to know Lawrence over the past few days, I realized he was quite an intelligent person and not as ditzy as I thought. I had grown to like him despite our differences.

We move through the field of tall grass, led only by the moonlight. Lawrence stumbles, and from the corner of my eye I see him fall halfway down before standing up quickly and brushing off his trousers.

"Tripped on a root," he says, running his fingers through his hair. Maybe my initial assessment of Lawrence wasn't so far off. He is still rather ditzy and kind of a klutz. I try to maintain my seriousness but can't help a cheeky smile.

"These trials are meant to discover what really happened," I say, forcing the conversation back to Tuor. "If I don't speak the truth, then how can the governor judge accurately?"

Lawrence comes to a halt just before we reach Rande Square. The flame from the street lamp illuminates his rugged appearance, a dirty shirt with the top two buttons undone and a pair of tattered trousers. Even his nice boots have taken the manual labor hard.

"Trials are rarely won with truth," Lawrence says.

His words settle between us like heavy incense.

"How can that be when the whole point of a trial is to—"

"Governor Harras is just another maidservant to the Supreme Ruler. My father is the same. They will do whatever is best for the Warwick reign, and what's best is to keep people like you and Tuor scared and submissive. They need you to keep this farm running, and if you feel a threat of being tossed in the dungeons, then you'll simply obey. Have you ever seen a peasant go to trial and return?"

Doubt seeps into my mind. Is what he says true? I want to reject his logic, but Lawrence has seen a side to the Warwick regime that I haven't.

Awkwardly, I clear my throat. "No."

"Be prepared to say whatever you need to say to get him released." Lawrence reaches out and touches my elbow. "A guilty plea may be your only chance."

"If I could only meet with the governor, I could speak to him and just explain the situation and how Tuor is . . . I think I could convince him to at least go easy on Tuor and maybe even see that he's innocent."

Lawrence's arms drop to his side. "If you plead to the governor, he may bend. Is there anyone you know that could grant the meeting?"

I realize immediately that I don't. I'm not anyone of significance, and I don't know anyone of significance.

"Supervisor Benedek," I offer meekly.

Lawrence laughs. "Best of luck. I haven't met a man that strict since my father."

I sigh. I don't know what to do, and the trial is in two days. Right now my only option is the guilty plea. I pause, fiddling with my dress.

"Will you be at the trial?" I ask. It's something I've been wondering all week. Besides the benefit of having Lawrence's testimony, it would put me at ease to know I have another friend there.

"Oh . . . "

"If we're going to say that Tuor is guilty, but that it's his mind that fails him, I need as many people as possible to vouch for his character. You knew him well while he served in LilyAye. You'd be the perfect person to explain how kind Tuor is."

"I want to come to his trial, very badly in fact . . . but I abandoned my post in LilyAye. What if someone finds out who I am?"

"But you said no one here knows you."

"Yes, but it's a bit like walking into the lions' den."

I scrunch my eyebrows, regretting that I asked the question. "It's fine. I understand." I turn around quickly so that Lawrence can't see the wetness forming in my eyes. I was depending on this, depending on another person to vouch for Tuor. Pinching my lips together, I'm determined to not speak of it anymore. It's not right of me to ask Lawrence to put himself in danger like that. I just had hoped . . .

"Good night," I say, beginning my walk into town.

"Wait."

Lawrence reaches out, taking my arm in his hand, and spins me around. A tear falls down my cheek and I brush it away quickly.

"I'll come," he says.

"You don't have to do that." I stare at my feet.

Lawrence drops his hold on my arm but takes a step closer to me. Slowly, I tilt my head. He's close, close enough that I nervously tuck a lock of hair behind my ear.

"I'll *come*. I'll testify on Tuor's behalf. Even if you don't need me to. Even if you find another way to prove his innocence, I'll still swear to my death that his character is solid."

"You will?"

"Yes. No one here seems to care who I am anyway. If they were looking for me, they would have posted a notice like they did for Tuor. I'll use a different name at the trial and . . . "

"And?"

"We'll get Tuor freed."

I smile, brushing another stray tear off my cheek.

"Besides," Lawrence says, shifting away from me slightly. "Even if they do figure out who I am, what's the worst that will happen to me?" He crosses his arms across his chest. "They might throw me in jail. But the worst that can happen to Tuor is—"

Lawrence stops suddenly.

"He could die." I say it so he knows I understand.

"Yeah . . . I'll be by your side. *I promise*."

I practically leap, closing the gap between Lawrence and me, and pull him into a tight hug.

"What time is the trial?"

"Daybreak, at the Justice House."

"Daybreak . . . I will be there."

"I should get home," I say, thinking of Malcolm.

"Of course."

I call to Lawrence as he starts to step away. "Hey."

"Yeah?"

"I was thinking. Since you don't really have a place to stay, Mirabelle might let you sleep at her house."

"Oh, thanks, but don't worry. I've finally earned enough rings this week, I'm staying at Lindon Place. I haven't slept in a bed in a while."

A laugh erupts from my mouth, loud and boisterous. "You're spending your rings on a room at Lindon Place?"

"Yes," Lawrence says, his cheeks growing red. "A warm room and a hot meal . . . "

"You've been eating hot meals at Mirabelle's most nights."

"I'm very hungry," he says, shrugging his shoulders.

I shake my head slowly. I suppose habits of the wealthy don't die easily. "You still have a lot to learn when it comes to living in Bear Gap."

"I hope you stick around long enough to teach me," he says before flashing me a wide smile and jogging down the street.

***

Deep resonant voices pour from the cracks and crevices of our shack as I approach the front door. My father has friends over, I realize. I've never been able to decide if I'd rather come home to just my father or my father and his visitors. When his buddies are here, he usually doesn't hit me, simply because he's preoccupied. But these men, Vincent, Boris, and a few others, are loud, obnoxious, and narrow minded. A ripple of laugher floats through the room. I walk in, keeping my eyes pointed toward the ground, hoping I won't draw their attention. The room is warm with candlelight.

"Camilla." My father's rough, slurred voice calls to me as I creep along the wall to get to my bed mat.

"Yes, Father?"

Two other men sit across from Malcolm. The one, Vincent, I recognize. He's brawny like my father, but taller and more fit. I wonder how he's managed to keep so trim with the gallons of mead he consumes. He leans back on a chair and balances it on its back two legs, all while guzzling a long drink from a dark amber jug.

"Get me my... get me my... " Malcolm blubbers.

The second man, Boris, a scrawny fellow with a shrunken face and a short mustache, laughs uncontrollably at my father's stuttering. Malcolm is far more drunk than the other two.

"Is that Camilla?" Vincent asks, dropping his chair to the floor with a big creak.

I nod, pursing my lips in annoyance. Malcolm points a finger at me, his big eyes swimming.

"That's my kid."

"You're looking less and less like a little girl every time I see you."

Boris is bent forward, elbows on his knees, a mug of mead in his hand. He laughs at Vincent's comment even though Vincent's hungry gaze doesn't indicate that it was meant to be funny. I roll my eyes and start to move away when my father calls my name again.

"Camilla . . . come here." Malcolm reaches out an arm as if to draw me closer, but I hold my ground. "Come here."

"No," I say meekly.

Boris breaks into a laugh again and Vincent looks on, equally humored. "You ought to listen to your father," he says, taking another swig. "He's raised you all by himself."

"I raised myself," I say. I can hardly believe the words have left my mouth. A few days around Lawrence and I have started to feel less sympathy for my father.

"By the moon and stars!" Vincent shouts, pounding a hand on the table so hard that the legs jump off the ground. "You have quite a fiery daughter!"

Malcolm chuckles along with slow guffaws.

"Come 'ere," he says again, keeping his arm outstretched. "Come 'ere!"

His eyes grow big in a moment that almost resembles clarity, but I know it to be rage. Vincent gives me a scolding look, his bushy gray eyebrows raised. I sigh, slinking over to my father as he wraps me in a rough, sweaty embrace.

"This is my kid. This is my *good* kid." His breath reeks of the sour-smelling drink in his hand. The other two men look on in glee as Malcolm holds me tight to his paunchy middle. "The other one is no good . . . no good," Malcolm mumbles.

"We know about your brother," Vincent says. My body tightens. Does Malcolm know about Tuor's arrest? "Workin' for that Warwick scum, all high on himself living up there in LilyAye."

"He left me because he loves that fool Quinten Warwick better than me!" Malcolm moans in agreement. "That man rode in here, took away everything I owned, including my boy."

Malcolm jostles me around as he talks. Vincent and Boris look on, nodding at my father's drunken babblings.

"Get off me." I say, pushing Malcolm's hairy arm away. I take a step back, the group staring at me. "Tuor didn't leave because he loves our Supreme Ruler. He left because you're a dirty drunk!"

My heartbeat speeds like a galloping horse. There's a moment when I wonder if Malcolm will break tradition and reach out and hit me in front of his buddies. Instead, the three erupt into laughter as if I was just a bit of entertainment for them the whole time. I chance a few steps away from them before dropping my bag on the floor and plopping onto my bed.

"Eh, how's that delivery?" Boris asks, a laugh still on his lips.

"Near done," Vincent says. "Needs two more nights, then it'll be ready to sell. Hey, Malcolm?" My father grunts in response. "How 'bout we use your place this time for the selling?"

They're talking about the drink in their hands. Vincent makes the vile stuff.

"Mmm, sure." My father nods his head vigorously.

This isn't the first time Vincent has used our house for his business. He knows the governor is always looking for illegal producers, so Vincent changes his sell location often. Every couple of months, Vincent comes by, fills my father up with as much mead as he wants, and then asks him if he can sell here. It's dangerous, Vincent knows that, and he knows that my father will be arrested if he's caught with a house full of liquor.

"In two nights' time, we'll bring 'em by," Vincent says. My father nods. "Good. Well, nothin' better than your company." Vincent slaps my father on the back. "Boris, we ought to go."

As if this conversation were rehearsed, Vincent and Boris stand from the table. Vincent reaches out a hand to shake with my father, but Malcolm is so drunk he struggles to place his hand in the right place. Vincent settles for another friendly slap on the back before winking at me and walking out the front door.

I watch my father's soft blurry eyes as they look for an object to focus on. How pathetic, I think stretching out my legs and lying down on my side. Malcolm brings his cup to his mouth and takes four big swallows to empty it.

I could report him, I think to myself. I could report my father and all of his friends so easily to the governor. They're stupid enough to talk about their criminal acts around me. Maybe I should. Maybe I should turn them in. I'd look like a traitor to everyone in the swamps, but I've grown so tired of my father, I'm tempted to actually do it. I roll over to lie on my back and stare at the ceiling. Maybe I should . . . I nearly gasp out loud as an idea enters my head.

CHAPTER SEVENTEEN

"SIR, I NEED to talk to you."

Supervisor Benedek rounds the corner of his booth and marches past me. There's a glint of excitement in his eyes now that his morning duties are complete. "I told you, girl, the corn fields are that way." He throws a hand up to point to the farm as he steps onto the white stone path that winds through the back flower garden of the governor's manor. It's a pathway I'd normally never dare traverse, but my mind is focused on Tuor.

"Why are you acting like you don't know me?" I ask. Benedek is walking so fast I nearly break into a run to keep up. I watch the back of his head as it weaves in and out between the tall bushes. "I've been working here my whole life. The least you can do is call me by my name."

The words come out of my mouth before I have time to think about what I've said and who I've said them to. It catches Benedek's attention though. He stops just a few feet short of the back door. Benedek's thin, lanky body slowly turns. He grips the not-so-thin ledger book tightly in his spindly fingers.

"What is it I can do for you, *Camilla Crim*?"

His voice is so thick with sarcasm I almost don't want to say what I came here to say. He could easily call to one of the nearby guards to have me flogged, but he hasn't done that yet.

"Do you know of my brother's . . . situation?"

Benedek tilts his head. "That scoundrel they arrested the other night? I know they tied his family name back to you and that's how they discovered that you were harboring an Elmyra fugitive. What I can't determine is why they haven't arrested you as well for playing an assistant to him."

That was not the answer I expected Benedek to give. I feel for a moment like I'm talking to one of the captain's wives, gossiping by the posting tree.

"He might have been a fugitive, but he's innocent of the crime they're accusing him of."

Benedek shifts on his feet. Over his brown pants he wears a tunic that's striped in black and maroon, Warwick colors.

"I suppose that will be determined at his trial. Fortunately, the governor has asked that I give council during the trial. I look forward to it."

I feel my heartbeat trip over itself. I shouldn't be surprised by this news. Of course Governor Leo would pick his most loyal attendant to be one of The Seven.

"I need to speak with the governor before the trial," I blurt.

"Excuse me? Who do you think you are that you can gain an audience with the governor?"

"My brother didn't kill the man that they say he killed, and Governor Leo needs to know that."

"If that's true, then you can present your evidence at his trial."

Benedek starts to turn on his heels, but I catch him by his baggy sleeve.

"I will do that," I say through gritted teeth. "But I have a very good reason why I think you should let me speak to the governor *before* the trial."

Benedek's face erupts in a look of horror.

"You do not speak to me in that manner. I am the appointed Grand Supervisor over this farm, and I deserve respect!"

Grappling with the door, Benedek finally turns the spiral brass knob and steps inside after giving me a reproachful look. I turn and lean my back against the now closed door. Hope fizzles away from me like steam drifts from a cup of hot tea.

A few feet away, a guard eyes me. I could do as Benedek says, go to work in the corn field today, wait for Tuor's trial, and present my evidence that he's innocent. But I have no evidence. I have nothing to prove that Tuor didn't kill that man except for the character I know my brother possesses.

No one will listen to that during Tuor's trial. I can just imagine Benedek rolling his eyes at me from the council seats. I have to have a surety from Governor Leo before Tuor is tried. He has to understand the type of person that Tuor is. He has struggles, but he'd never kill anyone. I start to feel sick in my stomach. If Mirabelle was here, she'd sigh and give me a chiding pat on my shoulder. I take a deep breath and turn around to face the door. No, Mirabelle would shriek in horror if she saw what I was about to do.

"Benedek!" I yell, letting my voice echo for everyone to hear. "Supervisor Benedek!" I bang my fists as hard as I can against the tall wooden door. "Open up this door, you stuck-up fool!"

The guard who saw me earlier marches across the lawn. I need Benedek to open the door before the guard gets to me.

"Benedek! Let me in! I'm not done talking to you!" My voice cracks as I hit top volume. "BENEDEK!" The guard's wide gait closes in on me fast. I place my hand on the door knob, but the door opens from the other side. Benedek's tight sour face is staring back at me. I manage a smug smile before the soldier grabs my arms from behind.

"I'll take care of her, sir."

"Wait!" I yell, kicking against my restrainer. "I just want to talk to the supervisor."

"Have you lost all your sanity?" Supervisor Benedek says with a raging fire in his eyes. The soldier pulls me away, but Benedek holds up a hand, signaling him to stop. "You seem determined to be put in the stocks today."

"Wait, listen. I have information you want."

Both my arms are held tightly behind my back. Benedek tilts his chin up and looks down at me like the scum he believes me to be. But he doesn't have the guard whisk me away. "I know Governor Leo has been looking for illegal alcohol production."

"What of it?"

"I can give names, locations, drop off times, whatever you want. I have secret information that the governor can't get ahold of."

"Governor Harras' task force has done a fine job of ridding this territory of those that choose to break the law." Benedek folds his arms across his chest. "Put her in the stocks."

"Wait, wait, wait!" I yell. The guard drags me away, ripping at the joints in my shoulders. "They still can't find the man who's producing right here in Rande and I know why." Benedek's body turns slowly toward the manor but stops halfway. A shimmer of curiosity shows on his face. "How do you think you'd look to Governor Leo if you were able to give him the information he needed to catch these men?"

The guard bears down on my arms. My knees buckle so I'm practically kneeling in front of Benedek.

"Halt," Benedek says, holding up the palm of his hand.

"You can take me and torture the information out of me, or I'll give it to you happily . . . " The words continue to spew out of my mouth as the pain in my back and arms grows worse. "As long as I get a meeting with the governor."

"Why would I bother to torture you? I can have you arrested now for harboring the information."

"Yes, but you know as well as I do that Governor Leo doesn't care about putting a measly little girl in the stocks when he can report to the Supreme Ruler that he's arrested another illegal producer in his territory. I can help you, you can help keep order in Bear Gap, and Governor Leo looks good in front of Warwick. This can all work if you grant me a meeting with the governor."

Benedek's jaw twitches as he glares at me. "Let her go." The guard is reluctant but then releases my arms with a snap so that I fall onto the ground, scraping the palms of my hands. "Return to your post," Benedek instructs the guard.

I listen to the footsteps of the guard as he stalks away. All the while, Benedek's eyes stay pinned on me and his hands are tucked tightly in the folds of his arms.

"Now, tell me what you know."

I stagger to me feet. "Will I have a meeting with the governor?"

Benedek's eyelids dip closed for a moment to show his annoyance. "Yes, I'll set up the meeting if your information turns out to be correct."

"It is. It's all true, I promise."

"Who is producing in Rande?"

"His name is Vincent, he's the leader. But he works with a couple of local men too."

"Why is it that we haven't been able to catch this Vincent?"

"He moves his operation around. Every couple of weeks he brews in someone else's house. I've even heard he buries his bottles out in the woods and covers them in leaves and branches and things. And then they choose a totally different location to sell the alcohol from. Whenever Vincent has a new batch ready to sell, he rotates between a few houses. Then they use a code word or something to tell their buyers where to pick up. They don't sell from someone's house for more than a day."

Benedek scoffs. "A code word . . . " he mumbles. "They're quite sophisticated, these cronies. So where is he producing now?"

"I don't know that." A condescending frown forms on Benedek's face. "But I can tell you where they're picking up from this week."

"And how do you know all of this?"

I swallow hard. "Because my father is one of those cronies." Benedek's face is unchanged. "Tomorrow afternoon Vincent will bring his supply to our house. The buyers have one day to come and get what they need. But I've seen this done before. They'll sell out soon after nightfall."

"Anything else?"

"No." I'm surprised by Benedek's response, or I guess it's his lack of response.

"Off to the fields with you."

"What about my meeting?"

"Let's see how tomorrow goes."

Benedek disappears into the home of Governor Leo Harras. I push away the thought that's bubbling up inside my head, the realization that I may have given up my father to the governor without any guarantee that it will help Tuor. I feel a bit dazed as I start the slow walk to the corn fields, where I know I'll be punished for being late.

CHAPTER EIGHTEEN

I'M JITTERY AS I round the corner out of the farm. Tonight is the night that Vincent will drop off the alcohol at our house. I haven't heard anything from Benedek about a raid, but I'm hoping desperately that it will happen. If it doesn't, I don't know how else I'll get a meeting with Governor Leo before the trial tomorrow.

The sick feeling in my stomach started after work yesterday. I had planned on going straight home, but the thought of seeing my father after outing him to Benedek caused me to change direction to Mirabelle's house. By the time I did make it home, he wasn't there. He was probably with Vincent, preparing for the sell-off the next day.

Why am I so nervous about this raid? It's what my father deserves. It's what Vincent and his buddies deserve. They're breaking the law, and they should be punished. But what about Lawrence? He technically broke the law by freeing Tuor and returning him home. Should he be punished as well? I shake my head, trying to knock these and other impossible thoughts out of my head.

Malcolm's sitting at the table when I get home. He holds a bottle of mead in his hand but still seems rather sober. The walls of our tiny shack are lined with dark green and amber jugs, corked and ready to sell. My heart skips a beat at the sight of them. This is really happening.

"I have dinner," Malcolm says, taking a forkful of something into his mouth.

"What is it?"

"Venison. My buddy Hecktor shot one and gave me a few pounds to split up the meat. We need to eat it up before any of those soldier pricks catch wind of a poaching."

Hunting, along with gardening, is illegal in Bear Gap. That kind of food isn't to be trusted is what we're told. But just like the alcohol, people still do it. Malcolm taught me as a child how to use a bow and arrow. I used to hunt food for us all the time until he bartered our bow for a bottle of mead one desperate night.

I drop my jacket on my bed and take a seat at the table. I can't say no, or leave like I want to, or Malcolm will grow suspicious. Act like you normally would, I tell myself. And normally I would eat with him because food is food and I eat when I can.

Malcolm cuts a chunk of meat off what looks like the deer's leg and plops it onto a plate for me. "Boiled onions are on the stove."

"Who else got some meat?" I ask, getting up to retrieve the pot of onions.

"Gave some to Vincent and the others."

My body tenses at Vincent's name. Malcolm scoops the boiled onions onto my plate and pushes it toward my chair. I take a bite of the venison, savoring its wild taste. It seems hard to swallow. I realize it's because I know that any minute a Warwick soldier will burst through the door and arrest my father. Someone knocks on the front door, causing me to drop my fork on the table. Malcolm looks at me with scrunched eyebrows before standing to open the door.

"Come," Malcolm mumbles to the visitor. A young man, not much older than me, enters wearing light brown pants and a gray knitted sweater, which he holds tightly across his chest. He leans in close and mumbles something to my father. Malcolm nods in approval. A gust of cold fall air blows through the house before Malcolm can close the door. "How many?"

"Just one." The visitor looks at me sideways.

"Two rings."

Malcolm picks up one of the dark green glass bottles. They make their exchange quickly and the young man exits without another word. Malcolm returns to the table.

"I thought Vincent liked to make the sales himself," I say.

Malcolm spears a boiled onion and pops it in his mouth. "He had to get another load. Asked me to cover for him until he got back."

I nod, ripping the deer meat apart with my fork.

"Father." Malcolm looks at me under his thick brows. I don't know why I feel I need to tell him this. Is it guilt? Whatever it is, I can't keep it inside. "Tuor's in town," I blurt.

Malcolm takes a bite of the meat and stares at his plate while he chews. "I know."

"You do? How do you know?"

He swallows deeply and shoves another pile of food into his mouth. "I saw his face in Rande Square."

I let my fork drop with a *thud* on my plate, gawking at Malcolm. "You mean you saw his poster? Then you know he goes to trial—for murder?"

Malcolm nods, taking a long drink from his bottle. "Serves the kid right."

I fold my arms across my chest.

"He's acting just like his mother," Malcolm adds.

"Mother?"

I'm so surprised by Malcolm's mention of my mother that I forget I'm mad for a moment.

"She was just like him," Malcolm shouts, pointing a fork at me. "Runnin' off, doing whatever *she* wanted to do."

"At least she had mind enough to get away from you," I sneer.

Malcolm returns to his plate of food. "She wasn't getting away from me, she was getting away from the two of you. It's your fault she left me. You and Tuor were the worst children. She couldn't handle you." Malcolm takes another bite, his jaw moving furiously. "If you have any smarts, you'll stay away from Tuor. He's trouble."

"Are you crazy?" I spit. "Tuor's the only family I have! I'm testifying at his trial tomorrow." Malcolm bursts out in a howl of laughter. "What's so funny?"

"Good luck testifying at a trial for fools."

I'd heard that phrase before, trial for fools, but I didn't really give it any thought until now. Is this trial going to be a farce? No. I'm determined that justice will be found.

"Tuor is innocent," I say, a hint of disdain in my voice.

"It don't matter if he's innocent."

"It's the only thing that matters."

The room is silent for a moment before Malcolm takes another bite of his dinner. "He's past our help."

"You can give up on him, but I'm not. I know you don't like Tuor, but don't you at least care about his life? He could die. Or at least be kept in prison for the rest of his life!"

"I told that boy the day he left here to join the Warwick Militia he was dead to me. He's a fool. What did he think would happen?"

"He only left to get away from you!" I stand, pushing away my plate of food.

Malcolm glances at my half-eaten meal. "It's too bad the kid's in trouble," he says. "Can't say I didn't warn him."

I see Malcolm's temper start to rise. This is how it goes—he seems fine, and then he'll explode in anger. Or is it me who's feeling the fire of hatred?

"I got you this nice meal, would you just sit down and eat with me?"

"Why do you even care if I eat with you? You don't care at all about Tuor, and he's about to be convicted of murder!"

Malcolm slams the palms of his hands onto the table and uses them to push himself up to a standing position.

"I stopped caring for that boy when he chose to trust Quinten Warwick over his own flesh and blood." Malcolm gnaws at his top lip, brushing his mustache down with his hand at the same time. "If he wants to go work for the devil, then there's nothin' I can do for him. I warned him that them Warwick soldiers were the slimiest people I ever saw in my lifetime. I'm not surprised they turned on him."

Malcolm takes another swig from his bottle before setting it firmly on the table. He moves to sit back down, but I grab the bottle, whirling it across the room so it slams against the opposite wall. The dark glass shatters and the pungent liquid oozes down our already dank wall.

"I hope you enjoyed that!" I scream. "It might be your last drink."

Malcolm squints in confusion. "What do you mean by that, girl?"

"Nothing." I realize what I've said and try to recover the blunder. "Only that I hope your body gives out on you."

Malcolm looks at me sideways, his hand curling in and out of a fist.

"Are you lying to me?"

"No."

"I swear if you—"

"You're an idiot for storing this stuff!" I shout.

In a flash, Malcolm's hand stretches out and his palm hits the side of my jaw. I cover my face. We stare until Malcolm sits back down, returning to his meal as if he'd never been interrupted.

The front door opens. I take a quick step backward, expecting to see a Warwick soldier, but it's only Boris. He carries two big jugs in either hand and sets them down with the others. Vincent is close behind with two more jugs. Malcolm jumps up from the table as if he's just been caught by his mother playing instead of cleaning his room.

"Help us out, will ya, Malcolm?"

Slowly I inch backward, slinking down onto my bed mat. The stinging in my jaw starts to subside, so I pull my hand away. I'm glad Malcolm hit me. I'm glad because it means I'll enjoy seeing my father arrested. I watch the three of them as they unload their illegal liquor, filling up the floor of our house so there's barely anywhere to walk.

As evening bleeds into nighttime, shopper after shopper filters through our house, exchanging rings for a bottle of this or a bottle of that. No one notices me, silent and bruised. Then it happens.

There's a tussle outside. Everyone inside the house stops. Vincent draws a short knife from his belt. Then the door swings open wide. Vincent and Boris are shocked. Their contorted faces and wide eyes bring me a joy I've never felt before.

My father, though, the moment he sees the black vests and the emblazoned Warwick crest, he knows what I have done. Soldiers raid our shack, like vultures on a dead carcass. Boris throws his hands up in surrender, but Vincent must be tackled to the ground by two men. Malcolm doesn't give up so easily either. Hugging my legs close to my body, I flinch as he spits obscenities at me while they drag him away.

***

A barrage of Warwick soldiers storm our little shack and start removing the jugs of liquor. I watch on, still frozen in the moment. The sound of clicking boots peppers the floor. I hear another pair of steps, though, quick and light, that sound familiar to me. Supervisor Benedek steps through the front door, watching the proceedings with a look that still speaks displeasure for some reason.

"Your tip turned out to be correct," he says, clasping his hands together.

I straighten my back slightly and look up at Benedek from my seat on the floor. "When do I get my meeting?"

"The governor is a busy man."

"But the trial is tomorrow."

"I know." Benedek looks down his long nose at me. "That's precisely why he's busy." Benedek scans the shack as if he's viewing a filthy horse's stall. "Let's finish up here, men," he instructs. Benedek turns back to me. "The governor will be quite pleased to hear the news of this raid. I rarely get the chance to ride along, but this has been quite thrilling. Good night then, Miss Crim. I suppose I shall see you at your brother's trial." Benedek turns around.

"You just arrested my father," I say. "Can't you at least promise me a meeting with the governor?"

I try painfully hard to keep my voice flat and not inject my words with the disdain that I feel for Benedek.

He breathes in deeply, turning his head just enough so I can see the profile of his face. "I'll do the best I can."

Benedek spirits away and within a few minutes I'm left alone. The room feels hollow. But it's better, I reason, than being here with all of those things and my father. After a moment I can't take staring at the bare floor any longer.

I rise, blowing out all the candles except for one, which I place next to my bed. I stretch out, ignoring the throbbing in my cheek and find my eyes mesmerized by the candle's flame. Tuor's trial is tomorrow. I must go to sleep. I must sleep and think clearly tomorrow. This may be my only chance to show his innocence . . . or his guilt, depending on which story I decide to tell.

Sleep seems far away. My mind buzzes with thoughts of tomorrow and thoughts of Tuor's future. I roll over on my stomach and reach out to pull our special box close to me. I run my finger over the edges, dreaming of a time when Tuor and I could be together and no one paid us any mind. Now, it feels like the whole country has their eyes on Tuor.

Opening the lid of the wooden chest, my stomach tenses. I shift onto my knees and pull the box closer to ensure I'm seeing what I think I'm seeing. Lying diagonally in the box is a short rusty dagger with a worn handle. Slowly, I pull the dagger out. It's dirty with dried dark red streaks all over the blade. Blood.

How in all of Elmyra did a bloody knife get in my box?

The only other person in this world who even knows this box exists is Tuor. Malcolm could have seen the box, I suppose.

My mind whirls and twists. The night Tuor was arrested, he saw the box. He held this box. But could he have—I don't allow my mind to go any further. I snap the lid of the box shut and storm out of the shack, dagger in hand. The night is cold, and the air prickles at my bare arms. I march straight in front of the shack, deeper into the woods, until I feel the squish of the swamp on my feet.

The swamp, speckled with tall slender trees, seems to breathe and belch under the thick stagnant water. I bring my hand up to look at the dagger. The moonlight casts a blue haze over its dirty blade. I lift my arm and snap it forward, letting the knife slip from my hand. I hear a gentle plop as the weapon joins the inky swamp.

My hand trembles. What have *I* done? What has *Tuor* done?

CHAPTER NINETEEN

DAYBREAK HITS BEAR Gap like a blacksmith pounds away at a horseshoe, hard and sudden. I'm awake in an instant, no tossing on my bed mat or lying with my eyes closed just to enjoy a few more moments of peace. Today is Tuor's trial. I move about the house with stiff, rote movements, not really thinking about what I'm doing.

I rush into town, my head low. I don't notice a single person that passes me. If I knew what I was going to say in defense of Tuor, I would practice it in my head. I'd go over it again and again, but I still don't know exactly what I'll say. Should I admit Tuor is guilty? What if he's not guilty and he receives punishment he doesn't deserve? But the knife . . . I can't help but think about the knife. The thought bubbles up in my head before I have a chance to stop it.

What if Tuor is guilty?

The steps to the Justice House stretch out in front of me. There are a few soldiers loitering around the entrance. One of them yawns. The sun barely sheds light on the village surrounding me. I'm early. No one else is here yet. I start pacing in front of the steps, feeling as though I'll burst if Mirabelle doesn't get here soon. I glance at the soldiers guarding the door. They smirk at me. My hands move and twist together in a nervous wringing motion.

"Camilla dear."

I exhale. Mirabelle pulls me into a hug without having to say another word.

"They arrested Malcolm last night," I blurt.

"What for this time?"

"He was selling alcohol at the house."

Mirabelle nods. She understands. She seems like the only person in the world who understands.

"I just hope it doesn't look bad for Tuor," I say.

That was a thought I didn't have until I woke restlessly in the middle of the night. What if turning Malcolm in actually *hurts* Tuor's trial? I take a shaky breath as Mirabelle rubs my back.

"Have faith." Mirabelle tilts her head to stare at the ground, but I can tell she doesn't see it. She's thinking about something else. "We'll get Tuor out . . . one way or another."

Mirabelle talks as if she knows of some cure to this problem that I'm not aware of.

"Did you eat anything this morning?"

I shake my head. "I can't."

A carriage pulls up in front of the Justice House steps. A boy servant hurries along to open the door to the carriage. Out steps a round woman adorned in a woolen jacket that's been dyed a shade of bright blue. Her hand glitters with many rings as the boy servant grabs it to help her out of the carriage. She's the first of The Seven to arrive.

Fear grips my insides. The woman passes through the Justice House door. I know her kind, rich and entitled. She'll have no mercy for a man like Tuor.

"I don't know if I can do this," I say, spinning around to face Mirabelle. "These council members, they're not going to care one bit about Tuor or what he's been through."

Mirabelle takes my face in her hands. I feel like I'm six years old again, crying to Mirabelle because I tumbled down the steps on her stairwell.

"Oh, child," she coos. "Unfortunately, you don't have a choice whether you want to do this or not. You must face what's beyond those doors. You'll have to accept Tuor's fate."

Her speech is quite different than the one she gave me when I was six. As I think on it, I realize she's right. I have to do this. It's no comfort to me. It's simply the truth.

Two more council members arrive, Benedek and another woman. This one is tall and dressed very businesslike with her hair spun up in a bun, thick streaks of gray striping her light brown strands. Other villagers begin gathering around the Justice House too. Tuor's is not the only trial today, I find out after talking to a woman who's there with her young daughter. She's here to attend the trial of her husband, who was arrested for poaching a few squirrels.

"If you're late, they won't let you sit in or be a witness," the woman explains.

"Truly?" I ask.

"That's why I'm here so early."

I look to Mirabelle.

"Perhaps we should go in," she says.

"Lawrence isn't here yet."

"I'm here." Lawrence jogs toward me. His hair's disheveled. "Sorry. I'm sorry," he stutters. "I overslept. The beds at Lindon Place are far superior to sleeping on the street." He runs a hand through his hair.

"It's time to go in," I say.

I walk toward the door of the Justice House, now overly anxious to get inside. Another carriage pulls up that causes me to stop. I recognize it as Governor Leo's. Out pops the governor, flipping his long gray-speckled hair over his shoulder. A servant is immediately behind him, his only task to spread out the governor's cape. Behind him, Tuor's captain emerges from the carriage. Ridley surveys the area as if he's a hawk searching for a lowly mouse to attack.

"Now we really have to get inside," I say, a rush of panic coursing through me. I march toward the door. "Let's go." Mirabelle is close on my heels, but Lawrence dawdles behind us. "What's wrong? We have to go in now."

His body jerks when I speak. He stares at the door as Governor Leo and Ridley pass over its threshold.

"Lawrence?"

His fingers rake through his hair as his eyes dart back and forth.

"Are you okay, dear?" Mirabelle asks.

The soldiers at the front door scan the steps as the final council member arrives.

"We have to go!" I shout.

"I-I'm sorry, Camilla. I can't go inside." Lawrence takes two steps away from me.

"What do you mean?"

"I have to go." Lawrence raises a hand to me. "I'm so sorry."

I drop down one of the steps toward Lawrence. "You promised me." My voice quivers.

Lawrence turns to walk away. "I can't. I'm so sorry," he says, looking at me one last time before breaking into a fevered run.

"You promised!"

I stand on the courtroom steps, staring as Lawrence's body disappears. He's gone. He's just gone, which means Mirabelle and I are the only ones to testify on Tuor's behalf.

CHAPTER TWENTY

THE JUSTICE HOUSE is dim and cramped with only the light of a few candle sticks to light the way. Its walls are lined with archways that appear to lead to different hallways and stairwells. Soldiers guard the archways with a wide stance. With the snap of his fingers, the soldier with the parchment instructs two men to take Mirabelle and me by the arm. Mirabelle is taken to the archway on the far right, and I'm pulled to one in the middle.

"Mirabelle," I yell with a shaky voice.

"It will be okay, sweetie."

I'm led unceremoniously down a dark corridor. The walls and floor are all made of the hard gray Catahli mineral. I touch a hand to the wall and find the stone cold and perspiring. As we walk, the hallway grows narrower. The soldier pushes me forward into the darkness, his hand still firmly on my arm.

The floor steadily declines. I try to slow my pace, but the soldier forces me to keep going, quick and fevered. We round a corner, then another. I nearly trip down a set of steps as we delve deeper and deeper into the pit of the Justice House.

I'm nudged around another sharp corner that opens up into a long corridor. At the end of it, I see an opening lit with dull orange firelight. We march forward, the walls closing in even further. Finally, we come to a halt just inside a carved stone archway. He releases my arm, and I snap it back quickly.

"What do I do now?" I ask.

"Wait."

I place my hands on the edge of the archway, leaning forward to look inside the Justice Hall. There's one large step down that leads into a grand cave with a high ceiling and torches all around the perimeter. Smoke settles heavily in the room, and my nose crinkles as the smell mixes with the dampness.

On the far right wall hangs an enormous flag, so striking it begs to be looked at. A blanket of black fabric nearly covers the whole back wall and bares the flashy red Warwick crest. In front of the flag is a raised platform of seats, almost three times my height, with a thick wooden railing around the front. Seven chairs sit on the platform, four on the back row and three in the middle, all covered in dark maroon fabric. Governor Leo Harras sits in the very front of the platform. He's propped up in a high-backed red-cushioned throne and picks at his fingernails absentmindedly.

His wife, Karla, sits next to him on her own throne with an expectant look on her face. A tiny white-haired dog is nestled on her lap, which she pets with long, pampering strokes. Her hair is stringy as it hangs over her eyes. Her lips are stained a deep crimson.

This is odd, I think. Karla is rarely seen outside of the Harras Manor, let alone in the courtroom. I've heard stories from her handmaidens that the governor's wife is known to be holed up inside her room for days, insisting that every necessity be brought to her bedside. But she's a Warwick, I remember, married off to Governor Leo so the two of them could build up the national farm and establish a Warwick presence in Bear Gap.

Behind Governor Leo and Karla, seven other men and women filter onto the platform. They're the council members that will advise Governor Leo on my brother's fate. I watch Benedek as he's the last to take a seat. He holds a stack of parchment, notes he's taken, it seems. And then there's Ridley Thatius, Tuor's captain, one of The Seven.

I glance around the room and notice that the wall opposite me has ten archways, like the one I'm standing in. They're for the witnesses, I realize when I see Mirabelle standing in one. I try to catch her eye, but she's too far away. Catahli envelops me at every turn. The tiniest of sounds echoes across this cavern.

A man stands up on the platform, the great Warwick flag casting a dark pall behind him. "Bring out the accused." His voice reverberates through the rotunda ceiling.

From the back of the room, opposite the platform, an iron-gated door cracks open. Tuor is dragged through the archway, his hands and feet bound with iron chains. His back is curved and slumped, and he stumbles across the floor as the soldier jerks his chains forward. The clatter of Tuor's iron bonds echoes across the length of the room. I grit my teeth at the sight of him. His hair is wet with sweat. It hangs limp, clinging to his sallow skin. His face is a mosaic of nicks and bruises, and he walks with a severe limp, dipping down low with every step.

"You've hurt him!" I say, spinning around to confront the soldier. His eyes flicker at me with a look of utter disinterest.

Tuor is dropped several feet from the foot of the council platform. The soldier latches his chains to an iron ring that's screwed into the floor. The chains on Tuor are just long enough that he's forced to kneel before the council. His eyes avert the council members' stares.

Governor Leo stands, bemused, in front of Tuor, the witnesses, and The Seven. The man who spoke earlier hands Governor Leo a scroll and bows before returning to his seat. The governor clears his throat.

"The trial for the accused, Tuor Crim, has now begun under my direction, Sir Leo Harras, governor and servant to our Supreme Ruler, Quinten Warwick. I will now read the crimes of the accused." Governor Leo shifts the parchment in front of his face. "Tuor Crim, of the house of Malcolm Crim, is accused of the murder of one Aiden Brookes. Captain Ridley Thatius has henceforth accused Tuor Crim of the killing of Aiden Brookes based on the following evidence. Tuor Crim was the only person present at the time that the body was discovered. He was also in possession of a weapon that is believed to have been used during the crime." The governor raises his eyes and turns to address the council. "Can the accuser confirm that the accusation has been read correctly?"

Ridley stands, his mouth set in a hard line and says, "I confirm it."

"Well then," Governor Leo shifts to face Tuor. "My council and I will now hear witness from those associated with the accused and examine the truthfulness of these charges. First witness, please." Governor Leo sits down on his throne with a quill at the ready. He then nods, and a moment later Mirabelle steps from her archway.

She is led to the center and stands just in front of Tuor. The platform is so high she has to crane her neck to make eye contact.

"Testimony will be heard from Mirabelle Pender," the reader announces.

"Mirabelle," Governor Leo says, running his eyes over the parchment. "You confess to having a relationship with the accused, Tuor Crim?"

"Yes, he's a good friend of mine and—"

"Just a yes or no answer will do." The governor seems to relish his power, savoring every snide comment. "Only answer the questions we specifically ask."

I can see drops of sweat forming on Mirabelle's brow despite the chilly air in the court room.

"How long have you known the accused?"

"Oh, well, it's been nearly fifteen years."

"Tuor tells us you were something of a mother to him. Is this true? And if so, why was such a relationship necessary?"

"Yes, yes, that's very true." Mirabelle seems to relax a little. She chances a sideways glance at Tuor, and I can see the tenderness in her eyes even from this distance.

"Tuor's real mother left him when he was just a child. He's always been a sweet boy, and I'm proud to know that he thinks of me as a mother." Tuor's chains rattle as he manages to tilt his head and give Mirabelle a weak smile.

Benedek stands from his spot in the gallery and addresses Mirabelle after a moment of silence from Governor Leo.

"In all truthfulness, Miss Pender, do you know of any instances since you've known Tuor that he has broken a Warwick law?"

His thin spectacles rest on the tip of his nose as he looks down at Mirabelle with an unrelenting stare.

"Well . . . he had no mother, and no money. There were things he had to do just to live."

"A yes or no," Governor Leo warns.

"Yes, there were instances." Mirabelle pauses for a moment. My hands grip the edge of the archway, feeling the raw Catahli mineral against my palms. Of course Tuor and I had to do some things when we were children that weren't legal. That was before the farm was built, before I could work to provide for us.

"He used to . . . steal things," she says flatly.

"What things?" Benedek pushes.

Mirabelle's eyebrows sag and she looks down at Tuor as if she's the one who attached his fetters.

"Clothes, food . . . "

"Anything else?"

"Rings. He used to steal rings from me. But it was only to survive," she adds quickly. "He had nothing!"

The council stirs as Governor Leo gives Benedek a nod to continue.

"I'm of the opinion, Sir Harras, that a man that can break the restrictions of our government at such a young age could certainly be capable of murder fifteen years later."

Benedek sits as nods of agreement ripple through the council.

"What?" I say loudly. "That doesn't mean he's a murderer." My words are absorbed into the vast room. The soldier reaches out and squeezes my arm tightly, signaling me to shut up.

Governor Leo waves his hand and Mirabelle is taken away, led through an archway and taken out of sight.

"Bring out the next witness." Governor Leo's voice booms through the Justice Hall.

"Is that me?" I ask.

The soldier just shakes his head. Who else would be a witness? Is it Lawrence? Has he come back? From one of the arches along my wall, a man emerges, struggling against his restraints. He's plopped in front of Tuor and bears similar chains, and even a similar countenance. His broad back is bent and his thick head hangs low.

"Father?"

The reader stands. "Testimony will now be heard by Malcolm Crim."

"Malcolm Crim," Governor Leo says, looking at his notes. "State your relation to the accused."

Malcolm brushes his nose with the back of his hand. "I'm the boy's father."

A man stands behind Governor Leo. He's tall and thin with deep wrinkles on his face. "Mr. Crim, can you please tell your governor, Sir Leo, myself, and the council why you're bound today?" Malcolm coughs harshly on the stone floor before looking up toward the platform.

"I guess you could say I'm something of a Warwick rebel." Governor Leo turns to his wife and rolls his eyes. "Think I heard someone call me that one time. I break any law that man makes." My father lets out a throaty chuckle, then turns his head and looks bitterly at Tuor. "So much like your father, ain't ya?" he adds before turning back toward the council.

The wrinkled man speaks again. "Mr. Crim, I find it strange that a man of your reputation and your past would encourage your son to join the Warwick Militia. Perhaps you used your son as a means to get revenge on the establishment that you've so often disparaged?"

Malcolm smirks before speaking. "You overestimate my intelligence, *sir*. Whatever my son did, if he did anything at all, was all on his own doing. I never told him to do anything except stay away from you Warwick scum."

The soldier takes two quick steps toward my father and hits him hard across the mouth. Malcolm pauses, then spews a splattering of blood onto the icy smooth floor. I shudder in surprise, but Governor Leo and The Seven look perfectly placid.

The wrinkle-faced man gathers together the fabric of his long tunic before sitting down.

"We understand your instinct to protect your son," Governor Leo says. "No matter how poor you may be at it, but I would be willing to permit you a level of . . . pardon, if you share with us all you know about your son's indiscretions." Governor Leo touches his long gray-streaked hair as one might pet the mane of a horse. "We have plenty of evidence to connect you with Vincent and his illegal activities. Perhaps we could just . . . forget about that if you confirmed our thoughts regarding Tuor's character."

My heart is pounding so loudly now, I'm sure the soldier next to me can hear it. Malcolm scoffs. Please don't do it, I beg. *Please.*

"I don't know of any *indiscretions* my son has committed . . . *sir.*"

I exhale. Governor Leo sighs, turning his eyes to the parchment sitting in from of him. He turns a page before asking: "It seems I employ a Camilla Crim from your house at my farm. Is that correct?"

"Yeah."

"So she supports you then? Buys you food, gives you rings for your illegal liquor, pays the taxes on your land?" Malcolm doesn't respond, but his silence is clearly a yes. "I have the power, Mr. Crim, to dismiss your daughter from employment if you choose not to comply with us today."

Malcolm snorts a laugh as he slowly shakes his head. I'm holding my breath, waiting for Malcolm to incriminate Tuor. He knows that being banned from the farm is as good as being sent to the execution block.

"I haven't seen my son in three years. I don't know nothin'."

Malcolm locks eyes with Governor Leo in a silent game of power. I'm in such awe, I can hardly move. He didn't take the deal.

Malcolm is waved away through his archway. He must truly hate the governor and the other Warwick supporters more than Tuor. I crane my neck to watch and listen as his shackles echo softly through the corridor.

"Bring out the next witness."

The courtroom goes silent and my breath catches in my throat.

"Let's go," the soldier says.

My body jolts, suddenly alert and buzzing. I feel frozen for a moment until the soldier takes my arm and firmly pushes me out of the archway. My footsteps echo across the hard floor. Tuor looks at me as I approach. His eyes say . . . they look . . . is it shame? His head turns back to the floor quickly.

I've underestimated the magnitude of this room. It feels as if I'm a tiny drop in a great lake full of water. I'm planted front and center where the others stood. A platform of quizzical, weird-looking council members peer down at me.

CHAPTER TWENTY-ONE

"WE WILL NOW hear testimony from Camilla Crim." The reader's voice bounces off the Catahli like the walls of a cave.

"Miss Crim." Governor Leo's voice snaps my gaze to the front of the courtroom. "Did you know your brother was running from the Warwick Army?"

The question is so presumptuous it throws me off. I hadn't expected it so early on. "No, initially, I didn't think so."

"But you met with Tuor at an abandoned church. You saw him there, and it was obvious that he had separated himself from his troop."

"Yes, but—"

"You must have known something wasn't right."

"My brother can be very paranoid, Governor. I just thought—"

"What you *thought* is that your brother was in trouble, and you were going to try and hide him to avoid capture." I bite my lip. He's right. Nothing he's saying is a lie. It just didn't happen that way in my mind.

"I'd like to remind you, Miss Crim, to tell the truth to the council. Honesty is vital to a fair trial."

"I did think he was in trouble," I admit.

"So then when was it that you reported your brother's break from the Warwick Militia?"

My hands begin to shake. I clasp them tightly together. "I didn't."

"I find that strange. Not only do you work on my farm, where there are a multitude of officials, but you could have notified any soldier in town of your brother's sudden appearance. Soldiers that you likely passed multiple times when visiting your brother at the abandoned church."

"I wanted to," I say. "I wanted Tuor to come forward. I tried to convince him to."

"Why didn't you come forward yourself?"

"I . . . " Seven pairs of eyes stare at me. "I thought it would be better if Tuor gave himself up. Perhaps you would show mercy on him if he had done that. I had no reason to believe he'd done anything like this, my brother has always been—"

"You had no reason?" Governor Leo's voice breaks into nearly a shout. "Didn't your brother tell you himself that he was . . . " Governor Leo picks up one of his papers to look at the writing closer. "Quote, 'being hunted down?' Doesn't being hunted down indicate a rather serious offense?"

"He . . . " My voice cracks for everyone in the room to hear. How do they know Tuor said that to me? I look to Tuor. His body is a bloody canvas of marks and bruises. They tortured him, I realize. "You tortured him," I say, still watching Tuor.

"Answer the question, Miss Crim."

I look back to Governor Leo and the others in the council. My eyes search their stony stares. Sympathy eludes them all. "He did tell me that." My voice is weak. I feel weak.

"Wouldn't you agree that such a proclamation would indicate a rather serious offense?" Governor Leo repeats.

"I guess."

"So the question I have for you then is why didn't you report this right away?"

"I don't know."

I look at my hands. I can't stop shaking. The dark smoke-filled ceiling feels like it's going to collapse on me. Everything around me is callous and cold. The Warwick flag seems to grow closer like a great dark monster.

"Miss Crim?"

"Because he's my brother!" I shout. "He's my brother and I love him and I . . . I suppose I was protecting him."

Governor Leo takes a deep breath and leans back in his chair. It's the governor's wife who speaks now. "Did you know your brother was a murderer?" she asks, stroking her dog who's sleeping peacefully on her lap. Her voice is queer and singsongy. It's like she's asking out of sheer curiosity.

"No! And he's not." My cheeks flush.

I bite down on my lower lip, begging myself to keep calm. The angrier I get the guiltier I look. I steady my breathing. "My brother loved being in the Warwick Militia. He would have never done anything to intentionally affect his status there."

"All right then," Governor Leo muses. "What do you have to say in defense of the overwhelming evidence against your brother?"

I want to ask, what evidence? Where was it found? Who else was there when Aiden Brookes died? But the look on Governor Leo's face is telling me I have one shot, one gift in this trial that I can use to speak what I think. I squeeze my hands tightly together as if the action will give me strength. I glance at Tuor one last time because I know once I start speaking, I won't be able to look at him. The image of the bloody knife flickers across my mind.

"Governor," I say. Leo's eyebrows raise. "My brother suffers from an illness of the mind." The courtroom goes silent. Every tiny noise, a cough, a readjustment in a chair, the scribble of a quill, it all stops. "He sometimes has thoughts and . . . outbursts that he can't control."

"What is it you are trying to say, Miss Crim?"

"I truly don't know what happened to Aiden Brookes in LilyAye. I wasn't there, and Tuor never mentioned this man to me. But if my brother is found guilty of his murder . . . " Tears silently spill from the corners of my eyes and flow down my cheek. "Please remember that he couldn't help it. Tuor is a kind and energetic person. He has always looked after me and I . . . " I brush a hot tear from my face. "I couldn't live without him." I make eye contact with Governor Leo. "Please remember, Governor, he's not a bad person. He's just a slave to his disease."

The room remains silent as The Seven look to each other. Governor Leo shifts on his seat, trying to keep his composure.

Please let this work. *Please let this work.*

"What would you have me do with such a man, Miss Crim?"

I look to Governor Leo and notice that his countenance has changed. Is it toward mercy? I'm not sure. "Put him out of society and entrust him to my care. I will watch his every move and ensure he never hurts anyone."

"And what if he does hurt someone?"

"Then you can have both of our heads."

A gasp rings out and I look to my left to see Mirabelle with a hand over her mouth.

Governor Leo clears his throat. "That's a very interesting suggestion." He looks at his papers. "Any other questions for Miss Crim?" The council shakes their heads sullenly.

The soldier has me by the arm again and I'm taken away. I'm keenly aware of the lump on the floor that's Tuor, but I can't look down. I'm led back to the archway, where I turn around, wondering what other possible torture they could have in store for us.

"You can leave," the soldier says. "You've made your testimony. It's up to the governor now."

"I'll stay." My voice is almost a whisper.

"We'll now hear from the accused," Governor Leo says, sounding exhausted. He turns to his council. "I think we'll refer to you as Tuor from now on, so as not to confuse you with your father."

Light laughter ripples through the seven council members behind Governor Leo. My father's notorious in town, I know that, but I didn't expect laughter at his mention.

"Tuor," Governor Leo continues, "where were you three Thursdays ago after dinner?"

From his crouched position, Tuor tilts his head to look at Governor Leo.

"Three-three Thursdays ago?" His voice shakes as badly as my hands. Governor Leo nods slowly. "Thursdays we always have chicken and radish soup for dinner with water and bread." Tuor is speaking calmer now, but his words run together. "I remember we didn't get bread that night because of the wheat shortage. The cook said . . . he said, 'no bread tonight, fellows!'"

"We're not interested in your dinner." Another ripple of laughter hits the room, including the soldier standing in the hallway with me. "We want to know what you did *after* dinner."

Tuor's body tenses. "I went to bed. I just went to bed, nothing else. I went back to my dorm, laid down, and went to sleep."

Tuor clutches the sides of his head like he did in the church.

"I checked with your captain, and he said dinner is served promptly at six in the evening. So even if you took an hour to eat your soup, with no bread, which I doubt, that means you could have easily been back in your dorms by seven, or maybe seven thirty. You must have been awfully tired to just go to sleep that early."

"No, no, no . . . " Tuor mumbles, his head still held tightly in his arms.

"What else did you do that night, Tuor?"

"Nothing—nothing happened!"

"What about Aiden Brookes? What about the man we found dead at the bottom of your dormitory steps?"

"It wasn't me. I didn't do it!"

Governor Leo stands and I grab at the cracks between the bricks on the wall for balance.

"Tell us what happened that night!" Governor Leo pounds his fist on the wooden railing that separates the council from everyone else.

Tuor's body convulses. I can hear his afflicted weeping from my spot under the archway. Is it guilt? Has Governor Leo broken my brother to the point where he can't take the guilt? Tuor rocks slowly on his knees, his face still buried in his hands. He's done speaking, I can tell, and so can everyone else.

"Pathetic." Governor Leo mumbles. "We'll now have our final witness." The governor signals to Tuor's captain with the flick of his finger.

"We will now hear witness from Captain Ridley Thatius."

Ridley steps down from the platform. His back is firm and he holds his arms tightly to his side. Turning swiftly in front of Tuor, he faces the council members as if they're the ones on trial. His fingers stroke the black pointed goatee on his chin.

"Captain Thatius, will you tell us what you know about Tuor and these unfortunate instances?"

"Of course. This man, Tuor Crim, was a member of my troop." Ridley purposefully stretches out an arm toward my brother. "A faithful member, I'd say. I very much liked him. But several weeks ago I noticed his demeanor became more erratic and disturbed. Then with the death of Aiden Brookes . . . " Ridley drops his eyelids in an apparent gesture of sadness, but it feels forced. "Well, I did not travel all the way here from LilyAye to speak well of the boy. As much as it troubles me, I make witness today in front of Governor Harras and The Seven that I found this man standing over the bloody dead body of Aiden Brookes with a knife in his hand that evening three weeks ago."

***

I feel my legs go weak as I grip harder to the wall.

"Captain Thatius," Governor Leo says, "do you believe Tuor murdered Aiden Brookes that night?"

"Yes. Tuor had blood stains on his uniform. We searched the area and found no one else in the vicinity that held any evidence of having been involved. We also found several of Tour's comrades who testified that he hadn't been in his dorm room for nearly an hour."

"This can't be true," I say.

Tuor shakes his head back and forth furiously.

"There was a bloody knife that was to be presented today, but it was unfortunately stolen. I'm confident, however, Governor, that Tuor's guilt is still obvious without the presence of this knife. His escape from the LilyAye prison further solidifies his guilt."

"Yes, Captain, thank you for bringing up the prison escape," Governor Leo says, flipping over a piece of parchment. "How can you explain a man freeing himself from the great dungeons of LilyAye?"

For the first time it appears that Ridley is uncomfortable. He shifts on his feet and reaches up to brush his nose.

"Captain?"

Lawrence. It was Lawrence. I want to scream that out loud just for the pleasure of seeing him arrested like Tuor.

"We don't know," Ridley says.

"You don't know?"

"We're not sure how the accused managed to escape."

Governor Leo leans back in his throne, letting out a deep breath. "That's unfortunate," he says. "Because if Tuor had been held as prisoner in LilyAye, his trial would have been there, in your home territory, Captain."

"That's correct."

"That is all the questions I have." Governor Leo smiles, pleased with his performance. "Oh, one more thing . . . "

"Yes, Governor?"

"Curiosity is overwhelming me. How exactly was Aiden Brookes killed?"

"I'm afraid his throat had been cut."

Governor Leo makes a face that expresses his disgust. "How heinous," he says. "That will be all for the trial of Tuor Crim." Governor Leo speaks to the whole room now. "I will take advice from my council and ponder the testimonies I heard today. We shall convene again in two days, when I will make a judgment. Thank you."

The tension in the room instantly loosens. The council members stand and stretch. Governor Leo leans over and whispers something into his wife's ear. Tuor's chains are unhooked from the loop on the floor and he's led across the Justice Hall floor.

"Time to go." The soldier behind me takes my arm and tugs me backward.

My fingernails dig into the Catahli. I picture Tuor, soaked in blood, standing over the lifeless body of another man. I whip my arm away from the soldier and sprint into the courtroom.

"Tuor!"

Tuor's head pops up. His eyes are alarmed and sunken.

"Stay back." shouts the soldier holding Tuor's chains.

I take Tuor's face roughly in my hands. "Did you kill that man?" I screech.

"No."

"Tell me the truth!"

"I didn't!" he weeps. "I swear I didn't."

Tuor's chains hit the floor with a clunk as his soldier rips my hand away. I'm spun around just in time to see my soldier approach. He raises a fist and punches me squarely in the jaw.

CHAPTER TWENTY-TWO

THE DARKENING STREET in front of Lindon Place is empty except for a few remaining villagers. Warm firelight glows through the foggy windows, and a thick cloud of smoke billows from the chimney. It wasn't easy ditching Mirabelle after the trial, but she wouldn't approve of what I'm about to do.

The temperature is starting to turn for the season. Evening grows cooler and cooler every day. My body seems to be doing the opposite though. I'm hot with anger, pacing in front of the inn with a ferocity that feels like fire might burst from under my feet. Every step I take sends bolts of pain through my temples. I rub my chin where the soldier hit me.

Swinging the door open, I march into the lobby. Straight in front of me is the smoke-laden dining room that's set down low by a few steps. To my left is a dark stairwell that leads to the upstairs bedrooms. I peer up to see only one dim torch flickering at the top.

As if she's guarding the patrons upstairs, a woman sits on a stool jotting something onto a piece of parchment. She wears a round embroidered pin on her lapel that reads *Eve*. Eve's head, dressed with thick, shiny blonde hair slowly tilts up to look at me.

"Can I help you?" she asks with a dull yet sour tone.

Her eyelids look heavy, but her posture is straight and narrow. She's befitted with a tight, blue cotton knitted shirt and woolen skirt, equally as snug. She catches me glancing upstairs. I fiddle with my fingernails, and I'm tempted to just run up the stairs immediately and chase down Lawrence.

"Why do you keep looking up there?"

Her boldness surprises me.

"I . . . " I look up the steps again. "I'm supposed to meet someone who's staying here."

"You can sit in the dining room and wait."

Eve points to the dining room with her quill and puts her head down to return to her work.

"No." I inch closer to her hostess podium. Eve looks at me again, her eyebrows scrunching together in great disgust. "I need to meet him upstairs. Can you just tell me what room he's staying in?"

Eve reaches into the cubby of her podium and pulls out a wide ledger book similar to the one Supervisor Benedek uses. She flips open the cover.

"What's his name?" she asks, dropping her quill precisely in the inkwell.

"Lawrence."

Eve runs a finger down the page.

"Lawrence has said nothing to my staff about a visitor." She slams her book shut. "I'm sorry, I can't let you upstairs."

I'm feeling even more agitated. How is it possible that little Lindon Place is exercising the highest standard of security? Eve bows again to her parchment. I'm getting tired of looking at the top of her head.

"Anything else?" she asks without looking at me.

"It's supposed to be a surprise," I say with a forced laugh.

Eve sighs, setting aside her parchment and ledger book.

"It's policy. I don't let strangers upstairs." She brings her eyes up to mine, pausing a moment to let her intensity settle over the rest of my body. "It's unsafe, and I don't allow that type of visit here."

She stares at me while pursing her lips. I feel as though Eve disapproves of every part of my character. I try and judge her age. Her features are delicate, but the faintest glimmer of wrinkles at the corners of her eyes hints to someone a decade older than me.

I could challenge her. Maybe she just works here. Maybe her great-grandfather owns the place and she doesn't really care who comes and goes, she's just following the rules.

Slowly, Eve lifts her arm and directs a pointed finger behind me. I turn my head to see where she's pointing: the front door. She's throwing me out! I place a hand on her podium, feeling the wood's grain beneath my fingernails.

"I've been pushed around all day today," I say through gritted teeth. Eve seems unfazed. "I'm not going to let a light-haired twit tell me who I can and can't see!"

I'm tired of following the rules, whether it's at Lindon Place or the farm or even at the Justice House. I fly up the steps, making a sharp right turn at the top. There are four doors with four rooms behind them. I don't know which one Lawrence is in, but that doesn't matter.

"Lawrence!" I yell through the dank wooden hallway.

I stagger down the hall, banging on the door to my right.

"Lawrence!"

The tattered rug on the floor does little to absorb my cries. I reach to my left to hit the next door when an enraged man opens it. His sweater pulls tightly across his chest. I move forward a step when the door at the very end opens. Lawrence looks down the hall at me, nervously biting his bottom lip. My mouth is set, and I scrunch my eyes. I feel a crease in the middle of my forehead that I'm told I get when I'm angry.

"Hey!" A voice echoes behind me.

I turn around to see Eve rounding the corner.

"Stop!" she yells, her voice solid, without a hint of fear, as if she deals with crazy people like me every day.

I ignore her, marching down the rest of the hallway toward Lawrence's room.

"Camilla, I—" Lawrence raises both of his hands as if he's surrendering, but surrendering is not a choice I'm willing to give him.

"Shut up!" I scream, pushing him roughly over the threshold and into his tiny room.

"Camilla, please, let me explain. I . . . "

I hear the quick determined foot steps of Eve coming down the hall. I shut the door and turn the key that Lawrence has left in the lock.

"How could you leave me?" Hot tears burn in my eyes. "How could you?"

Lawrence backs up and hits the frame of his bed that's just big enough for one person.

"You said you cared for him," I continue. "But you abandoned us both!"

"I-I know," he stutters. His face is a sheen of horror. It pleases me that a man double my size and trained by the Warwick Militia for combat seems terrified of what I might do.

I raise a shaky finger at him. "Tuor will probably die now! They don't trust Mirabelle. They think I'm guilty too. I needed you today! I needed you to tell them that Tuor didn't do it!"

I hear knocking on the door behind me, but I ignore it.

"Why weren't you there?" My voice cracks. I close my eyes for a moment, feeling that I'm falling apart. "Why?"

"I'm sorry. I'm so sorry."

Lawrence's mouth hangs open. His eyebrows dip into a long crease. It's the mark of a man heavy with guilt. I look around the room at the dirty curtains and the pitcher in the corner. A burlap sack sits on his bed, half packed with clothes.

"You're leaving town," I say between sniffles.

"I have to."

The pounding on the door subsides and for a moment it's quiet in the room. I swallow hard.

"Why didn't you stay for the trial?" I say, my voice weak. Lawrence hangs his head.

I stare, my face twisted and tortured. Lawrence tries to speak, but the words never leave his mouth. He bites his bottom lip. A tear runs down his cheek. He wipes it away so quickly I'm not sure it was actually there.

"I'm finished with you," I whisper.

I turn around to leave.

"My father's here." Lawrence's voice is clear but riddled with pain.

I turn around slowly. My arms hang weakly at my side.

"He's come here to take me home, Camilla, and I can't go back there. I can't go back." Lawrence turns from me, his back hunched and his shoulders sunken. His sits down on the bed but barely looks at me. "My father tried to control everything about my life. He was the one who forced me to be in the militia. Anytime I spoke of leaving, he'd make me feel as if I was the town fool." Anger seems to bleed into his sorrow. Lawrence bares his teeth, but it's not his usual charming smile. Instead he reminds me of a mother wolf. "Can you even imagine what it's like to have the constant disapproving gaze of your father every single time you step into the room? The worst part is he kisses the feet of Quinten Warwick, and I can't bear to look at the man."

Lawrence glances at me. I hold my gaze with his fiery eyes. "My father always spoke of duty," he continues. "It was all I ever did—my duty, duty to my family, duty to my country." Lawrence breaks my gaze. "Before I left LilyAye he was insisting it was time for me to marry, time to bind our family with another Warwick dignitary." Lawrence laughs derisively. "My father even has a bride picked out for me. She's fine. She's lovely. It's just, I don't want that life anymore!" He takes in a deep breath through his nose. "I'd rather work at that farm than go back with my father. I saw him at the Justice House and I had to leave, Camilla. I had to."

I hear a clicking at the door. The knob turns. I comprehend nothing Lawrence says.

"Your testimony might have made the difference," I say.

Eve pulls her master key out of the lock and flings the door wide open. Blood pounds through my chest like a stampede of horses.

Lawrence rushes toward me, taking my hand in his. "Camilla, please."

I rip my arm away from his touch.

"Don't ever talk to me again."

Lawrence nods. His face is sallow and he looks defeated, which is the greatest encouragement I can feel right now. Eve wraps her long bony fingers around my arm and tugs me away. I'm shoved out the front door without even a word from her. But when I turn around to take another look at Lindon Place, I spot Lawrence looking down at me from his room's window.

***

A yawn escapes my lips as I run my finger along the wood grain of Mirabelle's kitchen table. It's barely dawn. I didn't talk to Mirabelle after seeing Lawrence last night so I decided to stop before work so we could discuss the trial in private.

I'm depending on Mirabelle's normally upbeat demeanor to lift my spirits after yesterday's devastation, but Mirabelle's acting strange. She's holding her emotions close to her. I'm not sure if she's angry with me, annoyed maybe. Perhaps it's something else entirely.

"Where did you go after the trial?" she asks, busy at the stove, more fidgety than usual.

Mirabelle briskly stirs a pot of oatmeal. Her shoulder bobs up and down as if she's frustrated with the contents.

"I'd rather not talk about that."

Mirabelle breathes out through her nose and begins stirring even faster.

"I can't help you, dear, if you don't tell me what's going on."

"I'm beginning to think no one can help me."

The stirring stops.

Mirabelle's arms drop to her sides. She then folds them across her chest only to release them a moment later to return to her pot.

"I'm going to leave," I say. "I'm leaving Bear Gap once I get Tuor out of prison."

"How do you think you're going to do that?"

"I don't know. I'll figure something out. I'm done following the rules, Mirabelle. I tried to do the right thing and Tuor is still . . . " I brush a wisp of hair out of my face. "It doesn't matter. We'll leave, both of us, get out of Bear Gap, and go somewhere away from all of these Warwick soldiers."

Mirabelle wipes her hands on her apron. She shakes her head slowly. "I don't like the idea of the two of you out there on your own."

"But I'm taking your advice. That was your idea in the first place."

"I know." Mirabelle sighs. "A couple of days ago I thought I'd get you two out of Bear Gap and then you'd be able to return. But now it seems like you'd just be fugitives."

"Maybe that's just the way it has to be."

"You're forgetting that you actually have to get him out of prison before you can run away with him."

I bite my lower lip and flex my fingers in and out as I make a fist. What Mirabelle doesn't know is that I feel like I could rip the iron bars right off Tuor's prison cell. A heavy clunk shakes me out of my thoughts as Mirabelle places the lid on her pot. She spins around and places the pot on the table in front of me.

"Camilla . . . " she says, letting out a great exhale of air.

Her face contorts in a sort of agony. Is this because I didn't tell her about going to see Lawrence? I lean back in my chair, crossing my arms over my chest. I hate it when Mirabelle scolds me.

"There's something we need to talk about."

I scrunch my eyebrows together. "There is?"

"It's something I heard at the trial about how Aiden Brookes was murdered."

My body tenses. *The knife.* Does Mirabelle somehow know that I had the knife? Or that Tuor had it?

"It made me remember something," she says. "Something about a person that you—"

"That I what?"

"It's about your . . . " Mirabelle looks at me, her eyes strained, her hands wringing together. She shakes her head. "It's very complicated."

"What are you talking about?"

"You need to understand that I avoided this for many years."

"Avoided what?"

Mirabelle takes a deep breath as if to calm herself. Her eyes close for a moment, and then she says, "I think it's time you meet Knox Duffy."

CHAPTER TWENTY-THREE

"WHO'S KNOX DUFFY?" I ask.

"I'll try to explain, dear." Mirabelle hurriedly brushes her hair behind her ears. "Do you know the story of The Battle of Bear Gap?"

"I think so. It happened when I was just a little girl."

"That's right." Mirabelle takes a seat across the table from me. "See, Quinten Warwick had just become the Supreme Ruler, but many people in Bear Gap didn't want to recognize him as the new leader."

"Why?"

Sighing, Mirabelle says, "He had just murdered Supreme Ruler Bradac. It seemed he grew incredible wealth and a huge army in an instant. People didn't like it. So Warwick rode down here himself to claim this territory . . . and he brought his army with him."

"Hardly anyone survived, right?"

"All were either killed or imprisoned. All except for *one*."

I look at Mirabelle, my eyes squinting in confusion.

"Knox Duffy?" I ask. She nods. "How is he going to help me get Tuor back?"

Mirabelle purses her lips. "Ohhh . . . " she moans. "I had hoped you'd never have to find this out."

"Find what out?" I jump to my feet, no longer able to take Mirabelle's cryptic tone.

"This is very hard for me, Camilla."

"Tell me what you're talking about!"

Mirabelle bites her lower lip. "Get your coat."

"We're going now? What about work? I already missed yesterday for Tuor's trial."

"This is more important," she says, rising from the table and placing the pot back on the stove.

"More important than eating? Malcolm will have my head when he's released from the stocks."

Mirabelle spins back around to face me. Her eyes grow intense. "Do you want to help your brother or not?"

"You know I do."

"Then get your coat before I lose my nerve. The farm will have to go on without us today."

I pull my jacket off the back of the chair and button it while Mirabelle hurriedly rips off her apron. She dashes up the steps. I follow to the front hall, where Mirabelle dons her own coat and scarf. Pushing me out the front door, I'm given no chance to ask any more questions.

"Where we're going isn't the safest place to be," Mirabelle says, linking her arm into mine.

We follow the front walk through the woods. Bright, morning sun rays pierce through the leaves.

"What do you mean?"

"Knox is known to . . . lose his temper from time to time." Mirabelle gives me a sideways glance as we enter the field with tall grass. "That's a kind way of putting it, I suppose."

"I'm used to that," I say, thinking of my father.

Still, I actually start to feel nervous. Mirabelle has always exploded stories for the sake of being dramatic, but it seems for the first time that she's trying to downplay this Knox fellow. What I can't figure out is why.

We take a left before entering town. Staying in the woods, Mirabelle leads me through the forest as if she knows this trail by heart. We're heading east, upriver from the swamps. The water is clearer there, but the landscape is steep and craggy. We descend deeper in the woods until it becomes so rocky that I take Mirabelle's hand to keep her from falling.

"I'm fine," she fusses. "I've done this before."

I notice her reach for her lower back. She's in pain, but pushing forward anyway.

"How long has it been since you've been here?"

Mirabelle's eyes meet mine. "Quite a while."

When we reach the water, Mirabelle leads me to a tree that's fallen across the river, creating a natural bridge. It's fat and tall with spindly roots that stick up taller than me.

"Jump on up there," Mirabelle says.

"This is where we're crossing?"

Mirabelle nods. She places a foot in the crevice of the thick trunk and hoists herself on top. On all fours, she waves for me to join her. I follow, jumping onto the tree with only slightly more ease than Mirabelle. The tree looks old and well assimilated with the earth around it. I imagine it could have fallen a hundred years ago.

Carefully, Mirabelle and I rise to our feet. The river below rages, bathing us in mist and cool air. The tree is wide enough to walk across, but it's riddled with knots and divots.

"Take my hand," Mirabelle says, reaching back.

I take it, and the two of us inch forward across the tree. The sound of the water crashing against the rocks is so loud it fills my ears completely. Halfway across, I look up the jagged coastline. I want to pause, close my eyes, and soak in the vastness, but Mirabelle pulls me forward. The sky is clear and filled with wispy clouds. I breathe in what feels like fresher air than I'm used to.

Mirabelle's foot sticks in a rotting hole and she trips, falling forward on her hands. I'm jerked down with her. My heart leaps as I stare at the foaming white rapids below. The rough tree bark scratches the palms of my hands.

"Mirabelle?"

"I'm all right." She moans, pulling herself into a standing position again. Her hands shake as she brushes off her skirt. "We're almost there."

I take her hand again, and we finish crossing at a much slower pace than before. The forest rises on the other side of the river, forcing Mirabelle and I to hike uphill. Mirabelle holds up her dress to keep the thorns and branches out of her hem. I place one foot after the other on rocks and roots as we climb. I wonder if there really is a pinnacle at the top of this mountain. We stop before I can find out.

Nestled between two boulders is a little cabin that I would have never seen if Mirabelle hadn't pointed it out to me. Whoever built it carefully carved a cave-like foundation among the rocks. The front is built up with trees from the surrounding forest so it blends in. There are no windows, and the door is barely visible. If it weren't for the front stoop and the smoke billowing from the chimney, I'd say it wasn't even a house.

Mirabelle approaches cautiously. There are two horses tethered out front.

"What's wrong?" I ask.

Mirabelle hesitates. "I think someone else may be here." She bites her lower lip. "Perhaps we shouldn't—"

"We didn't come all of this way to turn back."

"I know. You're right." She nods.

We take careful steps toward the cabin. The forest feels eerie all of a sudden. The river beckons in the background. There's a rocking chair on the front stoop. A small book sits on its armrest. Strange, I think. How dangerous can a man be that sits on a rocking chair and reads?

A crashing noise thunders through the door. It sounds like a table is being turned over. A deep guttural shout follows the crash. Mirabelle pauses before knocking on the door.

"How do you know this man?" I ask, suddenly panicked.

Mirabelle swallows hard before tapping three times.

"We were friends once."

"Go away," comes a voice from inside.

Mirabelle knocks again, more determined this time. "It's Belle," she says.

The yelling and tumbling inside stops. *Belle?* I've never heard Mirabelle refer to herself as Belle before. Heavy steps march toward us. The door is ripped open. Over the threshold stands a man, tall and stocky with a thick neck and long unkempt beard. He looks down at us through bushy eyebrows set over heavy eyelids.

"What do you want?"

"We need your help," Mirabelle says.

Knox's eyes shift toward me. He looks at me like Governor Leo looks at his workers, with great distaste.

"You shouldn't have brought her here."

"Knox, please. Something has happened with Tuor and . . . " Mirabelle looks to me as if she doesn't want me to hear what she's about to say. "I think it has something to do with Portia."

"I told you, I never want to speak of her again." His eyes nervously dance between Mirabelle and me. "Now leave."

Knox swings the door, but Mirabelle catches it with her hand before it fully closes. She pushes it open just enough to catch Knox's eye.

"Please." It's nearly a whisper. "Do this for me."

Mirabelle's hand rests on the edge of the door, only a finger's length away from Knox's hand. His eyes settle on their closeness for a moment before looking Mirabelle in the face.

"No."

Mirabelle barely has enough time to pull her fingers out of the way before the door is slammed shut.

"I shouldn't be surprised!" Mirabelle shouts. Her voice startles me. A pair of ravens flutter away from the tree branch above us. "It should not shock me that you would turn your back on the one thing you can help with. You're such a coward, Knox Duffy!"

Mirabelle turns on her heels and steps off the front stoop. I've never seen her so mad. The door cracks open again before I can follow. Knox glares at me.

"Belle," he says. Mirabelle stops, her back to us. "What happened?"

She turns around but wears a heavy look of contempt on her face.

"Tuor is in trouble." She takes a step closer to the house. "And I think Camilla's life may be in danger too."

Knox sighs, deep and guttural. His fingers reach up to his chest and curl into a claw like he's trying to rip the heart from his body.

"Come in."

Knox lets go of the door. He disappears inside as Mirabelle joins me on the front stoop again.

"So hospitable," Mirabelle mumbles. She pushes the door the rest of the way open, and I follow her inside.

Although built with walls made out of tree logs, Knox's house feels like a cave, dank and dark with just a fire burning in the back. A heavy layer of soot covers everything, yet all of Knox's belongings are neat. Firewood lines the wall, cut and stacked edge to edge. Three swords decorate the space above the mantel. A pile of books sits on a side table. They look like they've been set there with as much care as Mirabelle has for her books.

I watch the back of Knox's wide shoulders as he stomps to the middle of the room and rights the table that has been knocked over. He returns four chairs to their spots at the table.

"Sit," Knox instructs us.

Awkwardly, Mirabelle directs me to take a seat. A man stands in the corner of the room, close to the door that we just came through. Although he's nursing a bloody lip, his posture is tall and confident. He steps toward us, pushing thick locks of blonde hair out of his face.

"I'll be going then," he says.

"You should have never come here."

The embers in Knox's dying fire spit and spark like the tension between these two men.

"Think about what I said, Uncle."

Knox barely looks at his nephew as he slips out the door. Knox walks to the table and places the knuckles of both hands on its surface. His body towers over me.

"I don't know what Mirabelle has told you about me but—"

"She hasn't told me anything about you," I interrupt. "I barely know who you are."

Knox leans in closer, and a heavy scowl stretches across his face. His stance, I assume, is meant to be intimidating. I straighten my back in response. He's just like Malcolm, big, grumpy, and mean.

Knox rounds the table and takes a seat at the head. He looks directly at Mirabelle. "What makes you think Portia's got anything to do with them?"

"Tuor was arrested a couple of weeks ago and—"

"For what?" Knox asks.

"For what?" I repeat. "How do you not know what's going on? The story of my brother's trial is all over Rande."

Knox shifts in his chair. "I don't make it into town too frequently." He turns to Mirabelle. "What else?"

"He's been arrested for murdering a man named Aiden Brookes."

"I don't know an Aiden Brookes."

"I know that," Mirabelle says. "Just listen. Tuor's trial was yesterday, and they said this man who was killed . . . had his throat cut." Mirabelle pauses, letting the impact of her statement settle.

"Many a man has died by having his throat slit."

"Maybe," Mirabelle says. "But the murder happened in LilyAye. At the very least Tuor was close by when it happened. What if Portia is involved?"

"So what if she is? What am I supposed to do about it?"

"Knox, you know Portia better than anybody. If she's the reason that Tuor's been arrested, then I need your help."

I struggle to keep up with the twists and turns of Knox and Mirabelle's conversation. What in all of Elmyra are they talking about?

"Who is Portia?" I ask.

They both turn to look at me.

"She doesn't know?" Knox asks.

"Know what?"

"I haven't told her anything," Mirabelle admits, hanging her head slightly.

Knox hits his fist on the table. I jump back. "You brought her here to see me and she doesn't even know about her own mother?"

"My . . . mother?"

Knox leaps to his feet. His chair skids across the wood floor. He walks to the back of the house by the fireplace. Resting a hand on the mantel, Knox clutches at his heart with his other hand. I squint and watch as he seems to rub away an ache in the center of his chest.

"How do you know my mother?"

Mirabelle's the one to answer. "Knox grew up here in Bear Gap with me and your father and your mother too."

"I thought you never knew her. I thought you just took us in when you saw we had no mother."

"No." Knox's deep voice reaches me from his spot by the fire. "We knew her before she left."

I lean back in my chair. "What does my mother have to do with this?" Mirabelle holds her lips tightly together. "Why won't you tell me?" I ask her.

Mirabelle reaches across the table and takes my hand in hers. I jerk my arm away though. What is this secret that Mirabelle's been keeping from me?

"I never wanted you to have to know the truth about your mother. But I'm afraid . . . " Mirabelle bows her head. "I'm afraid now you must know."

"Tell me," I say through gritted teeth.

"I'll tell you," Knox says, turning around to face us. Mirabelle looks up, tears glistening in her eyes. "I don't care about protecting you like Mirabelle does." Knox takes two steps toward us. His hand still rests on his chest. "You think life in Bear Gap is terrible. You should see what's outside this territory. Mirabelle doesn't have the heart to tell you that your mother left, ran away from Bear Gap with some woman and her husband. You were practically a baby. Years later she returned home, but she had a new lover with her."

The gap between Knox and me closes. His heavy footsteps feel like they're drawing the question out of me.

"Who?"

Knox comes to an abrupt stop. "Quinten Warwick."

My laugh echoes in the quiet hollow room. "Are you saying my mother and the Supreme Ruler were—"

"Yes," Knox interrupts me. "She traipsed back into town during The Battle of Bear Gap, but she wasn't fighting on our side."

"So all this time my mother has been living with the Supreme Ruler?"

I feel like I've just been told that I'm a princess. That I've been living my life as a pauper all while really being royalty. Of course, my mother being Quinten's romantic plaything hardly makes me royalty.

"She's with him when it suits her," Knox says.

"But I don't understand." I look to Mirabelle. "This still doesn't explain her involvement with Tuor."

"Well," Mirabelle's face is tight with agony. "I think your mother may have killed Aiden Brookes."

"Portia tends to leave a trail of dead men behind her," Knox says.

The words hang in the air as queer and disturbing as a child's scream at midnight.

"What?" A hot flush falls over my face.

"Her signature kill is to slit a man's throat from behind." Knox stands over me again, a fist resting on the table.

"My mother's a *murderer*?"

"She also has quite a penchant for witchcraft," Knox adds.

Witchcraft . . . I place my hand on my chest. My thundering heartbeat feels like it will break through my ribs.

"All this time I've been wondering if Tuor actually killed an innocent man . . . But it's not Tuor, is it? It's my mother. But why? Why would she do that?"

Mirabelle shakes her head. "I'm sorry, dear. I don't know."

Knox drops down into his chair. "She probably doesn't have a reason," he says simply.

Knox's arm rests on the table. Blurred on his tan skin is a Warwick brand. Why would he have a brand? I've never seen him at the farm before. I realize suddenly that I've been taking the word of someone I don't even know.

"How do you know all of this?" I snap. The pitch of my voice elevates. "Were you her lover too?"

Mirabelle's face blushes a soft crimson.

Knox laughs. "No. I was one of the few men who wasn't."

"It's of no importance," Mirabelle says quickly. "Knox, please. Can you help us? If it is Portia's fault, then you know they're going to find Tuor guilty and he'll be . . . he'll be punished for what she did."

"How do you know she didn't seduce Tuor onto her side? Maybe he really did kill this man?"

"He didn't," I shout.

Knox stares at me intensely as if little girls like me are not allowed to speak.

"You want my help?" He glances between Mirabelle and me. "Get out now while you still can. If you get even a whiff of Portia . . . " Knox leans in close. Deep wrinkles beset his rough weathered face. "Run away . . . and fast."

I hold his gaze. "I'm not leaving without my brother."

"Then you're a fool."

"Stop telling me to leave my brother. Why do people keep saying that?" I push my chair away from the table. "He's not dead!" I scream, rising and staggering backward. Tears burn in my eyes. "You know nothing about my brother. You're just an old bitter man with nothing to live for!"

Knox jumps to his feet. His chair falls onto the ground with a crack.

"Get out," he growls.

"Knox, please," Mirabelle begs, standing and coming to my side.

His eyes are fixed solidly on mine.

"I've never asked anything of you," she weeps. "All I have are Tuor and Camilla. Please, help me save them. Do this one thing for me."

Knox pretends he can't hear Mirabelle's desperate words.

Her voice drops low. "The things you've done in the past, you make them right if you help us."

Knox bares his teeth. He slams his fist onto the table. "Get out!"

***

I rush down the craggy slope away from Knox's house.

"How dare he," I mumble.

Mirabelle focuses on her feet as she tries to keep pace with me.

"He's not as bad as he seemed just now."

"Are you defending him?" My voice practically screeches.

"Knox has been through a lot in his life," she says.

"So have I. So have you. That's not an excuse to call me a fool for wanting to save my brother."

We come to a stop at the river. Mirabelle pauses in front of me.

"I know. He lost his father many years ago and—"

I grab Mirabelle's arm. "How does he know all of that about my mother? They were in love once, weren't they?"

"No," Mirabelle says quickly.

"He was lying about that. Is he the real reason my mother left?"

"No, Camilla, you're wrong."

Mirabelle tucks a strand of hair behind her ear.

"Knox and your mother were never in love—he and *I* were."

My face contorts in disgust. "But you were married to Neil."

"I was."

"You had a daughter . . . " I glance up in the direction of Knox's house. "He wasn't the father, was he?"

"No, Neil was the father."

"Then what does it matter? He's mad at me and everyone else in this world because he couldn't have you?"

Mirabelle rests a hand on my shoulder. She's so calm I feel the anger drip away from me.

"It's more complicated than that."

"Why did you take me there? What could Knox do that you and I can't do?"

"I don't know, dear." She hangs her head. "I thought he would help."

Mirabelle's face seems to tell a long, complicated story. She looks exhausted.

"The Knox I used to know stood up for what was right. It doesn't seem that he exists anymore."

Mirabelle takes my arm and leads me to mount the tree to cross the river.

"I suppose you're glad you didn't end up marrying him," I say.

I put my foot on the tree trunk's knob and pull myself up. Mirabelle follows.

"I am," she says solemnly. I take a step, staring down at the white waves. "But Knox was my soul mate."

I pause, listening to the dull crashing of the river rapids. I look behind me just as Mirabelle brushes a tear away from her eye.

CHAPTER TWENTY-FOUR

I WALK WITH Mirabelle to her house, but I don't go inside. Surprisingly, she doesn't fuss when I say I need to get home. She wants to be alone, I suppose, which is both unusual and sad. I've never known Mirabelle to not want me at her house.

Rande Square is oddly empty, filled with only a few vendors preparing for the flood of farm workers that will assault the streets this afternoon. There's no point in trying to go to the farm now. I'll just be barked at for being late. I don't feel like going home yet either.

I'm thinking about my mother more than I'd prefer. Everything Knox said, or didn't say, about my mother has my mind reeling. I should be upset at finding out my mother is a murderess, but . . . I'm not. It's the same as if someone told me that a man who lived in Billage had just died. It's irrelevant to me. I don't know the man, and I don't care what happens to him.

I wander down Reaper's Way on the route that I usually take to get to the farm. It sickens me to think of Tuor locked up for something he didn't do. It hurts even more to think he could be being punished for something our mother did. *Mother*. How strange that word sounds in my head. I've always thought of Mirabelle as a mother, but I've never called her that.

The Justice House stands to my right. I pause, thinking about how close Tuor is to me right now, how close he was during his trial. So close but so unattainable. The Justice House is abuzz with Warwick soldiers. Ten or so villagers and farm workers line up outside of the Justice House's door. Those poor people are headed into a trial for their loved ones which will likely have a similar outcome as Tuor's trial.

A man stands a few yards back from the Justice House steps. His horse waits obediently next to him. He's not here for a trial, I can tell. His stance is too tall and confident for such an affair. From behind I see him lift his hand to his mouth to chew on a piece of long grass. He turns to look at me.

"Those people are going in for a trial, aren't they?"

I look around to see who else this man could be talking to.

"Those people there, going into the Justice House, what are they doing?" he asks, gnawing away on his blade of grass.

"Oh yeah. They're witnesses." I roll my eyes. "I should know. I was one of them just yesterday."

The man scoffs. He shifts to look at me more fully. Recognition fills his face.

"You were at my uncle's house, weren't you?"

I blink slowly until I notice the red cut on his lip.

"Yeah." Without thinking, I throw my arms across my chest.

"What's your name?"

"Camilla."

"I'm Johnny."

I nod. Johnny looks down at me and smiles. Thick locks of dusty blonde hair fall into his eyes. He has a strong square jaw and a nose that protrudes like a mountain peak, but I realize I find him handsome.

"Your uncle is a vile beast," I spit.

The words burst from my mouth before I have a chance to think about them. A moment of silence passes between Johnny and I, and I suspect that the two of us may break into a quarrel as well. Johnny pulls the grass from his mouth, then leans back and laughs loudly.

"He's awful," Johnny agrees. I smile. "My uncle . . . he doesn't lose an argument. If he's about to, he'll just get up and leave."

I laugh. In the short time I was with Knox, I understand what Johnny means.

"He's my family though." Johnny shifts on his feet and tosses the chewed piece of grass onto the ground. "I have to love him, right?"

Family. How odd for that word to come so soon after I learned about my mother. "No. You don't have to," I say.

Johnny laughs again. He thinks it's a joke. I don't have the energy to tell him I've never just loved a member of my family because they were a member of my family.

"Uncle Knox wasn't always like that. He used to fight against men like them." Johnny points toward the Justice House.

"Warwick soldiers?"

"Warwick *himself*." Johnny's arms open as he talks. "My uncle and grandfather started this whole group back when I was just a kid. It was like their own little militia, called The Duffy Rebellion. They started it right here in Bear Gap. Built an army to defend the territory from the Warwick invasion."

"I know about the battle," I say. "The one that happened here."

Johnny turns to look at me squarely in the eyes. "That was all because of my grandfather."

I nod. "Knox was the only survivor, right?"

"No, not technically."

I glance up at Johnny, scrunching my eyebrows in confusion. His face is scruffy with blonde stubble.

"He was the only survivor that was able to go home. His father, my grandfather, along with other men from Bear Gap were captured, taken up to work camps somewhere in LilyAye."

"I never heard that part of the story before."

"People stopped talking about it." Johnny rests his hands in the pockets of his rough brown jacket. "My grandfather could still be alive. His name was John too actually." I nod. "I hate those men. They're so smug about wearing the Warwick crest." Johnny chuckles as he peers at the soldiers. "I hate Quinten Warwick."

I almost scoff. Saying something like that in a territory like Bear Gap is very dangerous. I could turn Johnny into the Warwick soldiers we're watching, have him arrested for treason or some other ridiculous claim. But as I stand here staring at the women and men that are being ushered into the Justice House, I realize that I, perhaps, hate Warwick as well. It's Warwick law that has placed my brother in the bowels of this hideous building.

"My brother's in there," I say.

Johnny shakes his head. "I'm sorry."

"Don't feel sorry for me." Johnny gives me a quizzical look. "Those soldiers are puppets. They do what they're told and obey blindly."

"I'd love to do to them what they did to my grandfather."

I take a step back. "I'd love to just talk to my brother. It's so simple, I know. I just want to talk to him, ask him if he's okay. But I can't."

I find myself seething at the sight of those tight black vests and the crimson Warwick crests. It's like I'm suddenly realizing what I've been frustrated with this whole time. So what if the mother I never knew killed a man? The point is that Tuor *didn't* kill him, and our government failed to find that truth.

There's a hand in my hand. My body tenses. I turn to look at Johnny's mischievous grin. "So go talk to him," he says. "Let's go in there right now and talk to him."

"Wh-what?" I stutter.

"Let's break into the Justice House. C'mon!"

Johnny pulls me toward the Justice House, leading his horse with his other hand.

"What are you doing?" I shout.

He releases my hand to tie his horse at the post in front of the Justice House.

"I know what those people are doing," Johnny says. "They're going in to testify for a trial, right?"

"Yeah."

"Do you want to see your brother?"

"Yeah, I do but—"

Without another word, Johnny takes my hand again. He jogs up the Justice House steps and jumps in line behind a middle-aged woman who holds a little boy by her side.

"State your business," the soldier asks.

It's not the same soldier that was here for Tuor's trial, but he stands by the door holding a parchment in his hand.

"For my husband," the woman says. "Peter Schlapler."

"Go through those doors," the soldier instructs. "They'll show you where to go from there."

Johnny pulls me so we're right in front of the soldier. He looks us up and down.

"State your business."

"We're here to serve as witnesses for the trial of Peter Shraper."

The soldier squints his eyes at us. "Schlapler?"

"Right," Johnny says. "Schlapler."

The soldier nods us on and Johnny urges me through the Justice House doors. My skin instantly prickles at the sight of this dim, hollow room. Another soldier approaches us, his feet moving swiftly. I take a step back. I'm certain we'll be kicked out any moment. He points a finger at me.

"You come with me. You," he points to Johnny, "go with him."

"No, no, no. That won't work," Johnny says.

My eyes widen. I can tell he has no plan. Johnny looks assured nonetheless.

"She has to stay with me."

"She comes with me and you go with him."

The soldier points to another soldier standing in one of the far right archways.

"No. No. You don't understand," Johnny says. "She's blind. I have to stay with her to lead her."

His hand tightens on mine as the soldier grabs my forearm. "*I* will lead her."

The soldier pulls me away and I feel my grip on Johnny slipping.

"That's not a good idea." Johnny says, his voice rising in pitch. "She doesn't like strangers." He winks at me as he feigns a worried look.

"Let go of me!" I say, unsure what Johnny wants me to do. I can't scream or they'll surely kick me out, or worse, I'll be recognized as the troublemaker from the other day. So I do the only other thing I know how to do. I cry. I pull my hands over my face and start to weep, sad, pathetic weeping.

"I warned you," I hear Johnny say.

The soldier lets go of my arm. I pull away my hands and give him a look of utter terror.

"Please, sir . . . " I beg, reaching out my arm as if I can't see where Johnny is. "I need to stay with my friend."

Johnny takes my hand again, pulling me close to his body. I peek around the room as attention starts to fall in our direction. I let out another wail that could be heard from a dying horse.

"Fine," the soldier says through gritted teeth. "Both of you come with me." The soldier turns on his heels. Johnny looks down and gives me a quick smile. *It worked.* Johnny's unplanned and poorly executed plan actually worked.

I find myself cracking a smile too as we follow the soldier through one of the stone archways. I have no idea what Johnny and I will do now, but for the moment I feel we've beaten the Warwick system, and that thrills me.

CHAPTER TWENTY-FIVE

JOHNNY AND I are led down the dark stone hallway. Torchlight flashes past us every few yards as we intermittently pass through parts of utter darkness. I look to Johnny. His square jaw is extra-pronounced in the deep shadows.

"Hey!" Johnny shouts suddenly.

He lets go of my hand as the soldier takes a few paces in front of us.

"What's your problem now?" the soldier says, turning around.

Johnny takes a step forward, reaches out his fist, and punches the soldier hard in the nose.

"What are you—"

Johnny hits him again and the soldier drops flat on his back on the hallway floor. My mouth gapes open.

"What are you doing?" I whisper.

"How do we get to your brother?" Johnny asks.

I can't think and I can't get my eyes off the still body of the soldier. "Is he dead?"

"No, he'll just sleep for a while. Camilla, listen, where's your brother? I'm not from Rande. I've never been in this Justice House before."

I tilt my head up to look at Johnny. I suddenly realize I know nothing about this man I've followed into the depths of a Warwick courtroom. In the silence I hear the ever-so-quiet murmuring of Governor Leo's voice down in the trial room.

"Your brother," Johnny reminds me, taking my shoulders in his hands.

"He's in the dungeons," I say. "They're to the left of us, I think. When I was here for his trial, they brought him in from that way."

I point down the corridor and toward the left, remembering the big gate in the back of the room. Johnny releases my shoulders, stands up, and looks around.

"Follow me."

He hops over the soldier's motionless body and jogs down the hallway, running his hands along the walls. I follow, tiptoeing gingerly past the soldier. We run the rest of the way, twisting and curving until we take the last few steps that open into the trial room.

"Johnny!" I say, trying to get his attention before he stumbles into the light.

He halts just inside the archway. I come to his side, and we both peer into the trial room. Governor Leo sits atop the platform, listening as a man pleads his case. I feel a shudder of nausea rush over me.

"He came from over there," I whisper, pointing toward the back of the room.

Johnny and I stand for a moment, squished together in the tight archway. I feel his body's warmth where his arm and leg brush mine.

"All those other archways," he says. "They all feed from that room upstairs?"

"I think so."

Johnny backs up through the hallway. He goes slower this time, feeling along the wall. What is he thinking? He seems more determined to see Tuor than I am. Then I see it, the same time he does. Johnny's hand suddenly drops off the wall into an open doorway. I'd never seen it before because I was always moving through these halls so quickly. And even if I hadn't been, it's so dark in here, even now it blends in.

"I thought so," Johnny says, grabbing a torch from the wall.

The torch brings to light a small alcove in the Catahli, inlaid with an iron door. Johnny grabs for the handle.

"How did you know this was here?" I ask, feeling along the iron rivets that line the door.

"I didn't know, for sure. But I think all of these hallways lead to the dungeon. So I knew there had to be a corridor or a secret passageway."

Johnny jerks on the door to open it. It budges only slightly as a puff of dust ekes from its edges.

"But why?"

"They must have designed it this way so that prisoners can be taken to and from the dungeons from any hallway. Here, hold this."

Johnny hands me the torch. With both hands he yanks on the handle of the door. It's tight to the wall. I glance up the hallway, feeling like someone could walk down any moment. Johnny pulls and pulls, and the muscles in his arms tense and bulge. Every drip of moisture that echoes against the walls sends a note of fear down my spine.

"Ughhhhh," Johnny groans. "Lock's too tight." He drops his arms.

A voice echoes down the corridor toward Johnny and me. I crane my neck around the alcove's corner. The voice booms against the hard Catahli mineral.

"Someone's coming!" I whisper. "They're gonna see the soldier's body!"

"Come on."

Johnny whips past me and runs full tilt up the hallway. The sound of our footfalls mixes with the echoes of two men who seem to be barreling toward us. We reach the soldier's body. Johnny grabs him under his shoulders and drags him back down the hallway. Shadows crisscross on the wall.

"Hurry!" I hiss.

I drop the torch, snuffing it out on the ground, and take one of the soldier's arms from Johnny so we're both pulling his body as fast as we can. My back aches as I feverishly tug the full weight of a grown man.

"In here." Johnny drags the unconscious soldier into the alcove.

I fall back onto the cool floor, exhaustion tingling through my arms. The footsteps grow louder. I reach across the soldier and pull his legs into the alcove so the three of us are hidden in the darkness. Johnny's breathing is heavy.

"Be . . . as quiet . . . as . . . possible . . . " he says as the voices grow closer.

"They're going to see us."

Through the dim light, I notice Johnny freeze and turn stiff. I move my legs, brushing along the belt of the soldier. It makes a jingling noise. Johnny and I look at each other as if to say together, "What was that noise?" I reach for the soldier's waist, feeling along the belt to a key chain.

"Keys," I whisper.

I jump to my feet, scrambling to shove a key into the lock. There are only three, and one of them has to fit this door. I turn the key but feel no movement in the lock.

"They're close," Johnny says, his voice even but stern.

I push the second key in and feel the rusty lock pop.

"I got it," I say.

"Shhh!"

Johnny touches the small of my back, pushing me as close to the door as we can get. A flash of torchlight passes us as the two men march down the corridor. Together we exhale.

"It won't be long before they realize we're not down there."

Johnny steps out of the alcove and takes another torch from its perch on the wall.

"Take this," he says. "The dungeons can't be too much farther past this door."

"You're not coming with me?"

"I'll stay here and guard the door. Make sure you come back this way, or we won't be able to get out of here without being caught."

I nod. I don't fully understand what he means, but he must have a plan. Or maybe he's going to think of one while I'm with Tuor. Johnny shoves the torch in my hand as I jerk open the door. A sheen of dust envelops my body. Johnny pulls the door closed behind me as I pass over its threshold.

The ceiling drips with muddy water. My torch casts the only light in the room onto a set of stone steps that curve sharply downward. The sound of quiet muffled moaning ekes its way up the dark stairwell. Only for a moment do I consider if this is a foolish decision. The dungeons are close, which means Tuor is close.

I run my hand along the wall to steady myself as I take the slippery steps. The moans become more pronounced, and they're mixed with the sound of distant tapping. It reminds me of the blacksmith at the farm, hitting his hammer on his anvil over and over. This sound is quicker though with a tinny quality. Carefully, I creep down the steps, following the curve until I'm only a few steps from the bottom.

At the bottom is another iron gate that reaches floor to ceiling. From a few feet back, I look past the bars and stare into the dungeon. It's a maze of dirt-floored tunnels with moss and vines snaking their way up the walls and across the curved ceiling. I take a step closer, keenly aware of the tapping sound that's growing louder. Straight ahead is a tunnel lined with iron-barred cells. It curves hard to the right so that I can only see a few cells. One man hangs on the bars, his arms flopped outside his cell door as if he's literally reaching for his freedom.

Turning my head to the right, I peer down the long main corridor of the dungeon. The tapping sound reaches its peak as a guard, walking in my direction, runs a wooden club along the bars of the prison cells. I step back quickly into the shadows as he turns around and starts his march in the other direction. The tapping sound starts to diminish.

I look again down the main corridor. At the end on my far right, I see three soldiers sitting casually atop old wine barrels, playing a game of knucklebones. But there are no other guards around. I touch the gate, trying to push it outward, but it doesn't move. There's a chain wrapped around the gate. A rusty padlock hangs from the chains. Locked. *It's locked.* I set the torch down and pull out the keys I'm still clutching in my hand. I push in the first key and feel no give. The second key doesn't work either. I try to shove in the third, but it won't even go in the keyhole the whole way. Glancing up the stairwell, I realize I'm trapped. I have to get past this gate.

The soldier with the wooden club turns about and continues his patrol in my direction. I jump back again to hide myself in the darkness. I wait until he turns around and heads back down the row of prison cells. A guttural moan wafts through the gate.

I wrap my fingers around the rusty bars. I'm probably the only person who wishes they were on the other side. I rest my forehead between two bars. How stupid could I be? I'm stuck. I'm stuck when Tuor is so close! The thumping of wood on iron returns. Frustration bubbles up inside me. I want to scream out Tuor's name. Ugh! I push hard against the iron gate. The tapping noise stops. I stand firm, my hands still digging into the rough bars.

The noise returns, and I relax slightly. I've moved the gate, I realize, as I look down at my feet. The chains are loose enough that I've managed to push the gate outward a few inches. I wait until the guard turns around again and then slowly push the gate as hard as I can. It inches open with thin, high-pitched screeches. I continue to shove it until the chain is taunt, unable to stretch any further. It's wide enough, I think, wide enough that I can push through.

I snuff out the torch, remove my jacket, and hang the keys around my wrist to get rid of any excess items that might get in my way. The guard turns around. I watch his back for a moment before sticking my leg through the opening. I duck under the chains and push the rest of my body through. The rusty bars leave a shallow scrape on my chest which I ignore because I'm now standing fully exposed in the dungeons buried deep beneath the Justice House.

CHAPTER TWENTY-SIX

I SPRINT STRAIGHT ahead into the hallway lined with cells. The man standing slumped on the bars of his cell cocks his head as I run past. I look left and right into every cell, searching for Tuor. The stench of death and dung overtakes me. I'm forced to cover my mouth and nose with my hand. The prison cells are mere caves, as cold and confining as a tomb. They're stocked with motionless men lying on the ground or propped up in seated positions. I pause to catch my breath. This place is meant for monsters, I think to myself, not men.

The torchlight from the main corridor fades as I move deeper and deeper into the pit of the dungeon. I come to an intersection where the hallway splits left, right, or straight ahead. I run to the left, checking face after face, begging to see Tuor's. A man reaches through his cell and yells out to me for help. I'd be worried that the noise would draw the attention of a guard, but muffled screaming seems normal in this place.

I turn around and return to the intersection, veering right this time to avoid the guards playing their game. I pause halfway down. A rat scurries across my foot. I shake it off. Its furry body retreats to the nearest cell where the prisoner doesn't even notice its appearance. The tunnels seem to rope around each other in an infinite loop. Cell after cell, I look past the bars to search for the familiar image of Tuor.

I come to the end of this hallway, where it connects with another. Still no guards. The prisoners are simply left to rot. I turn left to search the next hallway. I walk slowly now, making sure I haven't missed him. I fear that his visage has become unrecognizable.

"Camilla?"

Tuor's quiet strained voice calls to me. I double back a few paces.

"Tuor."

Tuor crawls across the floor of his straw-covered cell and meets me at the barred door. He stands, and I wrap my hands around him, feeling the cold that's permeating his body.

"I'm so sorry. I'm so sorry you're here," I mumble.

My eyes instantly water. I stare at my feet, barely able to look at the puffy bruise around his eye or the deep gash on his lip. He's skinny, so skinny that his clothes hang from his limp body.

"Are you here to get me out?" Tuor croaks.

His voice is child like. He looks mystified by my appearance as if he doesn't truly believe I'm here. A tear falls down my cheek. Yes, yes! I want to tell him, yes, I've come to rescue you! I pull the keys from my wrist.

"Let me try," I say, fumbling with the keys.

The cell has a lock by the door handle. I crouch down, my hands shaking as I try the keys. The last one slips from my fingers as I realize they're not for opening the cells.

"I-I can't get you out," I stutter.

My tears fall slow and steady. Why does Tuor seem further from me when this is the closest I've been to him in days? The truth of Tuor's fate sinks in fast and hard. He may not make it to an execution, if that's what Governor Leo's sentence is. He's so weak. He'll die right here between these crumbling walls.

"Are you really here?" Tuor asks, stroking my arm.

"I am. I'm here." I speak through the tears. "Tuor, what happened that night? Tell me the truth." Tuor bows his head. "If you tell me exactly what happened, I could still try and get you freed."

I brush a cluster of tears from my cheek. Tuor stares at the ground. He's completely still, as if speaking the truth causes his limbs to not work.

"There was a woman," he whispers. "There was a woman there the night he . . . died."

"Tuor, did this woman *kill* Aiden Brookes?"

Tuor nods his head slowly. My hands clutch Tuor's shoulders through the cell bars.

"Why didn't you tell me that?" I beg. "Why didn't you tell me that when you first came back into town?"

I can't help but give Tuor a desperate shake. I'm relieved but angry.

A fresh set of tears falls from my eyes. "Why didn't you tell me?"

Tuor's head slowly turns upright. He's crying too, and for a moment our eyes meet in shared agony.

"I was afraid."

"Afraid of what? Afraid I wouldn't believe you?"

Tuor grips my wrists as if he might rip my hands off him. "You don't know the power she has."

My crying ceases at the sight of Tuor's imploring face. His hands tighten around my wrists, and his eyebrows tilt upward in strain and utter fear.

Nerves tingle through my whole body. I'm almost not able to form the question. "Who?"

"Mother."

A cell door clanks shut down the hallway.

"Mother? Why didn't you say this at the trial, Tuor? You could have told them it wasn't you."

Tuor releases my wrists and stares down at his own dirty hands. "I was too scared. I-I thought if I blamed her, then she'd be angry and . . . come after you."

"What about the knife? I found a bloody knife in our box." My voice shakes horribly as I interrogate him. "I have to know. I have to know what happened. How did you get that knife?"

"She gave it to me!" he blurts. "She made me take it. My captain took it from me before they threw me in jail. Then—"

Thudding footsteps march toward Tuor and me. Muffled voices echo down the corridor.

"Then what?" I beg.

"They're doing their rounds," Tuor says. "Get out of here!"

CHAPTER TWENTY-SEVEN

MY EYES DART down the hallway.

"I will come back and get you out of here. I promise."

Tuor and I hug through the bars of his cell. I take off in the other direction. I run, but more cautiously this time, keenly aware that there are now guards wandering these tunnels. Turning right at the end of Tuor's hallway, I pass two more intersections that branch left and right. I keep straight to head in the direction that I think the main dungeon corridor is, but I skid to a stop at a wall. The tunnel curves left and soon I'm running full tilt down a narrow tunnel with no prison cells and barely any torches.

I'm emptied into another section of the dungeon with a whole new set of hallways that branch out like a cancerous vine. I look left and right before creeping around the corner. Far to my right is the center gate where earlier the guards sat whiling away their day playing games. Those guards are gone now, on rounds, I assume. But there is still one soldier who continues to pace up and down the main corridor. I wait for him to turn his back to me and then I sprint toward the large gated door which Tuor was brought through for his trial.

For a moment I stare into the vast Justice Hall, imagining the terror that many a prisoner has felt while standing at this vantage point. Governor Leo's voice is only a mumble from this distance. I shake the barred door, thinking I can run from here to the tunnel where Johnny and I first came through. But it's locked. Of course it's locked! I reach for the keys but—I've left the keys back at Tuor's cell. Panic ripples up my back.

The soldier turns around to start his march in my direction. Our eyes lock and I break into a run only a moment before he does. I pass cell after cell, leaving the main corridor and continuing into another tunnel without cells. The damp air whips past my warm cheeks, and even my feet can feel the cold permeating up through the ground. I'm moving farther and farther away from Johnny. The wall curves ever so slightly as I follow along the tunnel.

Where is this taking me?

I come to a stop at a wall with four archways. I'm breathing heavily, and my lungs sting with the rank air. I look behind me. There is nowhere else to go. It's like a game, I realize. I must pick one of these four archways or stand here and be arrested, doomed to rot in one of these cells along with Tuor. But I can't do that. I have to rescue myself before I can rescue Tuor.

The shadow of my pursuer flashes on the wall. I spring into the tunnel on the far left. The first torch I come to I steal from its perch on the wall. The floor is stone now, and for a moment I run in total silence. It's as if I've been buried in the deepest hole. It's quiet, peaceful even, but I'll surely die if I stay here.

Then I hear the deep sarcastic trilling of Governor Leo's voice. It booms through the tunnel, engulfing my head with its vibrations. A soft light glows in the distance. I chase it with all the energy left in my legs. The light grows bigger. I slow slightly, still hearing the distant thumping of my pursuer's boots. I step to the edge of the tunnel. It's another archway. I'm bathed in warm light as I stand on the Justice Hall floor.

I've followed a tunnel that has led me to an archway right next to the platform where Governor Leo and The Seven sit. I stare upward, Governor Leo's dignitaries a head-and-shoulder's length taller than me. The Warwick flag looms down on me, somehow seeming more enormous from this angle.

No one notices me at first until my heavy breathing catches the ear of a woman who's acting as one of the seven council members.

"Uh," her voice cracks. She seems unsure of what to say about a loose prisoner. Then she screams, a high-pitched and terrified sound.

My eyes dart across the Justice Hall to the tunnel that Johnny and I came through. He runs into the archway. I watch him as he looks behind himself. He's waiting for me. But I have no way of getting to him. There's a soldier standing in the middle of the courtroom and another one close to the gated door that leads into the cell tunnels. I hear my pursuer run the last few paces of the tunnel, his feet like a galloping horse that's riding right toward me.

I scramble up the set of steps that leads to the platform. The soldier empties out of the tunnel and yells, "Stop her!"

The governor cocks his head, and collectively the gallery of council members gasps. I leap over the platform chairs until I'm all the way in the back. One of the council members holds a hand to his chest as if I might strike out and kill him without even touching him.

"Can someone please take care of this?" Governor Leo shouts.

The soldier follows me up the platform. He pushes members of The Seven out of the way and is met with more gasps and screams. I step back against the wall, feeling the magnitude of the room. I touch the Warwick flag. Its fibers are thick and rough. Knowing what it stands for kindles a fire in my belly ten times brighter than the torch in my hand. I hold the flame to the black and red fabric. It catches quickly, like a field of dry wheat. I drop the torch, stumbling backward from the growing fire.

The room erupts in panic. Governor Leo is ushered away by one of the soldiers, valiantly saving his governor. The seven members of the council trip and tumble their way off the gallery pedestal. I'm mesmerized by the fire. It eats away at the flag. The Catahli wall begins to crumble like sand. Hot embers pop from the flag and land at my feet as if to warn me that soon it will engulf my body too.

I leap from the platform, running toward the tunnel where Johnny still stands, waiting for me. People scurry in all directions, like a nest of mice that's been disturbed. The archways nearest the platform are flooded with council members as everyone begs to be taken out of here.

Johnny leans out of his archway, holding a hand out for me. I take it, and we climb the tunnel toward freedom. At the top, the front door hangs open. Soldiers run through, holding buckets of water as someone screams, "Fire! Fire!"

Johnny pulls me through the door. We flee the front steps of the Justice House. Johnny jerks me toward his horse. He rips the rope away from the post, mounts his beast, and pulls me up with him. Passing through Rande Square, we tumble past the tree line into the woods before finally coming to a stop. I jump onto the ground, leaning hard on my knees to catch my breath. My eye blink as they attempt to adjust to the bright sunlight. Johnny dismounts and doubles back a few paces to look out into the village.

"Is anyone searching for us?" I croak, my throat dry from heaving in and out.

"I don't think so." Johnny turns back toward me. He puts his hands on his waist. "Your brother is in there."

"Yeah."

"You lit the building on fire where your brother is being held."

I stand up straight. "They'll get the fire out," I say. "I had to get out of there. I thought a distraction was my best option."

Johnny glares at me.

"Plus, I hate that big ugly flag."

Johnny's mouth curves into a smile. His lips part and he lets out a chuckle. "Imagine what they'll put on the posting tree tomorrow," he says. "Justice House burned to rubble by lowly farm girl." I giggle. "Torches no longer permitted during trial proceedings."

I break into a laugh, letting the stress of seeing Tuor melt away. We stand in silence again.

"I think your uncle might be right," I say.

Johnny scoffs. "About what?"

"He said my mother killed the man that Tuor is being held prisoner for murdering." I cross my arms over my chest. "Tuor just said it's true. I don't know how it's true, but . . . I guess it is."

"Uncle Knox is unbearable." Johnny smirks at using my term. "But he's also smart."

I nod, understanding fully what he means. "Thank you by the way." Johnny gives me a confused look. "Thank you for helping me see my brother."

I feel a tear growing at the corner of my eye, but I push it away. My eyes meet Johnny's. He has no idea how important it was for me to see Tuor. This man I barely know, a stranger really, has given me something that I couldn't get myself. Even if I never see Tuor again, I had those few moments with him.

"Thank you for destroying one more Warwick flag from this land."

I smile, taking a step closer to him.

"Hey, Camilla?"

"Yeah?"

"Today when I was at my uncle's house . . . " Johnny brushes a lock of hair from his forehead. "I was trying to convince him to start up the rebellion again, the Duffy Rebellion."

"Oh."

"I think we should take our territory back. Make it what it used to be."

"I don't even know what it used to be."

Johnny shakes his head. "It was better than this."

"What did Knox say when you brought it up?"

"He doesn't want to be bothered." Johnny shifts away from me, placing his hands on his hips. "But what about you?"

"Me?"

"Yeah. Do you know what you just did back there? That's more damage than I've ever been able to cause." Johnny's smile broadens from cheek to cheek.

"Oh, I don't—I just want my brother back."

"Right. Well, maybe you can think about it." Johnny glances around the trees. "We should part ways," he says. "In case they're looking for us."

"You're right." I start to turn. "Where are you from anyway?" I ask.

"Billage, next town over."

"Oh. Good luck . . . getting home." I brush a piece of hair behind my ear. It's strange, but I don't want to walk away.

Johnny shakes his head slowly, looking as if he's holding back a full-blown smile. "You too."

I turn on my heels and take a few steps into the woods.

"Camilla . . . "

I turn back around quickly.

"The girl who set Warwick on fire," he exclaims.

CHAPTER TWENTY-EIGHT

MY AFTERNOON IS spent huddled away at home. I peer out the back window frequently, waiting for that moment that a band of Warwick soldiers will come marching down to the swamps to arrest me. I laugh to myself. Imagine it, the whole Crim family locked away, all for different reasons.

After my escape from the Justice House, I thought about why I didn't see Malcolm in one of those cells. It's possible that I just missed him. But it's more possible that they have him, Vincent, and Boris all locked up in the stocks at the farm. It's not uncommon to see men or women hanging in the stocks. There are usually whispers around the farm as to what their crime was. Sometimes I think Governor Leo reserves the stocks for those particular crimes that he'd like to discourage us from.

At nightfall, I sneak back into town to see how the Justice House fared in the fire. Unfortunately for Johnny, the building is still standing. Things seem back to normal; two soldiers guard the front door, and the village is quiet and calm.

My walk home is slow and silent. I hate spending the night by myself, but I suppose it's better than spending it with Malcolm. I curl up tight on my bed mat, blowing out the candle so that the only light in the shack is the cool blue light of the moon oozing through the wooden slats.

What a strange day. To hear my mother spoken of just in a normal sense is strange enough, but to hear that she killed a man . . . What was she doing in Tuor's dormitory in the first place? I could have asked Tuor if I had been thinking. A few days ago I assumed my mother was dead, and now to hear that she appears to be alive and has had contact with Tuor . . . It's all a puddle of messy confusion that I'm too tired to sort through tonight.

***

My neighbor, Lina, is perched on her stool outside, shucking corn. I drop down the three steps from our shack to leave for work.

"Oooo . . . look at you, darlin', grinnin' from ear to ear!"

I scan the woodsy terrain that lies in front of our two houses. A couple of boys run past. One carries a large stick in his hand.

"Yes, I'm talking about you."

"Me?" I ask.

"Look at that smile!" she says, tossing a clean ear of corn into her basket. "All I ever see is you with your head low and your eyes all sappy. It's nice to see some perkiness."

I scrunch up my eyebrows. Smile? Was I smiling? My neighbor laughs a hearty belly laugh. I turn to run toward town before she points out anything else about me. Perhaps I *was* smiling, I think. I can't be happy with Tuor locked away. It wouldn't be right.

Rande Square bustles about with its daybreak crowd. I dismiss my portly neighbor and intentionally turn my mouth downward. Tuor needs all my attention. Now that I know that he did *not* kill Aiden Brookes, and that my mother, or at least someone who looks like my mother, did kill him, I can focus on getting the blame shifted to the right person.

I recognize the soldiers guarding the Justice House when I walk past. Maybe I'm being too bold to head to work today. Someone in that courtroom, guards especially, could recognize me. I keep my eyes down until I'm squished in with the other workers to approach the farm gate.

It was chaos yesterday, I think to myself. There's no way anyone was looking at me. They were looking at the fire. A soldier marches past our slow moving line, heading to his post, I assume. A trickle of fear flows through my body. How am I going to work today if I'm afraid that every soldier I see will recognize me?

An arm links through mine. It's Mirabelle. She's pushed her way through the crowd to stand with me.

"Hey," I say.

She smiles at me, but that's it, no cheerful hello or warm hug. The line inches forward. I have nothing to say either, I realize. I can't tell her about what Johnny and I did yesterday. She'd be furious. I look over at her face. It's sullen, and her laugh lines stick out harshly.

"Are you all right?"

Mirabelle smiles again. "Just fine, dear." Clearing her throat, she says, "I haven't seen Lawrence since the trial."

"I think he left."

"Left?"

"Yeah." We make eye contact. "He's gone. He told me he couldn't stay here any longer."

"But why?"

I tilt my chin up slightly and brush a wave of my hair over my shoulder. "Because he's a coward."

We move the rest of the way through the line in silence, just holding each other's arms. One of the soldiers guarding the gate waves me forward when it's my turn. I flash him the symbol on my arm and start to cross over the threshold.

"Wait," the other soldier says.

They lean close to each other, exchanging a whispered concern. I turn around to look at Mirabelle, who appears as confused as I do.

"Are you Camilla Crim?"

I feel my body freeze up. "Yes."

They've recognized me. They've recognized me as the one who defaced the Warwick flag.

"Come with me," the soldier says, handing off his ledger book to his comrade.

"What's going on?" Mirabelle asks.

"Stay back."

I'm ushered through the front gate, past the courtyard, and around the back of the Harras Manor. We pass the stocks where, just as I had thought, Malcolm hangs with the other men involved in the illegal mead production. His eyes are heavy with dark splotches. He yells muddled curses at me as if he hasn't slept in days. I swallow hard. I'll be next to him soon. Or worse, I'll be thrown into the dungeon.

The soldier pushes me through the back door of Governor Leo's home. The door swings closed, and it's instantly quieter. The yelling and grunting from the fields die away. Lined with floor-to-ceiling glass windows, the room is warm with sunlight. A sitting area with animal-skinned couches carefully encircles a giant bear rug. A shrill cackle of laughter echoes through the house from a distant room.

"Where are you taking me?"

"This way."

We take a sharp right, following along the wall that borders the field, until we enter the stairwell tower. It's a spiral set of steps that leads to all stories of the house. As we twist up the staircase, the laughter grows louder. The house feels hollow and haunted. We stop at the fourth landing, nearly the top, and walk down a wide hallway, passing even more vacant rooms. All the while the sound of feminine laughter laced with hysteria pierces my ears. The soldier seems oblivious. He whips me around to stand in the doorway of one of the rooms.

A man stands with his back to me and stares out a tall glass door that leads to a balcony overlooking the billowing fields. Karla's laughter comes to a sharp halt. She shamelessly glares at me from my feet up to the crest of my head. A dog squirms in her arms as she lovingly strokes its scraggly fur.

"Sir," the soldier announces. "The girl you requested."

With the turn of his heels, the man spins around to see for himself who has been brought to him. There is laughter on his lips when he finally looks at me. "That will be all. Leave the girl."

The soldier drops my arm and marches back down the hallway. I'm left standing face-to-face with the governor.

CHAPTER TWENTY-NINE

"DARLING, WILL YOU leave us please?" Governor Leo's wife gives him a sour look, then daintily crosses the room and gives him a light kiss on his cheek. "Find the captain, will you? Tell him he can't avoid dinner with us again tonight!" Governor Leo laughs as if he's made a joke. "And tell the kitchen I want the ham tonight, no more of that mutton."

A strong cinnamon smell trails Karla as she sidles through the door, all the while keeping a keen eye on me. A long deep-colored wooden desk stretches across the room. Governor Leo rests both hands on its surface.

"Come in, girl." Governor Leo summons me with the wave of his hand, which has been adorned with rings of gold and silver. Some are encrusted with green and yellow gems.

I step into the room, watching through the window as the farm below comes into view. The governor can see everything from up here. Every field, even the distant orchards, are visible. The high stockyard fence looks almost like a child's toy, wrapped around the fields, keeping all its inhabitants snugly inside. All the workers, thousands of them, scurry about the land like starving mice.

"Why am I here?" I ask.

"You called this meeting."

Governor Leo plops himself down on his leather desk chair. His eyes gaze in my direction. They seem to look past me as if I'm too inferior a creature to look upon. But mostly he seems . . . bored.

"My field supervisor said you're the reason we have a couple of producers in the stocks." Governor Leo waves his arm impatiently. "Now out with your request."

I open my mouth to speak but stop. This is my meeting with the governor? Benedek actually followed through? Maybe I'm not being punished for burning the Warwick flag.

"It's about my brother," I blurt.

Governor Leo picks at his fingernails.

"What is?"

"This meeting." I take a step closer to his desk. "My brother is being imprisoned right now for a murder he didn't commit." I take another step so that I'm right at Governor Leo's desk. "Sir, I will do anything if you let my brother go. I will work at your farm for less pay. I will work here in your home and be a maidservant to your wife if she wishes." I try to catch the governor's eyes, but he seems preoccupied by one of the paintings on his wall. "I will find the person who committed this murder and bring them to you so that you can have your justice."

Governor Leo leans back in his chair and rubs the bottom of his chin. "I preside over a lot of trials. The guilty often see themselves as innocent. How do you know your brother didn't commit this murder you speak of?"

"Because . . . "

What do I say now? I know because my brother told me when I snuck into the dungeons? Or I know he's innocent because some crazy man named Knox who lives on the outskirts of town told me it was my mother who committed the murder?

"I just know."

Governor Leo sighs and pulls himself closer to his desk. "What is your brother's name?" he asks while riffling through a stack of parchment.

"Tuor Crim."

The governor pauses, then drops his hands on the desk. Slowly, he tilts his head up to look at me.

"Crim," he muses, taking a good look at me. "I remember you now." Governor Leo nods his head. "Yes, you tried to convince me that your brother was sick in the mind. That was an argument I'd never heard before." He chuckles. "Out of the mouths of peasants, I say!"

I shift uncomfortably in front of Governor Leo as he fiddles with a silken scarf about his neck.

"I know now that he's not. He truly is innocent."

"Well, Miss Crim, I'm a rather merciful man, but I'm sorry to say that your brother will have to be executed."

"What? But I just told you he's innocent. He hasn't even had his sentencing yet."

"By my decree," Governor Leo bellows. "His sentencing has been cancelled. If you had looked at the posting tree today, you'd have seen that no meetings are being held in the courtroom because it has sustained fire damage. So I posted your brother's execution sentence to keep the process moving." Governor Leo shakes his head as he comes to his feet. "Blame the hooligan that tore through the Justice Hall yesterday carrying a torch. Don't these feral people know the building's made of Catahli?"

I hardly comprehend Governor Leo's insult. Tuor will have to be executed. The words slosh around in my head like a turbulent storm.

"But he didn't do it. He didn't kill that man, our mother did."

Hot tears pour from the corners of my eyes.

"It's quite irrelevant whether your brother is innocent or not."

Governor Leo moves to the glass doors, opening them as a gust of cool fall air fills the room. His shoulders broaden and his back straightens as he lifts his head to survey the fields.

"Irrelevant?" I shout. "What does that mean?"

Clasping his hands behind his back, the governor glances over his shoulder at me as if he's surprised I'm still standing there.

"Look," he says marching across the room to his desk. "Your brother is an unfortunate sacrifice that must be made."

"What do you mean?"

"It's not me that wants him dead. Quite certainly, your brother's future is of no import to me."

Governor Leo spreads his arms wide as if to absolve himself of any guilt. I wipe my face clean of tears. Perhaps Governor Leo is not the enemy I thought him to be. I look at him straight on again. The governor is actually looking me in the eyes now, and there's the slightest curious smile on his lips. He's suddenly no longer bored. I've become the audience that this man craves.

"Who wants my brother dead?"

There's silence. I feel as though I'm standing across from the town gossip, who has the juiciest news to tell but has been sworn upon death not to tell it.

"If my brother is to die, do I not at least deserve to know why?"

Governor Leo shrugs his shoulders. "All right. Can't hurt, right?" He sits back down at his desk, a gleeful, mischievous look on his face. "Who would you tell? Your brother?" Governor Leo chuckles to himself. "No one would believe you anyway." Pulling out the bottom drawer of his desk, Governor Leo produces a piece of parchment flecked in gold. Centered on the front flap is the seal of the Supreme Ruler.

My eyes grow wide as I lean in to look closer.

"It's political. It's as simple as that," Governor Leo says. He flips open the letter. "The Supreme Ruler simply stated that a fugitive, your brother, was likely fleeing to my territory and that it was of highest priority that I capture him and hold his trial here in Bear Gap."

"What else does it say?"

Governor Leo bites his lower lip. "Your brother *must* be found guilty, and he must be sent to the execution block."

My heart skips at the word execution. "And you never questioned why?"

"I don't need to," Governor Leo says, folding up the letter and returning it to its hiding place. "A man like me does not get to this position by questioning his authority." Governor Leo rises from his seat again. "When the Supreme Ruler asks you to do something, you simply *do it*." Governor Leo steps through the glass door and onto the balcony. "Come here, girl."

Slowly, I walk to the balcony where so many times I watched this man give speeches praising the morals of this farm and the Supreme Ruler, Quinten Warwick. "Look at what the Supreme Ruler and I have created. It's a system that not only provides food for the whole country, but it sustains our territory. Many sacrifices had to be made to make this happen." Governor Leo reaches his arm out and rests a hand on my shoulder. "Quinten once said something very wise to me. It was years ago, but I still remember it today. The sacrifice of few creates endless possibilities for many." Keeping his eyes high upon the fields, he says, "Your brother may be one of the few."

It feels like his hand is not on my shoulder but instead wrapped around my heart, squeezing and squeezing. In tandem we watch the workers bustling up and down the fields.

"Why Tuor? Why *my* brother?"

"I don't know," he says, letting out a long sigh. Governor Leo turns and takes my other shoulder in his hand so we're face-to-face. "You and I are not so different. We must obey our Supreme Ruler and continue on with our work."

Dazed, I stare at Governor Leo's crooked, wrinkled face.

"What is he giving you?" I whisper, my voice hoarse and strained.

Governor Leo cocks his head. "What do you mean?"

"What is the Supreme Ruler giving you in exchange for your cooperation?"

"It's not like that, child." Governor Leo chuckles.

If there is anything I've learned from working at the farm my whole life, it's that favors abound among the rich and powerful. It's how I knew to make a deal with Benedek.

"Politics is like bartering. You give him something and he gives you something. What did he offer in exchange for my brother's death?"

Governor Leo laughs again as if to shake off the uncomfortable question. He pats my shoulders before standing up straight. "Do you really want to know?"

I nod my head. My teeth clench and grind against each other.

"Did you know that there are four territories wealthier than Bear Gap? Think about how much happier my citizens would be if they had more money, yourself included. Less poverty. Less hunger. Less . . . people sleeping on the street. Maybe we can even make it to the top two territories if I can grow my fields." Governor Leo looks at me to respond, but I don't. A big smile grows on his face. "Quinten has offered our territory an influx of a hundred more soldiers for added security, a higher preference on wheat yields, and ten pounds of rings to use however I see fit. All just for following his orders regarding your brother." Governor Leo folds his arms across his chest.

I feel my breath quickening. Tuor is a commodity to Governor Leo and the Supreme Ruler.

"All for killing my brother," I whisper.

"That's right." His hands leave my shoulders, and he shifts his body toward the fields. "Think of all the people that this will help."

Not a single ring will makes its way to the farm laborers. Even if it did, Tuor will not be the reason. Hot anger pulses through my temples. A scream escapes my mouth. I sound like a lioness defending her cubs. I stretch out both my hands and ram them into Governor Leo. He flies backward so that his back hits the hard stone railing around the balcony. For a moment I think he might flip over and fall to his death, but instead he crumbles to the floor, howling out in pain.

Governor Leo's face is warped with anger. He bares his teeth at me. "You wicked girl!"

He tries to scramble to his feet, but slips and falls again with a new cry of pain. Slowly, I take a step back. My hands shake and I look at them as if I can't believe what they've done.

"I'll be happy now to see your brother die!" A furious roar explodes from his mouth. "Oh, I will have fun with him until it's time to take off his head!"

My body shudders as I take another timid step backward.

"No," I whimper.

"Yes. Yes! He'll have all of my attention," Governor Leo moans, grabbing for his back. "Guards!"

A soldier whips through the door and scans the room until he sees the governor and me on the balcony.

"Sir."

The soldier reaches out to help Governor Leo off the floor, but he waves the guard away.

"Take her!" he shouts. The soldier yanks me by the arm.

"Your brother will curse your name, Camilla Crim," Governor Leo screams. "I want her off this farm, permanently."

"No." I say. I'm pulled from the room and dragged through the hallway. "No, you can't do this!"

I struggle hard, twisting against the soldier's grip.

"You can't!" I beg. My voice echoes eerily down the hall. "I have to work!"

My eyes are a flood of tears. "Please."

Frustrated, the soldier picks me up and throws me over his shoulder. He carries me down the winding stairwell, out the back door, and across the courtyard to the front gate. He tosses me like one might toss a burlap bag of pumpkins onto the ground. The gate is pulled shut with a solid *click*.

"Please don't. Please don't!" I raise my arms in front of my face. "Have mercy."

I crumple like a baby onto the dusty road. The soldier pulls a dagger from his belt. He grabs my left hand, turning it around so my Warwick brand shows full on my forearm. He takes the blade of his dagger and lays a shallow cut directly down the middle of the brand, cutting a groove that splits the W. I scream out in pain and horror, holding my arm as the blood spills through my fingers.

"You've killed me!" I scream as the soldier wipes my blood from his knife. "You've killed me."

The brand is deformed now. I'll never be admitted to work at the farm again. Which means I'll never earn another ring or buy another piece of food.

CHAPTER THIRTY

MIRABELLE WRAPS A tattered bandage around my arm. I sit at her kitchen table like a child that's being punished. My dress is stained with splotches of blood, and my eyes are red and puffy. Mirabelle ties off the end of the fabric, then walks to the basin to wash her hands.

"What were you thinking?" she mutters. "I can't feed myself and you with the rings I make." Mirabelle spins around to look at me. I stare at the floor. "Camilla, I'd sell these books to take care of you, but they're worthless. I have that measly garden out back with a few herbs and mushrooms. There's not enough out there to even feed one person. On top of that, I could be turned in for that patch of dirt, and I'd be stuck in the stocks for endangering the health of this territory and using non-Warwick seed." Mirabelle smooths her frazzled hair. "I'm sorry." Her voice cracks. "I just don't know how I'm going to take care of you."

I look at her watery eyes. Standing, I cross the room to give her a hug.

"Maybe you won't have to."

***

At the posting tree, I rip off Governor Leo's notice with Tuor's sentencing. It's a small piece of parchment that fits easily in my hand.

Tuor Crim shall be sentenced to death by execution for the murder of Aiden Brookes in Rande Square two days hence.

I crumple up the notice and leave it to lie on the ground. The street is busy with people. Food vendors push their carts up and down Reaper's Way. Weary farm workers search for their dinner. Children run the streets with an energy that adults will never know.

But me? I have nothing to do. I don't have a job to go to. I don't even have a drunken father to go home to. And Tuor . . . Tuor's fate has been spoken. He will die. He will have to die. The question of why is simply irrelevant anymore. The Supreme Ruler wants my brother to take the fall for something our mother did. Perhaps he's protecting our mother?

I wander into the middle of the street, feeling the rush of the crowds bustle past me. I almost scream out in agony at the sight of all of these people. I'm sick of everything around me.

I turn about quickly, marching straight for the edge of town. I dive into the woods like someone might leap into a pond of cool water. Calm instantly surrounds me as the drone of the crowds gets eaten up by the calm sway of the large oak trees. After being banished from the farm, I feel worthless. Every person needs a purpose, I suppose. And I have lost mine. It wasn't a happy purpose or an easy one, but I had a mission every day. And now . . . now I have nothing.

The stirring sound of the river reaches my ears as I take long strides into the valley. I hop onto the fallen tree and cross it, walking with my chin up and my arms spread out like a bird. The breeze catches the folds of my skirt, and I feel like the wind could whisk me away like a feather. It doesn't send my stomach into a fit though. I like the feeling that I could leap into oblivion and fly away.

I ponder Knox's cabin intently. Even his house looks cross. What would Mirabelle say if she knew I was here? She'd be afraid that Knox would gobble me up like a monster. Mirabelle forgets that I have dealings with bitter old men everyday. I take a step closer to the door. My feet brush across the wood of his front porch. The rocking chair sways gently. I fold my hand into a fist and knock, three quick and hard raps on the door.

Heavy footsteps creak across the floor. The door is whipped open but only a few inches. The leathery face of Knox Duffy glares down at me.

"What are you doing here?"

His voice is low, strained.

"I wanna talk."

"You're a fool for coming here."

"I'm already aware that you think me a fool." I raise my eyebrows. "Please," I beg, placing my hand on the door.

"Get off my property."

He starts to close the door, but I hold it open with my hand. He's weak, I realize, when it's not too difficult for me to push against him.

"Please," I say again. "You're the only one who knows things about my mother."

"Ask Mirabelle."

"I can't." I try to meet Knox's eyes, but they shift away from me as if I'm an ugly thing to look at. "Plus, if Mirabelle has information about my mother that she still hasn't told me, then it means she doesn't want me to know."

Knox makes a huffing noise with his mouth and starts to close the door again. I catch it with my foot. "I don't want to be protected anymore. I want the truth."

"Leave me alone."

I force myself closer and give Knox a look that insists he meet my eyes.

"I need to talk to *you*."

The deep wrinkles in Knox's face look as if they might meld into the cracks of his door. He shifts away from the threshold and slinks into the darkness. The door hangs ajar, and I realize that this is Knox welcoming me inside. Darkness wraps around me like fog as I enter the cave-like cabin. Knox hobbles to the table.

"Sit," he instructs.

I take a seat opposite him at the table. The fire crackles lightly behind him, providing the only light in the room. His square jaw and ragged beard are highlighted by the firelight.

"What do you want to know?"

"I spoke to the governor today. He admitted to me that he knows my brother is innocent."

"So?"

"He showed me a letter he received from the Supreme Ruler." Knox's back straightens slightly. "He claims that Warwick told him to capture Tuor, hold his trial, and then sentence him to death." Knox rubs the coarse hairs on his chin. "Why would the Supreme Ruler care about the fate of my brother?"

Knox's mind seems to drift far away and search deep into his memories for the answer to my question.

I reach my arms across the table, unable to keep them still as I speak. "Tuor told me that *she's* the one that killed Aiden Brookes." I pause. "You were right. You were right about my mother."

"You're mother is a vile witch. It wasn't a far stretch to make that statement."

This is exactly why I've come to see Knox. He doesn't say much, but when he does speak, it's the truth, and he'll say it regardless of a person's feelings.

"That still doesn't explain what this has to do with Tuor." I shake my head.

Knox sighs. "It's obvious. Warwick is having your brother take the fall for what Portia did."

"But why?"

He shrugs his shoulders. "For love?"

"Are you telling me that this whole thing is because my mother and the Supreme Ruler are . . . in love?" Love doesn't feel like the right word to use.

"Maybe." Knox leans back in his chair, folding his arms across his chest. "Those two have done far worse."

We stare for a moment as if there's a challenge we're both trying to win.

"How is it that you know so much about me, and Tuor, and my mother, yet I never even heard your name spoken until yesterday?"

Knox says nothing, acting as if I hadn't asked the question.

"How do you know so much about her?" I ask. I'm willing to settle for this small piece of information.

Knox hesitates. "You said you didn't care about protecting me."

"I don't." Knox leans forward in his chair and spits something from his mouth. "Twelve years ago when Quinten—the Supreme Ruler—" Knox rolls his eyes. "When he invaded our territory, I set out to kill him. He got called back to duty in LilyAye shortly after the battle, so I followed his caravan deep into the woods. I waited until they had all fallen asleep. My plan was to sneak into his tent and kill him in his sleep, but instead I saw him and your mother . . . together."

"So you never fought him?"

"We did. I lost, badly. The only reason I'm alive today is because I made a bargain with him." Knox stops suddenly. He seems to choke on his words, breaking into a coughing fit. "I promised to track your mother and report back to him."

"Why did he want you to do that?"

"He couldn't keep ahold of her. He was heartsick for her, but she kept leaving." His eyes, distant and bleary, dart away from me. "She's more powerful than him, so he wanted to get an upper hand."

"Wait." I try to blink away my confusion. "My mother is more powerful than the Supreme Ruler?"

Knox rubs at a spot in the middle of his chest. "She's more powerful than most. I spent nearly seven years of my life following Portia all over Elmyra. I know what she's capable of."

I shake my head, a mixture of disbelief and an overabundance of information.

"I made one stupid decision as a young man," Knox continues. "And paid for it tenfold over these last twelve years."

"But why go after the Supreme Ruler like that? You must have known he'd defeat you with an army behind him?"

"I thought he had killed my father."

I remember what Johnny told me about Knox being the only survivor to make it home and how the others were taken prisoner.

"The truth of my father's fate turned out to be far worse. Quinten took him captive. To this day he's being held somewhere in LilyAye or . . . perhaps . . . he is finally dead."

I exhale. Understanding washes over me in a big wave. Knox wasn't holding back this story because he was trying to protect me. He was trying to protect *himself.* His sagging posture screams the proclamation of a man that's been defeated. The thought of his father, locked away, withering away, must torture him in the same way I ache for Tuor.

I stand quickly, pushing my chair back. I wander through the darkness, admiring the simple neatness of his home. I turn around and abruptly say, "Tuor is all I care about. I never knew my mother, and I don't care to ever know her." I hear the pitch in my voice rising. I'm growing angry, and I don't exactly know why. I take a step toward the table. "She killed Aiden Brookes, not Tuor. And the only way I'm going to get him out of that dungeon is to hold her accountable for what she did."

"How do you think you're gonna do that?"

"You tracked her before, why not do it again? I'll come with you. We'll find her and—"

"And what?" Knox challenges.

I step up to the table, poking my finger hard into the wood. The gash in my forearm stings. "I'll go to Quinten Warwick if I have to. I'll insist on justice."

Knox moves ever so slightly away from me as if he's scared to be this close.

"You'll never find your mother."

"Why do you talk about her like she's immortal? She's just a person!"

Knox chuckles to himself. It's the first lightness I've seen in him since I got here. He licks his lips and uncrosses his arms from his chest. Standing from his chair, he towers over me. It's as if he's suddenly been given his nerve back.

"Your mother *is* immortal, and you'll never find her. And if you did, your brother's fate will be long decided. I don't know why Quinten has decided to pull your brother into their tryst, but these two people are far too powerful for you or me."

"But what if we—"

"It won't work." He shakes his head. "Whatever idea you're coming up with in your head, it won't work." Knox spreads his arms wide apart. He inches closer, his hot breath on my face. "You're fighting against gods!" he shouts.

I swallow hard, backing away from a suddenly enraged Knox. I stumble to the door, open it, and watch Knox as he slowly returns to his chair. He doesn't stop me as I scurry away, tears bursting at the corners of my eyes.

CHAPTER THIRTY-ONE

MY BED MAT is wet and warm with tears. I roll over and over through the night, my blanket twisting between my legs. The wound on my arm throbs hot and sharp. Eventually, sleep envelops me. My dreams are a torment, riddled with nightmares and horrible images of Tuor. I will have to watch him die. I will have to watch my brother die. Like a fighter's mantra, that phrase repeats in my mind through hours of troubled sleep.

I wake early, desperate to escape my mind's fantasies. It feels like I've been in a horrible fistfight. My head aches, and my eyes are puffy and sore. I can hardly see as I scramble to my feet and cross the room. I anchor myself against the wall. All I'm aware of is air entering my body, then leaving as I take one breath at a time.

It seems like days ago that I spoke with Governor Leo. I'm certain it's been a month since I ripped that notice off the posting tree and saw for myself that Tuor would be executed. Then suddenly, like water spilling over a cliff, my emotions rush back to me. My body closes in on itself as I weep hot, stinging tears. I crumple to the floor, letting my hand scrape across the wall.

But there's too much pain in crying. So I force myself to breathe, in and out, just enough so that I don't fully collapse. Why do I stop myself though? I'd love to die right now. It would be a gift to simply wither away and not have to live through tomorrow. But even with me gone, Tuor would still have to live through his execution. What I do with my life doesn't affect his fate. I can't let Tuor experience it alone. I will be there. I will be there to watch them take my brother's life away just so that he won't be alone. After that, perhaps for me, death will come easier than life.

The load of knowing I must at least live through tomorrow creates a heaviness that feels like it could crush me. I crawl to the table and set my weary body onto a chair. The air is damp and musty, the way it feels after it has rained. My eyes glass over as I stare at nothing. The sound of soft raindrops finally reaches my ears. I simply . . . exist.

A dark amber bottle lies on its side between the wall and an overturned chair. It's left over from the raid. If Malcolm saw it, he'd scoop it up and guzzle its contents like they were essential. All my life I've lived around his foul drink, never once tasting it for myself. My father is a crippled man, broken and torn apart by things that happened when I was a baby, things that I've never cared to ask about. The drink *is* essential . . . to him at least. Perhaps there's a relief there.

I feel broken now, like him. For the first time, I'm tempted to find out what mystery lives inside those bottles. My legs straighten and I walk forward, tossing the overturned chair out of my way. I crouch down, taking the neck of the bottle in my hand. The rain outside picks up its pace. I stand again, leaning hard on the wall for support, and pop the cork from the bottle. The briny smell strikes my senses as I bring the opening to my mouth.

The fiery liquid assaults my tongue. I take a hefty swig, feeling it burn all the way down my throat. A cough explodes from my mouth. I take another gulp, wishing for relief through the pain. My stomach wrenches. The bottle slips from my sweaty hand. The amber-colored glass shatters, and dark liquid spills onto the knotted wood floor. There's something soothing about watching the drink slowly seep through the slats of the floor.

Numbness overtakes me, and I drop back onto my bed. I drift into exhausted sleep, feeling a temporary relief from my horror. My slumber is disturbed momentarily by gentle rapping on the door. Mirabelle comes to my bedside and cradles my head. She's heard the news, seen the notice on the posting tree. Why didn't I tell her? she asks. I want to explain that I couldn't speak those words out loud, but right now my mouth is mute. I lie on my bed in utter stillness. Soon she leaves.

I fall asleep, then shudder awake, then fall asleep again, all day and all night long. Hard knocking on the door pulls me awake. It's fast and firm, striking in quick beats. Sunlight bursts through every hole and crack in the house. The rain has stopped. It's morning, I realize, the morning of Tuor's execution.

Under the rickety door, I can see a pair of muddy boots. A soldier? Warwick soldiers wear thin black leather boots. These are wide, brown, and worn from use. The man with the boots knocks again. Leave me alone. Let me suffer in silence. I sit up in bed, drawing my legs close to my chest and burying my face in my knees. The knocking continues.

"Fine. I'm coming," I say, tumbling from my bed.

I pull the door toward me. My eyes sting as brightness explodes my vision. I make out the image of a tall blonde-haired man with a sharp square jaw.

"Johnny?"

"I brought you something," he says.

I open my eyes fully now. Johnny's shoulders are wide with confidence. "How did you find me?"

"I asked your neighbors where you live. Come with me, I want to show you something."

Johnny takes my hand and leads me down the steps. The air outside seems foreign. The swamp out front is no longer a swamp. It's a gentle moving river as it sometimes becomes when it rains enough. The earth feels spongy as my bare feet connect with it.

Johnny turns the corner of the shack. I let my hand slip from his. I follow, but slowly. There's nothing he could have that I would care about. He could have a chest full of rings, and they'd be worthless to me. When I finally round the corner, he's standing next to a white horse, stroking its mane. The horse shakes its head, which sends ripples down its light gray hair. I stare at the two of them stupidly.

"For you," Johnny says. I say nothing. "I named her Shea. *She's* for you."

"The horse?" I ask, confused.

"Yes."

He probably thinks I'm ungrateful because I cringe every time I blink—my eyes are swollen so badly.

"I don't understand. Why would you give me a horse?" My voice starts to rise. "Why would I want a horse when my brother is going to die? The governor has sentenced him to death. He'll be executed today, and there's nothing I can do about it but watch. I'll have to watch my own brother's life taken away right in front of me! *Why would I want a horse?*" I scream. I pause, catching my breath. "I'll have to watch . . . "

I bury my face in my hands because even in my grief I still feel ashamed in front of him. Johnny places both his hands on my shoulders. I look up quickly, surprised by his touch.

"I know about your brother." His voice is calm. "Knox told me. That's why I got you the horse."

I look up at him. Trying to understand why a horse would be the proper gift for someone in my situation.

"What do you mean?"

"Camilla, this horse is your escape from here, your chance to start over, away from Bear Gap." He pauses. "Leave here, *with* your brother."

"But he's—"

"You're going to get him back," Johnny says. He doesn't say it to encourage me. He says it like he can read the future, and he knows I'll get Tuor back.

I feel my knees weaken and the next thing I know I'm on the ground, being supported only by Johnny's firm grip on my arms.

"I can't do it!" I cry. "I've tried everything! Knox is right. Warwick is too strong."

Johnny squats down to face me, his firm hands still resting on my shoulders.

"This horse is a very special horse." Johnny pulls me up. He shows me, on Shea's left shoulder, a Warwick brand. It matches the one that used to be on my arm but is now scarred and mutilated. "She was a Warwick horse that I stole last year when I petitioned against the wheat shortage."

Johnny lets go of my shoulders. It feels like a test. Can I stand on my own?

"She'll help get you across territory borders with no questions," he says, rubbing Shea's back. Johnny's face is stretched in a broad smile.

I step toward the horse, running my fingers over the raised W on her skin.

"Why are you doing this for me?" I shift my gaze to his face.

"What Warwick is doing to your brother is disgusting. And your brother is not the only one. Look at that farm where you work." Johnny's arm flies from his side. "They make you think that the farm is a good thing, that it feeds all of these people, and that it helps people like you with a job." Johnny's passion seems to spill over and splash onto me. He comes in close, taking my shoulders in his hands again. "All they've done is create *slaves*."

I stare into the faint blue color of his eyes.

"Warwick has made you a slave," he says, pointing his finger at me. "I'll do anything to right the wrongs of Quinten Warwick." Johnny's hands move from my shoulders and scoop up both of my hands in his. "If freeing your brother is even a tiny needle prick against Warwick, I'd risk my life to do it."

My eyes are wide, and whether real or imagined, I feel the fogginess of my weeping melt away.

"Do you want your brother back?" Johnny asks, his voice firm now as he drops my hands.

"Yes." I run a hand through my tattered hair. "Yes, more than anything."

"Then let's go get him."

CHAPTER THIRTY-TWO

"BUT HOW?" I ask. "How can we rescue my brother? I've tried everything."

I've brought Johnny inside the shack with the explanation that if I'm going to fight against the Supreme Ruler, I at least need to change my clothes.

"We broke into the Justice House once already, we can do it again."

I hold an old pair of Tuor's trousers to my chest and give Johnny a signal to turn around.

"They'll recognize us," I say, slipping off my wool dress. I pull on a pair of brown animal skin pants that are snug around my hips because they were originally made for Tuor's slender frame. I don a loose blouse, a jacket I stole from Mirabelle since I lost mine at the Justice House, and my work boots. A dress simply won't do today.

"Getting inside will be tough," Johnny admits. I come to his side to show that he doesn't need to look away anymore. "But once we're in, I have a plan."

I pull my hair back with a piece of twine to keep it out of my eyes. "Then what's the plan?"

Johnny shifts to face me. "You already know how to get to the dungeons. We'll be forced to separate. We can't play that trick again. It will just be about getting back to the dungeons and pulling your brother out."

"But we need a key to open the prison cells. Last time I got all the way down there, and I couldn't even open the door to get him out."

"So who carries the keys then?"

"I don't know . . . probably the dungeon guards. They don't give the Justice House guards a key to the cells. I tried the keys that we stole off the soldier, and they didn't work."

I'm learning that Johnny's plans are fast and dirty, so there's little preparation. It unnerves me, but there's also a part of me that likes it. Jump first, think later. Besides . . . I have nothing to lose by throwing myself to the lions.

Johnny waves me out of the house. We drop down the three steps. "I'll have to teach you the move to knock out a guard." A sick thrill pulses through me. He wants me to fight a Warwick soldier? "Hop on," he says, pointing to Shea. "Do you know how to ride a horse?"

I give him a sideways glare. I shouldn't be offended that he asked that question. Most of the people who live in the swamps don't have funds enough to purchase a horse. But I'm well versed in this mode of transportation.

"Yes," I say with a bite of snark. "Mirabelle used to have a horse. She'd let me ride it all over."

I mount the white beast. She scuttles on her hooves at my invasion. "Shhhh." I rub her neck to soothe her. "She seems unsteady," I say.

"Nah." Johnny waves a hand at me. "I've been riding her for near four seasons, and she's still ornery. It's her personality."

"All right."

We kick off, Johnny and I, me on my horse and Johnny on his. *My horse*, I think. What a strange but amazing gift . . .

***

Rande Square is already busy with preparations for Tuor's execution. A stage is being built; its only emblem will be a block and an axe. I've seen enough executions to know the procedure.

"When will it be?" Johnny asks as we come to a pause.

"Sunset."

"We need to keep moving."

We gallop across town and stop just before the road curves into the Justice House.

"The trick is to surprise your opponent," Johnny says. He ties our horses off as he explains how someone like me can take down a war-trained soldier. "You're strong. You just need to funnel your strength. If they're behind you, take your arm like this," Johnny folds his arm in half so that his elbow protrudes. "And then just jam it in their face as hard as you can."

I try to mirror his moves, swinging my arm back at an invisible opponent.

"Good, good. Now if you're attacking from behind, just get a firm grip on their neck. If you hold it long enough, eventually they'll pass out."

"Okay, got it."

I nod confidently even though it feels like my whole body is shaking. My mind is telling me that what we're about to do is dangerous, really dangerous. Johnny and I may both rot away in the very dungeon we're about to break into.

Once, I saw a mother fly across Reaper's Way and grab her son before he was run over by a wagon. I feel like her right now, like I've been gifted with unnatural and temporary speed and boldness. I have a strength, rooted in anger, that's unexplainable, but it's there nonetheless.

"Ready?" Johnny asks.

"I'm ready."

We round the corner to the Justice House, but I stop suddenly. A man blocks our way, husky with a scraggly beard and a long animal skin coat. He leans conspicuously on a sheathed sword that's half as long as he is.

"Uncle Knox." Johnny sighs and paces ahead of me. "What are you doing here?"

Knox looks to me as if I should answer the question.

"You've come to stop us," I say.

"How did you know we'd be here?" Johnny asks.

"I told you, you're a blubbering fool," Knox says, pointing a crooked finger at Johnny. "You came to my house and asked me a mountain of questions about this girl and her brother. By the end of it, I figured you'd make a run at the Justice House."

The low drone of townspeople filling the street causes Johnny to glance up Reaper's Way and lower his voice.

"We're going in there." Johnny says it as if it's a declaration of his right to live. "I won't let you stop us."

"You can't keep me from my brother."

"I know." Knox sighs. "I haven't come to stop you."

Knox's tired-looking eyes settle on me.

"I've come to help. Why else would I have brought this?" Knox taps the tip of his sword onto the ground. "You'll need these too." He pulls out two short daggers from his coat and hands one to Johnny and one to me. "Hide those in your jackets. No nephew of mine is going to ride into a hive of Warwick soldiers without a proper weapon on him."

"Uncle Knox—"

"I ain't doing it for you, so just stop."

"Why are you doing this then?" I ask. "Why help me?"

Knox rolls his head around on his neck like he's a little boy whose mother just asked him an interrogating question.

"Mirabelle, she . . . she did everything she could to help you and your brother and I . . . " Knox looks as if he's forgotten how to speak. "You took all of her time and—"

"And what?"

"I never helped you. In fact I . . . " The lids on Knox's eyes slowly lift to look at my face. "I hated you," he says flatly.

"How could you hate her? She's never done anything to you," Johnny says.

Knox shifts on his feet. "You were the spawn of two vile people that took advantage of Mirabelle. I couldn't stand watching her give all of her time and money to two brats that didn't know how good they had it. And back then, I loved Mirabelle."

Love . . . it's hard to picture this man loving anyone. Knox reaches for his chest. His face contorts as if this very moment his heart is bursting with pain.

"Your mother," Knox continues, "took my life from me. For years I followed her bloody path for Quinten. And now, now I'm supposed to help *her* son and daughter?"

Suddenly, Knox doesn't scare me anymore. He's just a tired, pathetic man that's riddled with guilt. I take a step closer to him. "I am not my mother," I growl.

Knox bites on his lower lip. "I know. Why do you think I'm here now? If the last thing I do on this earth is help you rescue your brother, then maybe that will be penance enough for my sins."

I wonder momentarily what sins Knox speaks of. Mirabelle told me that once they were soul mates. If they were truly soul mates, then something ripped them apart. Could it be me? Perhaps Mirabelle's love for me conflicted with Knox's hate. Was I a part of their relationship and never knew it? I look at Knox's hunched visage and actually feel sorry for him.

"If we're going to do this, we better do it now," Johnny says. "When they come to make the transport, this Justice House will be inundated with soldiers."

Farm workers assault the street behind us. I turn around to see the crowds fill the already buzzing square.

"It's quitting time already?" I ask. "Sunset's in two hours."

"Johnny, tell me the plan," Knox says urgently.

I wander toward the road, watching as people hungrily await a village execution. I turn back around to see Johnny with his arm around Knox's shoulders, giving him the details of our very thin plan.

"Camilla!" I spin back around. A voice booms through the crowds. "CAMILLA!"

Carefully, I pace toward the screams. Lawrence bursts through the wall of bodies.

"Camilla . . ."

He runs toward me with flushed cheeks and dirty knees. I can't hide my surprise. He was gone. I believed I would never see Lawrence again. My face begins to light with a smile, but pride insists I stop. He comes to a gasping halt in front of me.

"I told you never to speak to me again." I carry an edge in my voice if only to mask the tears. Shaking my head, I turn to walk away.

"Wai-wai-wait!" Lawrence grabs my arm and spins me back around. "Camilla, please. I've been looking for you for two days, listen—"

"Camilla," Johnny calls. "It's time."

I nod in their direction.

"Who are *they*?" Lawrence asks, straightening his back as he scrutinizes Knox and Johnny.

"Don't worry about them. What do you want?" I snap. "Why have you been looking for me?"

"Tuor is not in the dungeons anymore."

"What do you mean?"

"I've been trying to find you to tell you—yesterday they moved him to the stocks on the farm."

Johnny and Knox ease up behind me to listen to Lawrence.

"I saw them drag him in yesterday. He's being held outside in the stocks, but he's heavily guarded."

"Why would they do that?" I ask.

"It's rumored someone broke into the dungeons. The governor apparently had six guards killed for compromising Tuor's security."

Johnny clears his throat. I look up at him, feeling a sinking in my stomach. "This is a trap. It has to be," I say. "They've *lessened* security on Tuor by moving him out in the open."

"Governor's scared," Knox says. "He wants to keep his charge close by. He's panicking, getting sloppy."

"I got kicked out yesterday," I say holding up my arm. "Could he be doing it because he knows I won't be admitted to the farm anymore?"

Johnny scrunches his eyebrows. "Maybe."

"What are you gonna do?" Lawrence asks.

"Nothing to concern *you* with," I say. "Let's get moving."

Lawrence blocks my way as I try to walk around him. He places a gentle hand on my arm. "I know about the death sentence. I wanna help. Let me help, please."

"Why would I do that? I can hardly trust you."

"Can't you forgive me for the trial?"

"We can't wait any longer," Johnny calls.

"Wait, wait, please, just give me a moment," Lawrence begs.

Knox, Johnny, and I turn around to mount our horses. Lawrence follows closely on my heels.

"I know I disappointed you." His voice is nearly a whisper.

"You left me when I needed you the most," I say. "Betrayal is a better way to say it."

I anchor my hand on Shea's saddle and place my foot in the stirrup, pulling myself all the way up.

Lawrence takes Shea's reigns and hugs them like a starving man begging for food.

"But Tuor is still my friend, and he doesn't deserve any of this." Lawrence leans in closer, his eyes turning soft like dough. "I want him freed too, not as much as you, I know that. But I can't stand by and do nothing. I won't. He's my only friend in this world." Shea shifts, taking a jerky step forward. Lawrence stays close at my side. "Camilla, I . . . I was running from my problems before, I see that now. That night we spoke in Lindon Place, I left, fled town like I was scared of my own shadow. But I came back because I realized that I can't run from my father forever." Lawrence looks down at the palms of his hands and then back up at me. "Besides all of that, it's wrong what the governor is doing. If I let this happen, then I won't be able to live with myself."

I swallow hard, remembering what Governor Leo told me about his orders to make sure that Tuor is executed. The thought on its own makes me feel cold all over. I want to be angry with Lawrence. I want him to feel the heartache I felt the day of Tuor's trial. Why does forgiveness feel like the hardest task I'll accomplish today? I look away from Lawrence. Knox and Johnny stand at the ready.

"We could use his help," Johnny says, answering a question I never asked.

My gaze drifts back to Lawrence's watery eyes. I can see that they're filled with hope, and although he looks terrified, he's still *here*. He hasn't run away.

"Get on."

I nod my head for Lawrence to join me on my horse.

"Thank you," he whispers as he scoots onto Shea's

back behind me. "Thank you."

CHAPTER THIRTY-THREE

WE BREAK INTO a spirited gallop on Reaper's Way, weaving through the last few workers exiting the farm. Before reaching the gate, I point, signaling to Knox and Johnny to break into the dense woods surrounding the farm.

"I think we should come in from the west, by the orchards," I say. "We can hop the fence there, and we'll have coverage until we can get close to Tuor."

The farm is equipped with a double defense. The stockyard fence is built of solid trees, double my height. It's for keeping the wildlife out. That's what they always told us. It's only now, I realize it was more to keep us in.

The farm is also buffered by a mile of thick brush and trees. We leave the horses tied just off Reaper's Way. The four of us push into the thick woods and begin our hike to the other end of the farm. Moss and vines have taken over these woods, even snaking their way up the fence. We move at a silent trudge through the trees. Knox hacks away branches with his sword.

The hem of my pants catches on a thorny plant. I rip it away, creating a little tear in the fabric. A web of prickly plants twists around my ankle. I stumble, but Johnny catches me before I fall. He holds my hand a moment longer than needed.

"This is like walking through honey," Lawrence says.

"We're almost there, I think. Stay close to the fence."

The fence begins a slow curve as we reach the far backend of the farm. I pause to look through a crack in the fence where the beams don't fit perfectly together. A row of short fig trees that have gone barren with the cold weather sit unguarded.

"We're there," I say.

Knox rests a hand on his thigh, trying to catch his breath.

"How do we get over?" Johnny asks.

Lawrence backs up into the woods a few steps. "I think I can jump it."

"You'll be impaled," Knox says, pointing to the spiky tips on top of each post.

Lawrence shakes his head. "I can avoid them."

"You need to get me over first," says Knox. "I'm the heaviest."

We agree, and Johnny, Lawrence, and I all lift Knox by his legs and hoist him to the top. He grabs a spike in each hand and lifts himself up. In one fluid motion he shifts his feet forward and drops onto the other side with a hard thump.

I look at Johnny with wide eyes, surprised that a man in his condition could move like that. "Is he all right?"

"Are you okay, Uncle Knox?"

"Fine," he mumbles.

Next, Johnny and Lawrence bend down to turn their hands into stirrups. I step up and follow Knox's move with not as much grace. One of the spikes catches on my jacket and I tumble down the fence. The only thing that keeps me from hitting the ground is Knox's thick arm reaching out to steady me.

"Thanks."

Our eyes meet as I brush dust from my pants.

"I can see your brother down there," Knox says.

"Where?"

Knox pulls me between a row of trees and hands me a scope from his jacket. Through the lens I see three rows of soldiers, all sword-equipped, shielding Tuor. The Harras Manor sits as a backdrop behind the stocks. It looks like a doll's playhouse from this far away.

"Why doesn't Governor Leo just kill him now?" I ask. "If the Supreme Ruler wants him dead, why not just do it?"

Knox gazes listlessly across the farm. "Quinten wants an execution. He wants to show it off."

"Why?"

Knox holds his lips tightly together. He's holding something back, not telling me the whole truth. And by the stoic look on his face, he's not *going* to tell me.

Johnny jumps down from the wall with a grunt. He steadies himself, then backs away to make room for Lawrence. I give Johnny a look that shows I'm questioning Lawrence's ability to make it over on his own. Then we hear a quick *thump, thump* as he runs up the other side of the fence. His hands claw around the spikes until he gets a solid hold. He breaches the top of the wall and leaps to the ground with a firm landing.

Lawrence beams at his accomplishment. "Easy," he says, brushing his hands together.

"Let's make a plan," Knox says. "We need to get as close as possible without being seen so we can make an ambush."

I look out across the farm. "I think we should move through the fields along the—"

"Sh-sh-sh-sh-sh!" Johnny places a hand on my back. "There's a guard down there," he whispers. "To the right."

The four of us crouch behind the grove of trees.

"Governor Leo doesn't usually have a guard in fields where no one is working," I say.

Lawrence sidles up close. "I noticed he started tightening up security a couple of days ago."

"It looks like there's a soldier pacing the perimeter every twenty yards or so," Knox says, looking through his scope again.

"So staying along the fence isn't an option," Johnny says. He turns to look at me specifically. "I don't think things are less secure here than the Justice House."

I shake my head in agreement, then take Knox's scope and look for myself. "Do you see those little buildings all over the field? Those are sheds. They hold tools and things that get used in these back fields. Instead of staying along the perimeter, if we can move from shed to shed, we can take cover, and hopefully the guards won't see us coming."

"Going through the middle of the field seems risky," Lawrence says.

Knox slowly takes the scope from my hand. "It's a good idea." He points to the first shed. "Let's stay together as long as we can. Then when we get down far enough, we'll split, Johnny and I, Camilla and Lawrence, and we'll ambush Tuor's guards from either side."

"Okay," Johnny nods. He jumps to his feet. Energy seems to be coursing through every limb.

I suddenly feel frozen. "We're so outnumbered," I mutter.

Knox tucks his scope away in his jacket and pulls the sheath from his long shiny sword. "This is a failed mission," he says flatly. "But this is your last chance to save your brother." Knox's eyes flicker between Johnny, Lawrence, and me. "We'll likely end up captured or dead. Does anyone want to turn back, hop over that fence, and run home?" The group is silent. "I have some wrongs to get right, and that's going to happen today."

No one questions Knox. Coming to a bent position, he leads us down the middle aisle of the orchard. We pass the fig trees and apple trees, then come to a pause once the orchard ends, and we're no longer afforded the benefit of branch cover. Ahead and to the right sits the first shed.

"Quickly and silently," Knox says.

The four of us scurry through a dirt patch that was once the corn fields but has now been pulled barren of any stalks. We duck inside the tool-lined shed. A bucket of dirty water sits on the floor. Knox peeks around the opening.

"Next building is only ten paces that way," he says. "There's a guard, but we'll wait till he turns his back. Be ready to move on my signal."

I aim to steady my breathing. *This is it.* With shaking hands, I reach inside my jacket and pull out the dagger that Knox gave me. It's short with a curved blade and a worn wooden handle. I pull off the leather sheath and tuck it away. I'm surprised by how comfortable the dagger feels in my hand. I grip it tightly, realizing I've drawn the attention of Johnny. He winks at me and gives me an affirming nod. I know what I've gotten myself into. I'm not innocent to the risk. But what is my life if I can't live it in freedom?

CHAPTER THIRTY-FOUR

KNOX COAXES US forward with the flick of his hand. We run past the first guard, hiding for only a moment in the shed until running to the next one. We zigzag across the field like a pack of blind rats. We catch our breath, hunkering down in the shed by the barley field.

"Someone ran in there," a voice booms from outside.

The shed door flies open. Knox lunges forward, elbowing the soldier hard in the nose. He falls straight back, hitting the ground.

"Move!" Knox yells.

We leave our shelter, now with eyes on us, and run full tilt toward the lower fields. Tuor comes closer and closer into my view. Three soldiers barrel toward us. I fall back from the group, the slowest of the four of us. I feel a frantic hand wrap its fingers around my jacket and pull me back. The guard throws me to the ground. My dagger falls from my grip. I crawl to reach for it as Johnny runs past me and punches the man two, three times in a row. The guard reaches for his sword, but Johnny flattens him before he can draw it.

Two more attack, their swords drawn. Knox is in front of me before I can even scramble to my feet. He draws up his long sword, colliding into one soldier as Johnny takes the other. The clash of steel on steel echoes across the acres. Johnny's hits are spirited, full of passion. He chooses not to use the dagger Knox gave him. Instead, his fists fly, one over the other in a desperate struggle. Johnny ducks to avoid a hit, then pummels the soldier until he falls to the ground. In one wide swing, Knox slices his opponent through the middle. A tingling feeling runs through my body.

"Let's go." Knox turns about swiftly, his face set and focused.

We huddle behind the last tool shed that sits on the edge between the upper fields and the lower fields. Before us lie the vegetable patches: broccoli, potatoes, carrots. Beyond that is Tuor. My father, along with Vincent and Boris, still hang in a set of stock separate from Tuor, but I don't care about them. They can rot. I'm here for my brother.

"I can almost see his face from here," I say.

Knox peers through his scope. "He looks injured. We should be prepared to carry him out."

I swallow hard. Johnny cracks his knuckles while Knox wipes his sword on the leaves of a lettuce plant. Blood smears across the bright green vegetation.

"Run straight out from here toward the corner of the manor," Knox says, using his finger to point. "You two take the north side. Johnny and I will take the south side, toward the front gate. Then charge in from the side and we'll make our attack."

Lawrence and I nod.

"Find speed," Knox says with the tip of his head.

Our two teams turn to face our targets. At Knox's signal we sprint in opposite directions. Lawrence and I run close to each other. The cool wind whips past my face. I focus only on the corner of the house. I hear distant shouts to my left, but I ignore them.

We tumble behind the northern corner of the house. I nearly collapse in exhaustion. Behind this wall is the stairwell I took to Governor Leo's office. A tall haystack sits here with a rickety ladder leaning against the pile. Lawrence peeks around the corner.

"Can you see Johnny and Knox?" I ask breathing heavily.

"Yes. They've been spotted."

Lawrence's voice is quick and panicked. I join him at the wall. The soldiers guarding Tuor keep their stance, but there's movement among them. We've disrupted their guard. Johnny and Knox take on a dispatch of soldiers.

"We have to attack!" I scream. "We'll have no chance if we don't go now."

"Wait," Lawrence says, holding me back.

My head flings to the left. A soldier from the upper field runs toward us.

"Look!"

Another follows closely behind him. I take a step back, feeling my heartbeat thump faster and faster.

"What do we do? What do we do!"

"Stay behind me," Lawrence says.

Leather boots pound the earth as the soldiers close in on us, sword at the ready. Lawrence stands with his arms out at his sides, spread ever so slightly. His fingers wiggle like they're preparing for something, but he has no weapon. I feel helpless with nothing but calloused hands and a borrowed blade that I don't know how to wield.

"Take my dagger!"

"No. I won't need it," Lawrence says coolly.

The first soldier, broad-shouldered with thick hands, swings his sword at Lawrence. Lawrence dodges, moving his body left and right, avoiding the blows. He crouches down, then shifts sideways, moving with a fluidity I've never seen before.

Like a snake striking for its meal, Lawrence grips the man's wrist. The muscles in Lawrence's arm convulse as he twists the soldier's arm. Lawrence growls, biting his teeth together until the sword drops with a clink. He kicks the sword with his foot. It flies upward, landing smoothly in his free hand. I stand awestruck as Lawrence's weapon soars gracefully with curving violent strikes. The blade cuts through the air, sharp and accurate.

The second soldier closes in. I take another step, but he doesn't even see me. He's rushing to the other soldier's aid. I glance to the right. Mayhem is breaking out among Tuor's guards.

Lawrence attacks the second soldier, but he's weakening. His strikes become more desperate. I grip my dagger hard, step back a pace, and spring into motion. I ram myself full on into the side of the soldier that lost his sword. He's like a sturdy forest pine that's just been sawed from the bottom. The two of us drop fast and hard. He rolls on top of me and wraps his sweaty fingers around my throat. I scratch at his hands as my vision grows cloudy, then flinging my dagger, I run the blade along his arm.

His hands snap back, blood trickling down his sleeve. I gasp for air. My head swims, and I claw at the raw feeling around my neck. The soldier leans forward, his hands spread wide to choke me. I swipe my dagger, splitting open his chest as he collapses on me. Screaming, I push his body off, feeling warm blood soak through my clothes.

Lawrence grabs my arm and pulls me to my feet. "You okay?"

"Yeah." I must look dazed.

"We need to help the others."

"Okay," I mutter. I'm unable to take my eyes off the man whose life I just took. He has a bow slung across his chest and a quiver of arrows on his belt. The bow string is soaked in blood, but I wrangle it off his body anyway along with the arrows. This is one weapon I'm used to using.

"This isn't going to work," Lawrence says, running back to my side. "We've been seen, and they have Johnny and Knox tied up."

Nerves shake deep in the pit of my stomach. Lawrence and I are trapped between the house and the fence. Lawrence swings his sword, ready to take on the crowd of soldiers barreling toward us.

"We need to get to Tuor," I shout.

"This is it. Get ready to fight."

My eyes shift all around in search of divine help. Without a word to Lawrence, I run to the stack of hay. It's three times my height. I touch the dilapidated wooden ladder that's leaning against the tower of dried strands.

"Over here!" I yell as I hoist the ladder into the air and prop it on the side of the house. It nearly reaches the roof.

Lawrence follows. "Oh . . . oh no . . . no way," he mumbles when he figures out my intent.

"Why not? If we get on the roof, then we have an angle to shoot them down." I show Lawrence the bow around my shoulder. "There are no guards on the roof. It's this or them."

I point to our pack of pursuers. Five, six, soldiers march our direction. Lawrence actually takes a moment to contemplate his options. I place my foot on the bottom rung, pulling myself up as the whole ladder creaks. Slowly but steadily, I scale the ladder, going one step at a time. I glance back at Lawrence. His face is contorted and strained. The soldiers round the corner.

"C'mon!" I scream.

With no other choice, Lawrence hops on the ladder. I feel a shudder ripple down its railing and rungs. We both freeze for a moment, then continue on. The farm is covered with scrambling soldiers.

We have to get on the roof before they do. The ground grows farther and farther away. I lock my focus on the crest of the roof.

The ladder groans as I reach the top most rung. I look below to see a pool of soldiers gathering at the bottom. One pulls his bow off his chest and reaches for an arrow but I'm faster. Matching his move, I set an arrow, and let it fly before he has a chance. He crumples, and the soldiers begin to climb.

Lawrence is at my heels. I place my foot in a crevice and reach up to pull my body to the peak. I swing my leg over and roll onto the clay-tiled roof.

I stand, stumbling on the slight pitch. My feet scurry across the tiles to the edge of the roof just above Tuor. He's a slumped, helpless mass locked in the stocks. A barricade of soldiers still stand mostly unmoved around him. Lawrence scrambles onto the roof. I watch as he kicks the ladder away from the wall.

I hear it fall with a crack and a shattering of screams. Lawrence's body crumbles onto the roof like he's been struck by a sword, but I see no blood on him.

"What's wrong?" I whisper across the roof.

Lawrence sits up, grabbing for his stomach. His face is pinched in agony. He looks like he might vomit.

"I'm coming."

On hands and knees he crawls across the roof to join me.

"Are you all right?"

Lawrence silently shakes his head.

"Being up this high makes me ill."

"You're afraid . . . pull yourself together! We have three people to rescue now."

On their knees and tied at the wrists, Knox and Johnny are being watched by one guard who's leaning on Knox's sword. They've been pulled a few yards away from Tuor. One of the guards marches back and forth, his arms flailing and his mouth spewing obscenities about everyone's lack of organization.

I need to act now, but we can't get out of this without Knox's and Johnny's help. Lawrence and I lie flat on our stomachs. I pull an arrow from the quiver and rest it gently on my finger.

"Once I start shooting," I whisper, "they're going to see us."

Lawrence nods with his eyes half closed, unable to speak in his discomfort. His hands clutch desperately at the edge of the roof.

I pull back on the bloody string, my fingers aching as it grinds into my skin. My eyes narrow around the soldier casually holding Knox's sword. Air passes out of my lungs and I release. The arrow hits the left shoulder of my target. He falls, dropping the sword.

Knox whirls his head to see me on my perch. With bound hands, he reaches back for his sword.

"Get it . . . get it," I mumble.

A soldier races toward Knox and Johnny from the cluster surrounding Tuor. I pull another arrow, set it, and release it with the flick of my hand. It strikes the man in his back and he falls forward. Knox is on his feet, breaking Johnny free as I pull my third arrow and aim it at one of Tuor's guards. I hit one, then another in the pace of a heartbeat.

"Your aim is impeccable," Lawrence says.

I pull another arrow and rest it carefully. "My father taught me how to poach deer," I say, forcing myself not to dwell on those memories.

Blood pulses through my temples. Newly freed, Johnny and Knox ambush the men surrounding Tuor. I let an arrow fly, saving Johnny from an attack from behind. I continue my strikes wherever they get overwhelmed. The wall around Tuor weakens, and confusion abounds.

Shouts echo from below as they discover our position on the roof. An arrow zooms past Lawrence and me, then another and another. We roll back onto the other side of the roof's peak so that we're facing the front courtyard.

"What now?" Lawrence asks, breathing heavily.

I lie on my back, the cloudy sky pressing down on me. A barrage of arrows soars over our heads and sticks into the clay tiles. We're peppered on all sides. I hug my arms close to my body. I don't know what to do. I truly don't know what to do next.

A harsh, angry voice breaks through the confusion with demands to stop the assault. The flight of arrows comes to a halt and the yelling below calms.

"Camilla Crim," the voice shouts in hysteria. "Camilla Crim!"

It's Governor Leo that calls me. I roll back onto my stomach and slowly scale the peak of the roof just enough so that I can see him pacing wildly in front of Tuor.

"I have had enough of this." Governor Leo pumps his finger in the air. He can't see me, but that's not stopping his rant. "You've killed half of my soldiers. Your men down here are injured, and it seems your poor brother has been hurt as a result of all of this." I scoff, trying to spot Johnny or Knox, but all I can see is Governor Leo, surrounded by men. I crouch down behind the peak. "Camilla, show yourself. Come out, give yourself up, and we'll come up with... an understanding."

Lawrence and I stare at each other. Is this my fight only, or is it his too? He could throw me to Governor Leo, giving the governor what he wants—but he doesn't.

"Come now, girl. You don't want your brother to suffer more than need be, do you?"

I bite my lip. Creeping back over the peak, I watch Governor Leo pace like a rabid dog. My fingers twitch on the handle of the bow, and I feel my throat tighten. I'm going to kill him. I'm going to kill him right now. I lift my arm into position and pull one of the last arrows out of my quiver. Before I can set it, Governor Leo's face explodes with a furious shout.

"We're going right *now!*" he commands, then dives toward the house out of view.

The remaining guards raise the heavy bar that's resting over Tuor's neck. His hunched body collapses.

Two soldiers grab him on either side and start dragging him away.

"They're taking him," I say.

"What?"

"They're taking him to the execution."

I run, crouched, along the roof toward the other side of the house, close to the gate. Clay tiles slip under my feet and roll to the ground. At the edge of the roof, I see Tuor being dragged toward a horse-drawn wagon with bars all along the edge.

"No! Stop!" I shout.

They can't take him away from me, they can't. But I'm suddenly ignored, somehow no longer a threat.

"Tuor!"

On the ground below me is a pile of dead, dried-up corn stalks. Lawrence finally makes it to my side.

"We have to jump," I say. I stand with my feet right on the edge of the roof.

"No." Lawrence's eyes are wide.

I pull off the bow and quiver and toss them over the roof.

"We'll break our legs," he says.

I whip my head around. "I don't care if you stay on this roof and bake in the sun! I'm getting my brother."

CHAPTER THIRTY-FIVE

I STEP OFF the roof, the wind flowing past my arms. I hit the pile of corn stalks hard. Pain shoots up my knees and into my hips. They load Tuor into the barred wagon. A soldier secures the door, then mounts the wagon and readies the horses.

"TUOR!"

My screams draw the attention of every guard as I bolt across the courtyard, dagger in hand. Tuor looks up. He clutches the bars of the wagon. A shimmer of a smile crosses my face as I run toward him. Tears moisten my eyes. I take his hands in mine and weep. A soldier rips me away. I slash my dagger at him, but he knocks it to the ground and brings me to my knees.

A captive audience of soldiers and servants slowly ease in. I thrash and struggle until the last bit of energy is drained from my arms and legs. The driver of the wagon pushes through the crowd. He pockets my dagger and turns to face me.

"Wait till the governor gets ahold of you," he spits, his voice low and gravelly.

Laughter ripples through the crowd. Any guilt I felt for killing their comrades starts to drift away. I have no idea where Lawrence, Johnny, or Knox are, captured like me most likely. I've been left all alone.

From the front door of the house, Governor Leo appears, pulling black leather gloves over his hands. His wife follows. She carries her little dog under her arm and is dressed in proper Warwick attire, a long crimson red dress with a black fur-lined coat. She boards a wagon parked in front of Tuor's. Governor Leo walks toward me, a jolly look on his face.

He takes a deep breath, kicking dust into my face as he comes to a stop in front of me. "Well." His tall, dark frame towers over me. "Look at what I have lived to regret. You peasants are all the same. You seem so sad and innocent, but inside you're all deviants." I hold my lips tightly together. Governor Leo bends over so he's eye level with me. "You're the one who broke into the Justice House, aren't you?"

I allow myself to smile at that accomplishment. "I decided it needed a change of appearance. Something about that flag disgusted me."

Governor Leo smacks me across the face with his leather-gloved hand. I revel in the sting.

"You're a problem, Camilla Crim. I can't have people like you polluting my territory."

"What are you going to do with me?"

Governor Leo smiles and stands up straight. He turns to address the expectant crowd. "We're going to have two executions today!"

The bloodthirsty onlookers cheer at the governor's proclamation. I'm picked up by both of my arms and dragged to the barred wagon through a tunnel of jeering Warwick soldiers. Governor Leo leans in close behind me, grabbing me around my waist. His hot breath prickles my neck.

"I think Quinten had big plans for you," he says. "Didn't you ever wonder why I never had *you* arrested?" I try to jerk out of Governor Leo's grip, but he holds me closer. "Something I didn't tell you is that as important as it was for your brother to die, you were to be untouched."

Together, Governor Leo and the driver shove me through the wagon door. Behind me I hear the click of the lock.

"Considering the circumstances, I think the Supreme Ruler will understand why I couldn't maintain that part of the deal. 'Tis a pity, though. I'm more curious than ever to know what he had in store for you."

I blink mindlessly at Governor Leo until he turns around with the sweep of his black cape. Tuor and I collide in a despondent embrace. I bury my face deep into his shoulder. My body convulses with the last bit of tears I have left. I feel the jerk of the wagon as it begins to move. I turn my head to the side and watch as Governor Leo and Karla's wagon passes first through the front gate. Ours follows. I close my eyes, determined to do nothing but simply hold Tuor in these last few moments we have together.

"Camilla," he whispers. "I'm so sorry."

I pull back away from Tuor. The skin around his right eye is deep blue with streaks of black. He's so thin it feels like I'm embracing bones.

"You have nothing to be sorry for."

"I should have told you everything at the beginning." His eyes glisten with tears.

"It doesn't matter. Don't think on it."

"There's something I didn't tell you." Tuor brushes a tear from his cheek. "It doesn't matter now, but I want to tell you. Sitting in my cell, I thought of all the things I wanted to do differently. I want to tell you the truth."

The wagon creeks and moans as we travel the bumpy road.

"I saw mother that night," Tuor says.

"I know. She killed Brookes, right?"

"Yeah." Tuor runs his hand across his forehead. His knuckles are scabbed and scarred. "There's more." His chest rises and falls, and each breath is labored.

"Camilla, she came to me every night . . . for weeks. Night after night she begged me. She wept on my shoulder and pleaded with me to come with her, to flee north." His face is riddled with anguish and guilt.

I cling hard to Tuor's arms as my eyes flood with tears.

"I felt I was going mad! I told her I couldn't leave. I couldn't leave my post, and I couldn't leave you."

My eyes search Tuor's face as realization overwhelms me about the torture that Tuor had been living through.

"Then one night, she changed."

"How?" I breathe.

"Brookes discovered us. Somehow he knew who she was."

"What do you mean?"

We continue down Reaper's Way, emptying into the village of Rande. Hordes of people are there to greet us.

"Mother started saying that she was sick of it all, sick of someone's meddling." Tuor's tears turn to weeping. "She killed him because he was spying on me."

"Spying? Why would he be spying on you?"

"I don't know."

Tuor's voice catches in his throat. He holds a hand to his mouth.

"It's okay," I say, pulling him into a hug. "It doesn't matter now."

"She just sliced his throat, Camilla. With no thought."

I rub Tuor's back to calm him. "I know." My voice is a whisper.

"She said there's a spy on you too."

I stop my movement. A spy? Someone has been spying on me?

"Why?" I ask, shifting back again.

"I don't know. I really don't know."

Who? Who is my spy? I think back on the last few weeks. Is it Mac? Someone living in the swamps? Perhaps it's someone I don't even know. A tingling chill runs through my body at the thought of someone watching my every move. The wagons come to a halt in Rande Square. A woman screams Tuor's name, and people begin banging on the bars of our wagon, shaking it on its wheels.

"We'll never understand it," I tell Tuor. "But that's okay. You just need to know that I love you. I love you so much."

"I love you too, little sister."

Tuor leans in and gently kisses my cheek as the door to the wagon is unlocked and flung open. The soldier reaches in and grabs Tuor by the arm.

"Please don't take him," I beg, knowing there's nothing I can do to stop it.

He slams the door shut. I grip the bars, watching as Tuor is forced through the crowd to the execution platform.

The crowd follows Tuor like a vulture stalking a dead carcass. "Killer!" they shout. No one is pleased to have a murderer in their territory. Tuor is tossed onto the platform. The soldier kicks the backs of his knees and forces Tuor to kneel, head down, neck exposed on a tree stump. The guard ties a rope around the base of the trunk, securing his arms. A man stands on the edge of the platform, silent and solemn. A wide axe swings from his hand. The executioner is waiting patiently for his talents to be called upon.

My hands dig into the bars. My fingernails split against the rough iron. I scream, rocking the cage on its wheels. The driver jumps from his seat and slams his sword against the bars. A *clang* reverberates through my head.

"Settle down!" he barks.

Governor Leo marches onto the platform, Karla and Ridley in tow. He turns to address the people, raising his arms as a hush falls over the crowd. Annoyance flickers across his face as he opens his mouth to speak.

"Today we witness the execution of one, Tuor Crim, who has been found guilty of the murder of a . . . a very innocent man." Governor Leo pauses, rubbing his hand across his chin. He looks for a moment like he doesn't know what to say. "So enjoy. And I invite you to remain for a second execution of his dear sister, Camilla."

Governor Leo gives a weak smile before approaching the executioner with what looks like a message to hurry this along. A surprisingly short speech for a man known to draw out his time in front of a crowd of people. The executioner crosses the platform. The crowd reels with excitement, but all I can hear is the sound of my own heart pounding in my ears. It's happening too fast. I'm not prepared for this. Panic rips through my body like a bad fever.

"Let me out!"

I shake the wagon door, willing it to burst open. The driver hits my knuckles with the butt of his sword and gives me another warning to shut my mouth. I look back to the platform. Tuor squeezes his eyes closed. The executioner raises his blade with a deep intake of air. At the end of his exhale, Tuor's life will be over.

"No!" I scream.

I close my eyes and sink onto my knees, clutching the fabric of my pants. The axe lands with a thump as a gasp rings out across the crowd.

CHAPTER THIRTY-SIX

SCREAMING SPLITS MY ears, and I'm surprised to discover that it's not my own. I hold tight to myself, terrified to behold the bloody scene. Around me, villagers push and squirm, rocking the wagon like it's a boat being flung to and fro on the high seas.

"Stay back." The driver scolds the disruptive crowd. "Stay back, I said!"

Why is everyone scurrying away? Why all the panic? I blink my eyes open and slowly rise to look upon the platform. The brawny executioner has dropped his axe and stumbles backward on the platform. An arrow sticks out of the middle of his chest. He takes it in his hand as another arrow whirls over the crowd and strikes him again. The driver draws his sword.

He's still alive. *Tuor is still alive.* He struggles desperately against his restraints, still hunched over the tree stump. Governor Leo's face is a deadly mixture of confusion and rage. He moves forward on the platform but is pulled back by a guard just as a third arrow strikes the executioner. His body falls like an old cypress tree that's finally given way to years of rot.

"Hey!" I yell. "Let me out of here."

The driver paces in front of me. Townspeople, terrified by an unknown archer, push and grapple their way out of Rande Square.

I rattle the barred wagon door. "Let me out!"

"Shut up."

The driver holds a hand to his pocket, looking unsure of what to do. I search for the source of the arrows. They continue to strike any soldier that rushes to the platform.

"Whoever is shooting those arrows is aiming at Warwick soldiers," I say. "Let me out of here, or we'll both die!" The driver turns around to face me. His eyebrows are scrunched tightly together. He can't abandon me, or he'll be sorely punished. "C'mon!"

His hand dives into his pocket. Then a pair of thick arms wraps around his neck and twists in a quick jerk. The driver collapses.

"Keys. The keys are in his pocket," I tell Johnny.

He fumbles with the keys, jamming them hard into the lock. "Are you okay?" He rips open the door.

"Fine," I say, jumping out. "You made it out of the farm. Where's Lawrence and Knox?"

A flood of people wriggle past us. Johnny takes my hand, and moves me to the other side of the wagon, his eyes continually scanning.

"Lawrence is the one protecting Tuor. Knox went to get Mirabelle."

"What? Why?"

"Camilla, pay attention." Johnny takes both my hands in his. His face is flushed with pride. "I have to keep these soldiers from finding Lawrence, or we won't have an advantage anymore. We have to get out of Bear Gap. Meet me at the church." He wipes sweat from his brow. "Now go get your brother."

Johnny dives into the chaos of the square before I even have a chance to ask any questions. I look to the platform, then down at the wagon driver. I pull my dagger from his vest and run to Tuor. A frantic woman collides with me. She scurries in the other direction. I nearly trample over a small child screaming for her mother. I'm coming, I say to myself, as if Tuor can hear it.

The spray of arrows ceases. I push past the last few frantic villagers and slide onto my knees at the base of the tree stump.

"You're okay. You're okay," I say, my voice scratchy and weak.

"Camilla . . . "

"It's going to be all right."

Using my dagger, I saw at the rope tied tightly around Tuor's wrists. A solider moves in on us from the back of the platform. Tuor's right wrist comes free. I switch to the left one, moving my arm in quick jabs. Footsteps click hard and fast across the platform. Governor Leo's dark figure explodes into my vision. His bony fingers grab the cuff of my jacket and fling me backward. My shoulder slams into the floor with a pop. I scream out. Numbness tingles through my arm and down to my fingers.

Governor Leo steps toward me. His body is a black tower, and his face wears a cruel, deranged sort of smile.

"Tuor," I cough.

He looks up, scrambling to untie his other wrist. I toss him my dagger just before Governor Leo leaps on top of me. I feel a sickening pressure on my chest. My breaths come in short desperate gulps.

"You piece of swamp trash, you're not going to get in the way of the future of this territory."

Governor Leo's hot breath beats down on my face. Like a serpent, his spindly fingers wrap around my neck. I claw and scratch, feeling as if I must escape a stone fortress with only my fingernails. Slowly, my throat closes and sheer panic creeps down my spine. Governor Leo's eyes bulge and his mouth quivers.

"How can such an insignificant creature disrupt the plans of the Supreme Ruler—how?" Governor Leo's eyes narrow in on my face. My head begins to swim. Black spots enter my vision. "Tell me!" he screams.

Tuor appears over the governor's shoulder, swinging my dagger at a soldier. He stumbles backward, the dagger slipping from his hand and landing on the ground.

Governor Leo lifts my head from the platform and slams it back down. "This execution *will* happen!"

Tuor crashes into Governor Leo. His grip loosens from my neck. I suck in air like I've been underwater for ages. I turn onto my side, coughing raggedly. Tuor throws a punch, but Governor Leo tosses his bruised body aside like a doll. Tuor lays motionless on the platform, arms splayed. I scramble onto my hands and knees, crawling for the dagger. Governor Leo's hand wraps around my ankle. I kick him off, inching closer and closer to the dagger. He comes back again, pulling my leg with a jerk until I fall flat on my stomach, unable to move any farther. Governor Leo flips me over. I fling my elbow, whacking him in the eye.

"I am *not* insignificant," I croak.

He groans, grabbing for my wrists and holding them against my chest. A cloaked form appears behind Governor Leo. In a calm fluid motion, a thin arm reaches around the governor's head and slices his throat open with a short blade.

I cover my eyes as blood gurgles from his neck and the full weight of his body drops on top of me. Blood soaks through my blouse, dripping down my arms and curling around my neck. I'm trapped in a puddle of sticky liquid like a soggy rag that's been used to tend a wound. Governor Leo's body is lifted off me and thrown aside casually.

Slender fingers lift the dark blue embroidered hood to reveal the pale, sensuous face of a woman. Her shoulders are blanketed in dark wavy hair. Long curled eyelashes blink down at me and sunlight catches on her red lips.

"What an idiot that man was. Don't you agree?"

CHAPTER THIRTY-SEVEN

I SIT, MY hands behind me for support. Tuor still lies on the platform. Rande Square has become deathly still. Soldiers' bodies litter the streets, and the last of the villagers have fled to safety. My lips are parted as I stare at the strange apparition before me.

Unfazed by the bloody scene before her, she lets out a long sigh and begins a slow pace in front of me. "Quinten thought he could use *this* man to find me?" A light chuckle floats from her mouth. "How amusing," she says darkly.

"I won't be made a fool of. Quinten-excuse me, I mean The Supreme Ruler- thinks he can dangle my children in front of me, and I'll just hand over the source of my power." The woman turns on her heels and faces me again. Her eyes, a bright emerald green, lock onto mine. "Is that what he thinks?" She laughs again. "He has no idea that this little game he's playing will be the end of him." She glances at the red-stained knife in her hand. "It'll be his neck next time."

A moment of silence passes where the world around me suddenly feels like a different place. It's alien to me, full of bizarre things and people.

"Mother?"

She shivers when I say the word. "I suppose I am."

From the corner of my eye, I see a stray soldier barreling toward us.

"Governor!" he calls.

Portia quickly turns her attention to the young man. She stretches out her arm, revealing the flat palm of her hand. The soldier stops abruptly. First, he looks confused, like there's a strange feeling inside of him. Then in a quick jolt, he reaches for his chest, clawing at his heart, falling to his knees, and gasping for breath.

I look toward my mother, her face cool and focused. Gradually, she bends her fingers as if she's clutching his heart in her hand. Tighter and tighter her fingers go until she has squeezed all of his life away. The soldier falls forward on his face, dead.

"What was it I was saying?" Portia asks, taking in a deep breath.

I scramble to my feet, Portia's eyes following me as I do. "You killed that man, Aiden Brookes. *You* killed him, and Tuor got blamed for it!"

"Aiden Brookes?" Portia places the tip of her bloody knife close to her chin as she thinks. "You mean that cretin of Quinten's that he sent to spy on Tuor? He did that to see if I'd show up. To see if I'd visit my only son."

"So Tuor was just bait?" I say, shaking my head.

Portia starts to pace again. "Bait to capture me, yes. Did Quinten really think that would work? Well, I suppose it did work because I paid a few visits to my son." Portia's feet move in long strides. "That was my own error for telling Quinten I wanted my children back." She stops suddenly and turns on her heels to face me. Her head sways back and forth as if she's gravely disappointed. "He thought he'd be able to catch me with a spy."

"So, this isn't about love, is it? This is a quarrel between you and The Supreme Ruler?"

Portia seems to not hear me.

"Do you know what I did? I approached that spy of Quinten's and told him to run and tell the master where I was." Her lips spread in a soft smile. "I didn't let him run very far."

"You were going to let your own child take the blame for his murder!"

"My child," she says, taking a step closer to me, "is pathetic. I gave him a chance to come with me. I told him that man was spying on him to get to me and that he had to be killed. I told Tuor if he came with me no one would accuse him of anything." Her gaze intensifies. "He started shaking his head and mumbling. He just went utterly mad in front of me! I shoved a knife in his hand, thinking it would toughen him up, force him to see that he was a part of this too, but he just . . . " Portia curls her lip and stares at the ground as if she's recoiling from something distasteful. "He crumbled like a baby bird. It was repulsive."

I'm barely able to form a word in response. I know now what Tuor went through in LilyAye because I've just experienced it myself. "It disgusted you that he didn't want to run away with a cruel person like you?"

"I'm not the cruel one, Camilla. Quinten Warwick is the cruel one." Portia tilts her eyes to the sky. "He's the one who enslaves you. How different your life would have been if I hadn't given that man a throne."

"Given?"

Portia uses the tip of her knife to point to her chest. "The only reason Quinten sits poised with the title of Supreme Ruler is because of *me*."

"How do you reason that?" I snap.

Her hand reaches up to curl around a turquoise stone that lies on her chest. "I possess powers you couldn't even dream of, and Quinten manipulated me into using those powers to help him." Portia clasps her hands together in front of her like a little girl. "Now, because he's displeased me, he's terrified he'll lose his throne. Quinten is weak." Portia rests a hand on my shoulder. I feel a chill run down my body. "But I am strong, and so are you."

"You don't even know me."

"Tuor is too much like your father, simpleminded. But you—you never give up." She points at me with her knife and shakes her head. "I've been watching you for the last fortnight. You never stopped trying to do something. There's so much fire inside of you, Camilla. I just have to help you channel that energy."

Despite my throbbing temples, I feel that fire my mother speaks of. "You've been watching me struggle to free Tuor, all while you just . . . you just what? Stood by and enjoyed the show?"

"I've actually been watching you and your brother your whole life. We have a connection, Camilla, whether you feel it or not."

"I don't understand you. You despise your own son, yet just now, you saved his life?"

"For you, Camilla." She takes a step toward me. "I did it for *you*. I'm not as terrible as you believe me to be. Only now do I realize how important he is to you. I want you, and if that means sparing your brother's life so that you don't have to see him die, then so be it."

The calm of the nearly empty Rande Square is suddenly disturbed. Down the road marches a new dispatch of Warwick soldiers. Ten... fifteen... twenty men move in on us quickly. Portia glares in their direction, then turns back to me and sighs.

"They're looking for me," she says. "Well, and the two of you I guess."

"Because they think Tuor killed someone!"

"You don't have to live this life, Camilla. I exist away from all of this. I follow my own tenets, and no one rules over me." Portia tilts her head and looks at me from under her thick lashes. "You can have that life too. You need only to come with me."

"Why would I ever want to go with you?"

"Because soon, Quinten will be dead, and I will be the one controlling Elmyra. Think of what you could have if you were on my side."

Soldiers begin flooding the square. I look over at my brother.

My eyes narrow. "I wouldn't come with you even if it meant certain death for Tuor and me."

Portia crosses her arms across her chest, the bloody knife still sticking up from her hand. Her eyes lock onto mine. I feel that at any moment she'll grab me by the arm and drag me with her out of the square. The corners of her mouth curl upward. "You are as strong as I believed you to be. Very well." She sighs.

My mother steps away from me, throwing her head back in mock defeat. She's letting me go, I realize. I give her a final glance before grabbing my dagger and shoving it in my coat.

"There's a war coming, Camilla." Portia shouts as I hobble across the platform to Tuor. "You need to be prepared."

I fall to the ground next to his battered body.

"Wake up," I say, smacking his cheek. "Wake up, wake up, wake up."

I hear a groan leave Tuor's mouth.

"Tuor? Tuor, wake up."

"What's—"

"Shhh, don't talk. We have to go."

I shuffle Tuor onto my left shoulder and pull him up. My other arm feels dead, and all I can do is let it hang. Standing up feels like a great pressure is pushing down on my head. I squint my eyes in pain as I look across the platform. My mother is gone.

CHAPTER THIRTY-EIGHT

SOLDIERS BARREL DOWN Soldiers barrel down Reaper's Way toward us. We stumble off the platform. I pull Tuor past the posting tree. Across the street, I duck into the closest alley and release Tuor's nearly lifeless body. He slides down the wall, closing his eyes in exhaustion. I peek around the corner of the alley. Portia is just gone. Like a ghost she seems to have simply disappeared, leaving a weird vacancy where she previously stood.

I watch as one of the soldiers in charge surveys the dead body of their leader. He points his hand down the four streets that branch off Rande Square.

"I want every house searched," he shouts.

"What's going on?" Tuor moans.

I return to his side, bending down to look into his face. "The governor is dead."

"Did you kill him?" A small smile spreads across Tuor's face.

"No." I reach out to stroke the mess of hair on top of Tuor's head. "But everyone thinks I did."

Tuor's hand leaves his leg, where it's resting, and touches the tops of my fingers. "We're the same now."

"Yeah." I laugh lightly. "We're the same."

"We have to leave, Camilla." Tuor's head sways side to side. His right eye can barely open for the deep bruise it bears. "Your spy . . . " he mumbles.

"We'll leave. I promise, we'll leave."

A shout wafts down the alley. The silhouette of a soldier passes across the opening.

"Can you walk?" I ask.

Tuor nods and I help him to his feet again. His arm lies limp across my shoulders. Two more bodies cross in front of the opening of the alley. I push us through to the other end. We empty into the back of a row of shops. To my left, at the other end of the street, a soldier spots us.

"This way."

I cut hard to the right. Tuor and I break into a hobbled run. The soldier's voice echoes against the shops with instructions for us to stop. But I'm not stopping. I will never stop as long as I have breath in my chest.

A great estate blooms into our view on the left. We scurry across the plush lawn. I pull Tuor into a hedge garden. We duck out of view and hide behind a stone statue. It shows the likeness of our Supreme Ruler. Despite my heavy breathing and throbbing head, I sense the irony.

The soldier stalks down the street on our right. I take a good look at Tuor now. He can barely sit upright. I can't risk a confrontation with that soldier. We wouldn't win.

I barely breathe as I sit motionless, waiting for our opening to run again. *We just need to make it to the church.*

I repeat that sentence over and over again in my head. Slowly, I turn toward the street. The soldier pauses at the end. He turns right, breaking into a jaunt.

"C'mon," I whisper.

At the end of the lawn, we run into the back of another stately house. We then cross another street and pass into the woods to avoid the main roads. We walk until I think we've walked too far and then curve back around to the left slightly. Our feet move at a slow trudge until we leave the cover of trees and return to a narrow dirt road. I swallow hard, feeling the panicked need to get out of Rande.

The road is deserted with tall tufts of weeds growing up in the middle. We turn right and walk down the road farther and farther into the outskirts of town. Then it appears. The hutlike church sits undisturbed at the end of Twenty-First Street. I run to it, seeing two horses tied up out front, but neither of them are my horse, Shea.

"Are you sure it's safe?" Tuor asks, grabbing my arm as I approach the front door.

"I'm sure."

I click the knob open and feel the shock of three pairs of eyes on me.

Mirabelle barrels toward us. "Camilla, Tuor, you're all right," she says. Her eyes widen at my blood-stained clothes.

"I'm fine. We're fine," I say as she takes me in one arm and Tuor in the other.

We're corralled into the church. It's calm inside but dark. The torches along the walls haven't been lit. Knox peers out the window. Lawrence walks down the aisle with a note of hesitation in his step. He musses his tangled hair and lets out a long breath as if all stress has been lifted from his back.

"You made it out," Lawrence says.

Tuor nods, and the two clasp their hands together. "Thank you."

"Sit down, dear."

Mirabelle and Lawrence lead Tuor to the back pew.

"How did you get the idea to meet here?" I ask.

"It was Lawrence's idea," Mirabelle says.

Lawrence helps his friend down onto a pew. "I remember that Tuor stayed here for days unseen. I suggested it to Knox and Johnny as a meeting place."

I nod, silently thanking Lawrence for his help. I bite my lip, still feeling that things are amiss.

"Where is Johnny?" I ask.

Knox answers while still keeping his eyes trained to the road outside. "Not here yet."

"We went back to the farm to get our horses, and then he and I headed straight here," Lawrence says.

"So where is he?"

Lawrence shakes his head. "I lost track of him when we crossed behind the Justice House."

"We can't wait for him much longer," Knox says.

"They're looking for us. It won't be too long before this church is found out."

Knox nods. "Maybe he went straight there."

"Straight where?"

"His house." Knox steps away from the window, impatiently moving between pews. "It's deep in the woods north of here. If we can get there, we'll be safe."

"Then just go," I say. Mirabelle looks up from her seat next to Tuor. "There aren't enough horses to carry us all. The four of you, go, get Tuor out of here. I'll wait for Johnny."

"But what if he has gone straight to his house?" Mirabelle asks.

"He hasn't." I pace toward the window, looking for myself at the vacant street. "I know he hasn't." I turn back around to face the group. "He'll come."

"Knox, you stay with her," Mirabelle says.

"I'm the only one here who knows how to get to Johnny's house and besides," Knox folds his arms across his chest. "I'm not going anywhere without you."

Mirabelle's cheeks blush ever so slightly.

I pace along the back of the church. "Just go, please. I didn't go through all of this just to have Tuor arrested again."

Mirabelle looks to Knox with pained eyes. She knows I'm right. Silently, they decide to do as I say.

"Let's go then," Knox says.

Lawrence and Knox lift Tuor, one under each shoulder, out the front door. Tuor is propped up on a horse with Lawrence while Mirabelle rides with Knox.

"You promise you'll be okay?" Mirabelle asks.

I nod. "I just want to see Tuor safe."

She takes my hand and squeezes it before Knox kicks off, taking the lead. The two horses bolt into the woods, absorbed by its cover of darkness. My heart starts to beat louder as I turn around in the emptiness of the road. I'm alone, completely alone, waiting on a person who may never come. But I made the right choice. I know I did. This was always about Tuor, and I'd never feel right if he wasn't safe. Even if it's away from me.

The emptiness of being all alone drives me inside the church. I sit on the floor underneath the window, turning around to look for Johnny every few moments.

My ears become overly aware of every noise around me. A gentle autumn wind hugs the wall of the church. It rustles the long grass outside. I look out the window again and again until I feel I'm going crazy. Is this how it was for Tuor, locked away in this church with nobody?

I pull my knees to my chest and rest my chin on top. How easy it seems to close my eyes and simply fade away. After all, I have done my job. I've rescued my brother. What reason is there for me to still exist? I imagine I hear the sound of pounding hooves on the ground. But I know it's just my ears deceiving me. Don't look out the window *again*, just don't. But the sound grows louder. I shove my legs down and spin around. At the end of the road, sunlight glints off a shiny blade.

Coming to my feet, I look harder out the window. The pounding is real. Galloping toward me is Shea, with Johnny atop. A long sword hangs from his belt, catching the sunlight as he rides. I fly out the door, stumbling to a stop in the middle of the road. My face brims with a smile. But it's short lived. Three soldiers stampede toward me, close on Johnny's heels.

Johnny pushes the horse hard. The space between her and the soldiers opens slightly until Johnny comes to an abrupt stop in front of me.

Breathless, he yells to me, "Get on." Johnny reaches out a hand and pulls me up. "Where's Knox?"

"They've gone. They've all gone ahead. Just go!"

We kick off. I grasp hard to his shoulders, feeling the bite of the cold air as we gallop into the trees. I chance a look behind us. The soldiers are still close. One inches closer and closer with each step. Heavy branches whirl past us as Johnny maneuvers Shea through the deep woods.

"You're going to have to fight them off." Johnny says, the wind muffling his voice.

I want to explain to Johnny that my one arm is practically useless, but I can't. Carefully, I pull the dagger from my jacket and look behind me again. The soldier urges his horse faster. I link my injured arm underneath Johnny's shoulder while gripping the dagger tightly with my other hand. The soldier creeps forward, like a rising river during a storm. Soon he's within arm's reach.

He claws for my wrist, trying to pull me off the horse. I recoil, but he grabs and jerks me sideways. A sharp pain shoots through my shoulder. I shake off the soldier's grip, feeling Shea sway as he lets go. My stomach plummets at the uneasiness. I twist my body farther as our pursuer returns. I stretch out my hand, revealing the dagger.

Up and down, I swing the blade, hoping he comes close enough to get clipped. My back aches as I stretch to reach him. Our horses run almost parallel. The soldier's teeth grind together in a determined scowl. He looks over at my dagger, and as he reaches out to take it from me, I lift up my leg and kick him hard in the hip. He wavers for a moment, almost correcting his mount, but then balance eludes him. He slips from his saddle, hitting the forest floor. In only a moment, his body is out of sight, along with any other Warwick soldiers.

The forest floor flashes past us in a blur of green and brown. I lay my head on Johnny's back and reach my other hand around his waist, pulling my body close to his. All I hear is Shea's thumping hooves and her heavy breathing mixed with the whipping wind. The danger is gone. I can finally rest.

We ride for miles across roads I've never seen, and through patches of woods I've never walked through. The cold air nips at my cheeks, and as the sun dips below the horizon, a chill engulfs my whole body. The only time Johnny slows is to take a few inclines or cross a narrow stream. Through dense, never-ending woods, a cabin appears in a small clearing.

EPILOGUE

FOUR WEEKS LATER . . .

I swing the axe up, feeling the full weight of its thick blade, then drop it down swiftly to the sound of a ringing *crack*. A bird, startled by the noise, flutters from its perch above my head. I retrieve another log, place it on the chopping stump, and split it in half. A twinge of pain strikes my injured shoulder. I'll continue to split logs, though, because there's always work to be done.

Johnny's house sits on a plot of land like I've never seen before. It's buried deep, very deep, in the woods surrounding Bear Gap. Johnny told me when we first arrived that we're well north of Rande and only a twenty-minute ride from the mountains that mark the edge of the territory. But that's not what astounds me. It's an independent homestead with a garden and animals and a creek nearby for water.

Everything is neat and tidy. It's not how I would normally describe a cabin in the woods, but Johnny's home is orderly from the stack of logs out front to the metal pots hanging in the kitchen. It seems that there's always something that needs tended to, whether the garden needs weeded, the fire needs tended, or like today, the wood needs split.

A light flurry of snowflakes begins to fall as I bend over to pick up the next piece of wood. Knox is rounding the corner to the back of the house. He spots me when he's just inside the tree line before crossing the yard. I ignore him, raising my axe again and bringing it down hard on the log. I'm not ready for what he has to tell me.

Knox runs a hand down his scraggly beard. "The cold is fast approaching."

I nod, tossing the two fresh pieces of firewood onto the pile. "Winter will be here soon."

He shifts his eyes away from me and onto the top of the trees. It feels like the first time we met, except this time I'm avoiding his gaze as much as he's avoiding mine. I pick up another log and balance it on the chopping stump.

"I've just returned from Rande," Knox says.

The axe drives hard into the log and it breaks in half.

"It is as you thought," he continues.

I swallow hard, adding two more pieces to the pile. "Did you run into any trouble?"

"No, I was discreet."

"Good."

I reach for another log to split.

"Camilla."

Swinging higher than before, I come down in a great swoop of frustration. My shoulder screams out in pain. I drop the axe and grab for the spot on my back where Governor Leo hurt me. Knox takes me by the other arm and forces me to sit on the tree stump.

"Camilla, we need to talk about this."

"We don't. I understand it."

"I don't think you do."

I try to roll my shoulder to work out the ache. Knox stands in front of me and waits for my cooperation. I look up at him through half-closed eyelids. His face is harder than normal, more stone-like and stern.

"Fine." I brush wood chips from my lap. "What did you see in Rande?"

"The governor's wife is looking for you," he says. "You and Tuor."

I sigh, picking at my fingernails.

"All of that, and Tuor is still being hunted."

"*You're* being hunted. Karla has wanted posters all over Bear Gap with your face on them too."

"She thinks I killed her husband."

"You were seen fleeing from his dead body along with your fugitive brother."

"Do they have any idea where we are?" I ask.

Knox shakes his head, shifting on his feet. "No. They don't know we're here."

In the days following our escape from Rande, we made plans that if someone happened upon this house, we would run for the mountains. It was only recently that we began to relax a little.

"What about anybody else?" I ask. "Are you being blamed for any of it?"

"They know there were others involved, but they don't know who. I went by Mirabelle's house. They ransacked the place, looking for you, I assume."

"What about . . . Portia?" I say her name with hesitation.

"It doesn't seem like anyone knew she was ever there."

I hold a hand to my stomach. Ever since this began with Tuor, I have felt as though the two of us were walking along in our lives, and our feet got caught in a sinkhole. We were innocent. It was just something random that happened. Today, I still feel that way, except now our heads are going under too.

I'm banned from my own town. I can't go home or run over to Mirabelle's house anymore. All of this because of my mother. After arriving at Johnny's house, the mystery behind Tuor's arrest began to make sense.

"When I came to your house that time without Mirabelle, you told me that my mother and Quinten were lovers."

"They are," Knox says.

"No, they *were*."

Knox's face is blank.

"And Quinten wasn't trying to win back my mother's affections. The two of them are fighting." I stand up from the tree stump. "Quinten used Tuor as bait to get to my mother. He's trying to capture her or something."

Knox looks at me with unblinking eyes. He reaches up and rubs the spot in the middle of his chest that I see him touch constantly. "He wants her powers," Knox says.

"This whole thing is because my mother supposedly has great abilities."

Knox folds his arms across his chest. "Quinten is just a puppet."

I pause, chewing on my lower lip. "I saw what she did to that man at Tuor's execution. She just stuck out her arm and . . . "

Knox shifts awkwardly on his feet.

"Is that what she did to you?" I ask. Knox purses his lips together and looks at me under heavy eyelids. "Is that why you hated me . . . because she . . . crippled you?"

"You look a lot like your mother. When I saw you up close, it . . . the memories returned."

I look at Knox as if I'm examining a complicated map. It feels like he's a deep chest full of secrets that are too horrible to uncover.

"Did you know that Quinten was spying on Tuor and me?" Knox looks down at his feet but doesn't answer. "Is Lawrence a spy?"

Knox shakes his head.

"Then how do you explain him?" I ask.

"Lawrence saved you and your brother. Without him we couldn't have escaped the farm that day, and it was his idea to stop the executioner and to meet at the church. All credit is due to him."

I plop back down on the tree stump. Ever since the execution, Tuor and Lawrence have been acting like the greatest of friends, which I suppose they are. But when I look into Lawrence's eyes, I still can't trust him.

The days we spent together in Mirabelle's attic were happy moments I used to dwell on. Once he abandoned me at the Justice House, the closeness I felt became a lie. I never again want to feel the way I did while standing on those steps before Tuor's trial.

"Perhaps he's running from something," Knox says. "Like we all are."

Our eyes finally meet, and I realize how similar Knox and I are. We've been hurt by the same people. I suppose when two people share in the same pain, they can only be fully understood by that other person.

"What are Tuor and I to do now?"

Knox unfolds his arms and leans against a nearby tree. "Move on," he says. "Why stay here? Tuor is well. He's almost completely healthy. Warwick may try to use you again, or worse, your mother may show up. Karla has her heels dug in that she's going to find the two of you and hang you herself."

I bite my lip.

"Go north, to the free territory."

"The free territory isn't a real place."

"I believe it's real," Knox says. "Warwick can't have power everywhere. If you and Tuor travel far enough north, you'll be out of his jurisdiction. It would be a long journey, but if you made it, you'd be free."

"I'd be leaving my home, and Mirabelle."

"This isn't going to go away. The country thinks you murdered a governor that our Supreme Ruler appointed himself. If you don't leave now, you'll eventually be captured, or at the very least you'll be on the run for the rest of your life."

"But we're safe here."

"Every day Karla has soldiers sweeping these woods. One day they're going to find us."

I look deep into Knox's cold features and realize he's right.

***

Mirabelle and I sit close to each other on the couch. Tuor and Lawrence sit in the corner at a small table playing a dice game. Johnny stands over them, explaining the tenets of how to play.

"How are you doing, sweetie?" Mirabelle asks.

"Fine. I like it here."

I flash her a smile to show her I truly am just fine.

"Knox told me what he saw on the posting tree today." She tilts her head, giving me a sympathetic frown. "We'll figure something out for you two."

Knox has found the only rocking chair in the house. He sways back and forth, moving his foot slowly. His elbow is propped on the armrest and a small book sits in his hand. I sometimes catch Knox and Mirabelle looking at each other in a way that makes me believe they really were in love once.

"You know," Mirabelle says, her jolly countenance back. "Johnny has been quite accommodating."

"He has," I agree.

Her voice lowers to practically a whisper. "I think he must care a great deal for you to have done everything he has to help Tuor."

I watch as Johnny gives another word of instruction to Tuor and Lawrence, then crosses the sitting area into the kitchen.

"He hates Warwick," I say. "He'd do anything to fight against him."

"Mmmm, maybe. But I think he likes you a little bit too."

I spin my head around to give Mirabelle a look of offense. She giggles and waves me off with the flick of her hand. Knox looks up from his book and eyes us in such a way that tells us to be quiet so he can read. Mirabelle ignores him.

Like a bolt of lightning on a peaceful summer night, a knock comes to Johnny's front door. Knox is on his feet. Johnny runs over from the kitchen. I reach for my dagger, which I now always carry on my belt.

"Who could that be?" Mirabelle asks in a whisper.

Knox crosses the room toward the door. "Stay there," he instructs Mirabelle.

I give Tuor a look, encouraging him to stay back, but he and Lawrence are on their feet too, swords drawn. Peeking out a window, I see the dark figure of a man standing at the door. Everyone looks to me for an explanation.

"It's only one person as far as I can see."

"Remember the plan," Johnny says as he reaches for the door handle.

Everyone braces as the door is pulled open. Johnny's face contorts in confusion. I hear the sound of boots stepping across the threshold. Ridley Thatius walks inside, closing the door behind him. His chin is held high as he surveys the room.

"Captain?" Tuor says.

"You hid yourselves nicely," Ridley says, pulling his black leather gloves from his hands. "I can't begin to explain the incompetence of Karla and her men as they search for you. It took me awhile, but I've finally found you." He takes another step inside.

Knox blocks him with a raised sword. Ridley looks down at the blade as if it's nothing.

"Stand down. I've simply come to retrieve what is mine."

"You're not taking my brother," I say.

Ridley strokes his short beard and continues to look each of us up and down.

"I don't want your brother," he says.

"Then who do you want?" Johnny asks.

"Lawrence."

I look to Lawrence. He stands, his mouth agape and his eyebrows knit tightly together in a horrified look.

"What would you want with Lawrence?" Knox asks, moving in closer to Ridley.

Ridley gives him a look of piercing arrows. "He's my son," Ridley says simply. "And I've come to take him home."

All eyes in the room move to Lawrence. He doesn't confirm or deny what Ridley has said. In fact, he doesn't speak at all. He seems suddenly unable to form words.

"Does he speak truth?" I ask.

Lawrence looks at me but still doesn't speak.

"Of course it's the truth," Ridley says. He moves to the middle of the room, and I grip my dagger harder. "The boy is my son. He and your brother were both stationed under me in LilyAye. Lawrence had a very high standing in the militia. I was quite proud of him until your brother got into these . . . troubles. Then, Lawrence became very disobedient." Every word that leaves Ridley's mouth has a sharp condescending bite to it. He takes another step closer to Lawrence. "My son broke this rebel out of prison and fled here before I could explain to him how this would damage his career."

"I don't want that life," Lawrence says through gritted teeth.

"We have talked about this, son. With me as your father, you'll have a long, prosperous career in the Warwick Militia. You'll never have to worry about having enough rings to support your family. You can live in a nice house and—"

"I don't want any of that!"

Ridley is taken aback. "But you make an excellent soldier."

"What of it?"

"Don't you want to serve your country in honor?"

"No." Lawrence seems to have broken free of his frozen shell. He handles his sword firmly and walks the rest of the way across the room to meet his father. "I don't stand for anything that you stand for. And I don't want to serve Quinten Warwick anymore."

"Then what shall I tell your mother?" Ridley asks, his brow wrinkled in concern.

Lawrence's face softens slightly.

"I'm willing to overlook what you've done. Dishonoring your position as a jailer." Ridley takes another step closer. "Stealing the knife I was to present as evidence at Tuor's trial."

"The knife," I say. "That's why Tuor had it. You stole it from your father and took it with you to Bear Gap."

Lawrence looks at me from under furrowed brows. "I told Tuor to hide it where no one could find it."

"We can forget it all," Ridley says. He waves his hand in a great sweeping motion.

"I can barely stand to be in the same room as you," Lawrence says. "I won't go back."

"That is truly how you feel?" Lawrence holds his ground. "That's unfortunate to hear." Ridley folds his hands neatly across his legs. He shifts on his feet to face everyone in the room. "If you don't return home with me tonight, I will be forced to reveal this location to Governor Harras, that is, Karla Harras." Ridley looks directly at me. "And before you think of tying me up or driving a sword through me, I have my own caravan waiting just a few yards from your front door.

You give me Lawrence, and we'll leave and not say a word. If not . . . well, I understand that the new Governor is quite bloodthirsty right now."

I feel a weight of guilt on me for how I've treated Lawrence. He truly is Tuor's friend, and he fled here to escape a man who's used to having control. I see now how a man like that can cloud the mind of the person they're torturing. It's what Malcolm did to me, and even though Mirabelle tried to tell me, I couldn't see it. I understand Lawrence now, better than I ever thought possible.

Lawrence's eyes are trained to the floor as Ridley examines him with what looks like indifference. Everyone stands, unable to move and unsure of what to say.

"Fine," Lawrence says through gritted teeth. "You have won."

"Don't do it," Tuor mutters from the corner.

"I won't let all of you be put back in danger because of me." Lawrence looks at his father. "I will go."

Ridley's mouth remains in a hard line. He places a hand on Lawrence's shoulder. "Your mother will be overjoyed."

Lawrence slips his sword back in its sheath and walks to the door, his head hanging low.

"We should be going," Ridley says, turning on his heels.

I look to Lawrence, begging for his eyes to meet mine, but he crosses through the door without a backward glance at anyone.

"Wait," I say. Ridley pauses, his hand on the door handle. "You'd rather lie to your Supreme Ruler about where we are than let your son live the life he pleases?"

"You misunderstand me, Camilla. My allegiance doesn't lie with the Warwick that sits on the throne in LilyAye."

"But you came here under his orders. You testified against Tuor because that's what Quinten wanted you to do."

Ridley tugs a glove back on his hand. "It is a mere illusion. I serve a greater power."

He passes through the door like steam evaporating into the air. Tuor marches across the room and bolts outside. The rest of us follow him onto a patch of grass in front of Johnny's house. Through the darkened trees, we watch as a member of Ridley's caravan hands Lawrence the reins of a horse. Father and son ride together into the woods. Their silhouettes disappear in moments as the black of night engulfs them.

I feel Knox's presence beside me. "I won't leave," I tell him. His head tilts down. "I'm not going to try and escape with Tuor to the free territory."

"You should try."

"No," I snap. I turn around to face the rest of the group. "As long as people like Ridley and . . . and Karla and even Quinten plague Elmyra, I just can't watch without doing something about it." I shake my head slowly. "I won't be manipulated by their sick desire to ascend some sort of tower of authority." I spit the words.

"This is my home. It's *our* home. We ought to be . . . " I stare at the ground for a moment. "We deserve to be free." My voice is nearly a whisper. I don't even quite know what being free means. I definitely don't know what it feels like. "We should not have to beg for food from the hand of our Supreme Ruler."

I look over at Mirabelle's tender face. "Mirabelle, Knox, you used to live in a world like that, before Warwick became ruler. So why can't *we*? Why do *we* have to live like this?"

"It's just the way things are," Knox says.

"I don't believe that." My voice is almost a growl. Johnny's eyes widen. "I won't leave," I say. "I won't leave and I won't run away. If I die, then so be it. I'd rather die than spend the rest of my life running."

I place my hands on my hips, feeling the pressure of four people staring at me. My chin is lifted slightly, and I feel the pull of the sinkhole lessening around my neck. Johnny catches my eyes. Without speaking, he praises me. I've joined his cause. I'm a rebel now, I suppose. Johnny's lips spread in a broad grin, and I feel compelled to smile back.

THE END

Pronunciation Guide

CHARACTERS
    Camilla: Kuh-mil-uh
    Tuor: Toor (like tour)
    Bradac: Bra-dak

PLACES
    Elmyra: Ehl-meye-ruh
    LilyAye: Lilee-eye
    Billage: Bill-ehj (like village)
    Rande: Randee (like Randy)

OTHER
    Catahli: Kuh-tah-lee

Want to know what happens next?

Camilla's story does not end here. Her story continues in the thrilling sequel, *The Bear Gap Rebels*. Flip the page to read a preview of book two in the Camilla Crim series.

***

Visit www.emilyfortney.com to explore the entire Camilla Crim series and grab a **FREE** eBook by signing up for Emily's email newsletter.

***

If you enjoyed this book, please leave a 5-star review on Goodreads or the online retailer where you purchased it. Also, pass this book on to a friend. Good books are meant to be shared.

Sneak peak of

The Bear Gap Rebels

CHAPTER ONE

I'M LOSING MY mind.

Like a parasite to its host, the voice echoing around in my head is attached so firmly that I'm utterly hopeless in removing it. Distraction works only for a moment and then I start hearing it again. I haven't told anyone, not even Tuor. I've tried everything to keep myself from going crazy, but I'm afraid it's too late . . . I'm losing my mind and I can't do anything about it.

I stand alone in the dark woods halfway between Billage, where I'm *supposed* to go, and Rande, where I *want* to go. A shiver runs its way up my back. I flex my hands in and out to fight against my body's cravings. Rain trickles through the leaves, falling in big droplets on my hair. Normally weather like this would drive me inside, but I've become like a rabid animal, unaware of and unimpeded by my surroundings.

They're all expecting me at the meeting in Billage. If I don't show up, they'll know something is wrong. I'm sure Johnny would come looking for me. He'd put his own life in danger. He could be arrested and killed and it would be my fault. I can't, I tell myself. I can't go to Rande, not now.

It's sheer pain turning my back on Rande, the one place I'm meant to be. Something in my home village calls to me. It feels wrong not to get it now. Resisting the urge to run to Rande is like refusing food after days of not eating. It's unnatural, but I do it. I push myself toward Billage, insisting to myself I'll ignore the voice until the meeting's over.

My contemplation in the woods has made me late. I jog through the trees until the street lamps come into view. I hurry nervously down a back alley, my wet feet sloshing from one dirty puddle to another. Rain gushes from the lightning-flecked sky. It's past working hours, but there's still a faint glow emanating from the window of a Warwick-owned leather shop. I stop outside the back door and pull hard on its thick wooden handle. The door doesn't yield to my tug.

I glance to my left, then to my right. No one wanders the alleys this time of night, especially not when days of rain have turned this street into a permanent mud slick. My feet feel as though they're sinking into the earth. Heavy droplets ooze from the crest of my head, around the back of my ear, and down my neck.

Knock, I tell myself, before the rain washes this row of buildings away. I raise a shaky hand, curl my fingers into a tight fist, and knock twice, very quietly. I hear nothing inside. The steady, muffled deluge of water drowns out all my other senses. The chilly air knifes me through my jacket.

The door eases open, and a tall, broad-shouldered man stares at me. He has a short trimmed mustache that curls ever so slightly at the ends. This must be Ivan. Knox described his acquaintance in Billage as *an honorable man that deserves our respect.*

Ivan's hard face and unflinching glare are certainly characteristics that Knox would be impressed by. Knox didn't say anything about Ivan's stern demeanor or that he has to be over six feet tall with a neck thicker than a maple tree.

"Leather shop's closed, ma'am," Ivan says coldly.

I clear my throat and remind myself that I'm stepping into a highly dangerous meeting that Knox didn't even want me coming to. "Pennies to pass."

Ivan watches me a moment longer before widening the door and allowing me just enough space to enter. Silence is heavy in the room aside from the light crackling of the fire. The tension is palpable. The last few months, Knox has been meeting with Ivan and other potentials, but tonight is the first time this many rebels have met in one place.

The leather shop is a square brick room with walls shared by neighbors on either side. From the outside, these conjoined buildings form a long row. Ivan closes the door behind me, running the dead bolt along its track. He stands with his back against the door and his legs spread wide in an upside-down V. The ceiling is low and I notice that Ivan's tall frame struggles to fit.

Knox stands opposite me. He leans against a thick square support beam, his long trench coat oiled dark brown from the rain. Tuor is close to Knox. His skinny frame shakes slightly. I'm not sure if it's from the chilly night or his nerves. Either way, he's putting on a brave face in front of the other rebel members.

The floor is soaked and muddy. A room full of skeptical men follows me with their eyes as I casually move from the door to stand next to Johnny. He brushes a lock of hair from his forehead and smirks at me as he scans my sopping visage. The edges of my mouth begin a half curve upward, but I stop before my lips become a full smile. Johnny's already been here for near an hour, so he's had time to dry off. The plan was for everyone to arrive separately to avoid being noticed.

When Knox told me we'd be meeting at the shop where Ivan works, I asked him why. This shop is not only surrounded on either side with neighbors, but it's Warwick owned. He explained that was actually the very reason it was chosen. The soldiers would expect us to be meeting in someone's home, but not here. We're hiding in plain sight.

Ivan speaks, his voice low and firm. "We're all here. Let's begin."

Laughter erupts from the street out front. Ivan holds up a hand, signaling all of us to be quiet. My body goes stiff. Water drips off my hair and onto the floor. The street grows quiet. Ivan gives another moment of pause before speaking.

"This is Linus and Munro." Ivan points to two men seated at a long table piled high with scraps of leather. "They work with me here." Munro is a short man with a bushy graying mustache and pink-tipped cheeks, while Linus' smooth skin and dark brown hair accentuate his youth.

Ivan points to another man wearing a pair of tan overalls. "Jol works at the canvas shop down the street. He represents four other men in his guild that support us. And these are my sons, Damion and Tommy." Ivan shifts his body to reveal two young men seated on a bench in front of the fireplace.

Men like Ivan and Jol work skilled jobs for the Warwick government. They make tents, saddles, and swords for the Warwick Militia. The pay is better than what I used to make at the farm, but I'm learning that this rebellion has nothing to do with compensation. It has to do with freedom.

"There are a few other supporters that do blacksmithing, but they stayed home to keep our numbers low tonight." Ivan turns to face me. "Gentlemen, these are Knox's people, Johnny, his nephew, Camilla, and her brother Tuor."

Linus looks directly at me and says, "You're the one that killed the governor."

Tuor stops shaking and his body tenses. I nod reluctantly. The statement does not surprise me. We discussed this before bringing me to the meeting. Explaining Portia's involvement in Governor Leo's murder was far too complicated, so I agreed to take responsibility for his death. It can't hurt our cause, having other members believing I offed the biggest Warwick supporter in our territory.

"What was it like?" Linus asks.

Tuor's eyes are on me.

"It was—" I hesitate. "He was trying to kill my brother. I just did what any of you would have done." It's quiet as everyone waits for me to expound on my story. I scan the room and decide to give their hungry gazes what they want. "He never showed us any mercy, so I didn't show any to him," I growl. "I slit his throat and watched his life slip away. I'm glad he's dead."

My last statement is not part of the lie. Governor Leo tried to have Tuor executed in exchange for a few hundred Catahli rings. I wish I had been the one to kill him. I sense Johnny next to me. He shifts uncomfortably while Linus gives me a nod of respect. It seems that I've satisfied his morbid interest.

"Our biggest challenge is numbers. I spoke with more shop workers this week. I have several that are interested but—" Ivan pauses, clasping his hands behind his back. "They're not ready yet to attend a meeting or to even know that meetings are taking place."

Tommy chimes in. "We're careful not to even say there's a group of us." Unlike his father, Tommy is slim with straight, greasy hair.

"When I recruit," Ivan continues, "I act alone. I talk as if I'm the only one who shares their concerns. So the risk of being caught is only to myself."

Munro nervously drums his fingers on the leather-strewn table. He continually looks to the front door as if someone will break through any moment.

"So how do we build our numbers? We've been at this for months. When are we going to act?" Jol asks. His voice is louder than makes anyone comfortable.

"Lower your voice," Munro scolds.

"Of course our numbers are low." Linus rises to his feet. "Ivan, you're doin' it wrong. If you told those people there was a rebellion forming, they'd be more likely to stand with us. Tell 'em we've got the girl that killed the governor!"

"Find your seat," Ivan warns, his tone still calm and steady.

Linus throws his arms up before sitting down. Ivan begins a slow walk across the room. Linus, now irritated, taps his foot furiously on the floor. The fire cracks and pops in response to Linus' temper.

"Why don't we ask Knox and his people what they think about our recruitment methods?" Ivan says. He comes to a stop only a few feet from Johnny and me.

Jol huffs. "Knox's people look like a bunch of children."

Children . . . I hate being called a child, especially by someone who doesn't know me. I don't hide my disgust. I glare icily at Jol before turning my gaze to Ivan.

"If we were found out tonight, the rebellion would be over like that." I snap my fingers and look directly at Jol. "There are too few of us to be acting loosely. What if tonight Karla discovered our location and sent a group of soldiers to flush us out? We'd be hanged at sunrise." Jol shakes his head at me. "Then who would remain to carry out the rebellion?"

"Camilla's right," Johnny says. "You haven't seen how bad it is out there. Until we have more men on our side—"

"And how are we supposed to have more numbers unless we get out there and rally the people?" Linus asks, looking as if he's ready to jump to his feet again.

"The time will come," Ivan says.

I hate to admit that Linus and Jol are right, but it's something of an impossible situation. We need a bigger group to make a stand, but how do we grow our numbers when we're constantly in fear of being caught?

"We need more people, right? What group of people has the highest population in this territory?" I ask.

It's Knox who answers me. "The farm workers."

"You people who work in Billage forget about the farm. You buy your food, but don't realize the amount

7

of people that it takes to plant and harvest it all. If we want to win this rebellion and take back our territory, we need the support of the farm workers."

"Aren't the people that work at the farm a bunch of oafs?" Damion asks.

I give Damion a look that makes it clear that *he's* the idiot. "No, I used to work on the farm. I know what it's like. They're probably scared. And if they're not scared, then they've grown complacent. For thirteen years people have become comfortable with their lives under Warwick's thumb, but I still think they're our best chance. If we can show them the possibilities of a life outside of Warwick rule, then maybe—"

A loud banging reverberates through the workshop. It comes from the back door, inches from where I'm standing. Johnny's hand touches mine and pulls me to his side. Ivan's sons are on their feet along with Linus and Munro. A symphony of swords is drawn. I reach for my dagger.

If Karla knew where we were meeting, she wouldn't knock before entering . . . right?

Jol steps away from everyone else and darts his gaze around the room as if he suspects a traitor. Ivan, calm as usual, moves toward the door. He gives us all a warning look.

"Weapons down," he whispers. "We're working late to catch up, remember?"

Reluctantly the swords are returned to their sheaths while everyone moves about the room, taking a stance that resembles work. I pick up a scrap of leather and try to appear as if I know what to do with it. Johnny stands behind me, blocking me from the door. Ivan clears his throat before unhooking the deadbolt.

The sound of pouring rain floods into the room. I turn and peer past Ivan's broad shoulders. I see a man, soaking wet and dressed in a full Warwick Militia uniform.

CHAPTER TWO

THE SLENDER SOLDIER pushes his way into the leather shop. I sense his cocky demeanor even from across the room. He orders Ivan to close the door. With the sound of the rain muffled by the heavy door, everyone ceases their fake work, bringing the room again to a tense silence.

"We've extended our work hours tonight," Ivan says confidently, trailing behind the soldier as he inspects the room. "More gear is needed for the recruits in LilyAye. Surely you've heard of the growing militia."

Johnny shifts in an attempt to further cover me. Linus just confirmed that I'm still recognizable in this territory as the governor killer. I continue to stare past Johnny's shoulder at the intruder. As a true Warwick soldier, his physique is impeccable. His waist is thin and the top of his black leather vest is drawn tightly over his chest.

The soldier stops suddenly. The wood floor squeaks as he turns on his heels to face Johnny and me.

He lifts his sword and points its tip in my direction, then lets out an awkward, sardonic laugh. Ivan studies the soldier with a perplexing eye.

"Sir?" Ivan questions. His voice doesn't betray any fear.

"You're not working late," the soldier says flatly. Slowly I move my hand so it's poised over the handle of my dagger. "This is a rebel meeting."

I exchange a glance with Knox.

"I'm afraid you're mistaken," Ivan says coolly.

Tommy casually slips from his seat by the fire. "A *what* meeting?" he asks stupidly. He comes to stand in front of the soldier, drawing his attention away from Ivan, who's moving fluidly to the back of the soldier. "We're doing what the boss just said; workin' late."

"I don't think so," the soldier says with a smirk. His grip around the hilt of his sword tightens.

A single moment passes where no one moves, and I wonder if Ivan will keep up the facade. But then in a blink, Ivan seizes the soldier from behind. As if father and son practiced the move, Tommy ducks and secures the soldier's sword by twisting it from his hand. Ivan clasps his thick arms around the soldier's elbows and pulls him to the ground.

The curtain has fallen. Everyone produces their weapon and circles around the intruder, including me. I expect to see the soldier's lithe body wrestling against Ivan's thick frame, but instead, the stranger squints his eyes and laughs jovially.

Linus cocks his head and looks at the group in utter bemusement. Even Ivan seems unsure of what to make of the display. The soldier attempts to raise his hands in surrender.

"Whoa, whoa!" he mutters, a laugh still on his lips.

"What is this?" Linus asks.

Ivan motions with his head. "Linus, check the door."

Linus obeys, first peering out the front window, then checking that the back door is secured.

"Put him down," Knox says.

Ivan tosses the soldier onto the floor like a hunk of meat being thrown before a pack of lions. Our circle closes in on him. The soldier pauses, staring at the floor before brushing dirt from his pants and rising to stand before us. He looks around the room, locking eyes with each of us. A queer smile forms on his face.

"I mean no harm. I'm one of you," he says.

"One of us?" Tommy barks.

"How stupid do you think we are?" Linus says. His post by the door isn't keeping him from the conversation. "They've sent a spy but haven't bothered to even change his clothes."

"That doesn't make sense. If he were a spy, they wouldn't have sent him dressed like the enemy," Johnny says.

Linus snaps back, "You don't know that."

"There could be more of them. What if this is an ambush?" Tuor says.

"The man might not know what he's stumbled in to," Munro says under his breath.

I stare at the Warwick soldier, standing among a dozen men that wish to see him dead, and he doesn't seem nervous. "He knows. He knows why we're here."

Ivan raises his sword to the man. "State your business, and quickly."

Tommy shakes the soldier's own sword at his side, eager to pounce.

"Wow. I'm impressed, truly." The soldier scans the room and the litany of weapons pointing back at him. "I never expected you to be so . . . well armored."

Ivan leans in, the tip of his sword close enough that if he breathed deeply, he'd poke a hole in the soldier's neck. Straightening his vest, the intruder glares at the blade. Dark circles encompass his sharp blue eyes. His thick black lashes only add to his striking gaze.

Like the flap of a bird's wing, the soldier suddenly turns his eyes to me. I feel uneasy and it has nothing to do with the Warwick crest on his shirt. The soldier is handsome, yet haunting to look at.

"You have ten seconds to explain yourself," Ivan warns, resting his sword just below the soldier's jaw.

"My name is Reed. I thought my reason for coming here would be plain."

Reed scans the room with a hopeful expression. It's like he's waiting for an ally to reveal himself in the crowd.

"I came here because I no longer serve the Supreme Ruler. I left the militia weeks ago and have been searching for your group ever since. It hasn't been easy finding you."

Reed is taller than every other man in the room, which makes him stick out like a carrot among tomatoes. His hair, black as tar, is slicked back and covers the collar of his shirt. "I've heard the whispers for a while now that the Duffy Rebellion was alive again in Bear Gap."

Knox stands like an unmoving stone edifice. He studies Reed with solemn eyes.

"How did you find out about this meeting?" Linus growls.

A long moment passes as Reed ponders the question and then shifts to face Linus.

"I have an informant who told me meetings were taking place in Billage, small meetings. I'm eager to align myself with the right side."

"What's his name, your informant?" Knox asks.

"Her," Reed corrects. "My informant is a woman, and I don't think she'd care for me speaking her name."

Linus scoffs from across the room.

"That's rather convenient, isn't it?" Johnny says.

Tommy speaks. "I say we kill him now."

Reed laughs awkwardly as he takes a shaky step away from Tommy. For the first time since his intrusion, Reed seems unsure of himself.

Tuor scrutinizes Reed as if he were a spider he just stepped on. "He's no defector. I don't trust him."

"It took us months to trust each other. He comes in here in one night and trusts all of us?" Munro says. "Doesn't seem right."

"H—hold on. I can prove it." Reed reaches a hand into the breast of his shirt. He pulls out a rolled piece of parchment. "I can prove I'm no longer in the militia."

"What's that?" Ivan asks.

Reed holds out the parchment, which Knox snatches out of his hand. "I grew up a Warwick supporter, but when I was stationed at the Bear Gap farm, I saw how the people there were treated and I couldn't stay any longer."

"What does it say?" I ask.

Knox shifts the parchment to the nearest flame. He reads in a monotone voice, "Traitor Notice: All Warwick personnel are notified of a deserter, Reed

Thrussell. If seen, take into immediate custody and report to your superior."

"Three weeks ago I left," Reed says. "I abandoned my post when I heard there were people in this territory planning to rebel. I found that notice posted in Rande Square and stole it as evidence of my loyalty. If I'm caught, they'll kill me."

Johnny says, "He could have just written that announcement himself and be using it as a way to gain our trust."

"Does it look real?" I ask my brother.

Knox hands the notice to Tuor. "It has the Harras seal," Tuor says.

"All that means is that Karla sent him here herself. Which makes him a spy." Linus sounds exasperated.

"Why would a spy come dressed as a soldier?" I ask.

"Why would anyone walk into a rebel meeting with that uniform?" Linus retorts.

Munro takes the parchment from Linus. "This notice could have been speaking of anyone. He might not even be Reed Thrussell."

"We have to get rid of him," Damion says, his boots scraping across the wood floor as he approaches Reed.

"Quiet," Ivan says as he stretches out an arm to steady his two sons.

A tremor ripples across Reed's hand and arm. His body jolts and then suddenly stops. "I'm wearing the uniform because I only left with the clothes on my back. I take off the vest in the daytime, but in case you didn't notice, it's raining hard tonight so I wore it for protection. This is the type of weather that can chill you to a point where you never warm up again." Reed glances around the room. "Not every man that wears the black vest is evil." Reed's eyes settle on Tuor. "You used to be in the Warwick Militia too. Does your sister question your devotion?"

"That's different," I say. My voice sounds mousy.

No one speaks. Johnny shakes his head. He turns to me, his mouth half-open.

"We have to do something about him," Johnny whispers.

"But he's right," I say, keeping my voice low. "Not only with Tuor, but Lawrence too. If anyone understood the draw of Warwick loyalty, it was Lawrence, and he still managed to break away." Only to be sucked back in, I think to myself.

"Camilla." Johnny's eyebrows furrow.

Tommy rises from his seat. "How long are we going to allow this piece of scum to take up our time?"

"I agree," Ivan says. "We have to kill him. If we let him leave here tonight, we'll all be hunted down."

"Wait," I say. The men, still clinging tight to their swords, pause to stare at me. "He was part of the militia only a few weeks ago. That might be helpful to us."

"I say we kill him. Get it over with," Linus says.

"I agree. What say the rest of you?" Tommy asks.

"I don't trust him," Johnny says.

Reed's eyes fall again to me. It's as if he wants *me* to free him from this hungry pack of wolves. There's something unsettling in the way he looks at me, but then again, his execution is being spoken of freely in front of him.

A familiar urge returns to my mind. In the same way I must go to Rande, I feel the need to save Reed. His presence is a risk. Every word he says could be a lie. We could be playing right into his hand, but my gut tells me that's not the case. My gut says he's an asset to our cause.

"I have an idea," I say. The room grows quiet. "The black vests, Warwick's soldiers, they sometimes get a brand too, just like us farm workers. Right, Tuor?"

Tuor hesitates. His fingers brush the spot on his forearm where his brand resides, given to him as a child when worked on the farm. "Captains do, and other elite. Many of the soldiers that work at the farm have a brand." Tuor gains courage as he speaks. "You have to say vows before they mark you, and once you receive your brand, you're considered nothing else for the rest of your life except a Warwick soldier."

The rain outside slows, bringing an eerie calm to the room.

"The brand for the soldiers is different than my brand." I hold out the underside of my forearm to show my mutilated scar, which keeps me from ever reentering the farm. "The soldier's brand is on their bicep, a symbol of power."

I signal Reed to show everyone his brand. He rolls up the sleeve of his cotton shirt to reveal a smooth, lean arm. At the top is a brand in the shape of a large *W*.

"Mine is on thin, tender skin," I continue, comparing my brand to his. "A symbol of submission. The soldier's brand is something to be proud of. Mine is something disgusting to hide and only be brought out when absolutely necessary." I let my arms hang limply at my side. "But one thing is the same, both brands represent property of Quinten Warwick. Tell everyone what your brand means."

Reed looks at me like we're two members of the same team. He's catching my signals.

"We're told to protect it. Once we receive it, it's a part of our body, a part of our nature. If it's destroyed—"

"Like mine."

"Yes . . ." Reed looks in the direction of my hideous scar. "Like yours. It means great disgrace. A damaged brand means a soldier . . . is no longer a soldier. He's executed."

"What of all of this?" Tommy spits.

"What of it?" I snap back, challenging his anger.

"We don't need a history lesson," Linus says.

I break away from the circle and take a step closer to Reed. "If Reed is truly a deserter, then he'll have no problem destroying his brand. Even a spy wouldn't do it. It's blasphemy."

I turn to look at Johnny. He nods, but he's not pleased. He doesn't need to say it. I know what we'll have to do if Reed doesn't cut his brand. I bring up my dagger, which I've been clutching since Reed's appearance. I recall the day that Knox lent it to me and how he never asked for it back. I hold it out to Reed handle first.

"Do you agree?"

Reed eyes me curiously, considering my offer. Then his lips curl into the faintest of smiles. He lets out a breathy laugh, then takes the blade with a look of relief.

"I agree."

Reed removes his black vest, tossing it carelessly on the floor. He then takes off his white linen shirt so he stands before the group bare from the waist up. His skin is perfectly smooth, except for a ragged scar on his right shoulder. Reed notices my staring. He runs a finger over the marred divot on his shoulder.

"Sneak attack," he says and raises his eyebrows. "The first of many in my life."

I say nothing, but sense that Reed has experienced a lot of pain in his life, perhaps more than just physical. The Warwick brand is formed perfectly on his bicep, a crisp *W*. Reed raises the blade to his arm. He pauses.

"Who do you serve?" Knox asks.

He pauses a moment longer before pressing the blade into his skin. He seems to revel in the feeling as he runs my dagger down the length of his brand. Reed's arm splits open and blood erupts from the cut, fully covering what's left of the brand. No one moves, as if we're all gazing upon something magnificent.

Reed looks up, my bloody dagger gripped tightly in his hand. "I don't know who I serve, but it's not Quinten Warwick."

Purchase *The Bear Gap Rebels* to read what happens next.

EMILY FORTNEY is the author of the Camilla Crim series. Currently living in Pennsylvania with her husband, Emily is passionate about dark chocolate, Earl Grey tea, and her cat.

Emily absolutely LOVES hearing from her readers! Connect with her over at www.emilyfortney.com